Children of
the Tide

Children of
the Tide

JON REDFERN

A Victorian Detective Story

DUNDURN
TORONTO

Editor: Laura Harris
Design: Colleen Wormald
Cover Design: Carmen Giraudy
Cover Image: © duncan/1890 istockphoto.com
Printer: Webcom

Library and Archives Canada Cataloguing in Publication

Redfern, Jon, 1946-, author
        Children of the tide : a Victorian detective story / Jon Redfern.

Issued in print and electronic formats.
ISBN 978-1-4597-2418-1 (pbk.).--ISBN 978-1-4597-2419-8
(pdf).--ISBN 978-1-4597-2420-4 (epub)

        I. Title.

PS8585.E34218C45 2015   C813'.6   C2014-904270-1   C2014-904271-X

1   2   3   4   5   19   18   17   16   15

Conseil des Arts du Canada   Canada Council for the Arts   Canada   ONTARIO ARTS COUNCIL CONSEIL DES ARTS DE L'ONTARIO an Ontario government agency un organisme du gouvernement de l'Ontario

We acknowledge the support of the **Canada Council for the Arts** and the **Ontario Arts Council** for our publishing program. We also acknowledge the financial support of the **Government of Canada** through the **Canada Book Fund** and **Livres Canada Books**, and the **Government of Ontario** through the **Ontario Book Publishing Tax Credit** and the **Ontario Media Development Corporation**.

Care has been taken to trace the ownership of copyright material used in this book. The author and the publisher welcome any information enabling them to rectify any references or credits in subsequent editions.

                                                            J. Kirk Howard, President

VISIT US AT
Dundurn.com I *@dundurnpress* I *Facebook.com/dundurnpress* I *Pinterest.com/dundurnpress*

Dundurn
3 Church Street, Suite 500
Toronto, Ontario, Canada
M3E 1M2

To Cecil William Redfern, 1917–2013

I'd like to thank the following individuals for their many contributions to this book:

my first readers — Kathy Eberle, Catherine Gildiner, Victor Pianosi
my gate-keeper and logician — Joan Redfern
my first critic — Jim Nielson, member of the Balfour salon
my fellow word-lover — Laura Ferri Forconi
my tireless and ever-supportive agent — Chris Bucci
my acquisition editor at Dundurn — Diane Young
my sharp, smart Dundurn text editor — Laura Harris
my one and only Gladys
my readers

LONDON, 1841, a teeming metropolis, a city of gaslight, new railroads, and steam-powered factories. Gangs roam the night streets; child thieves prey upon the old and the naive. The Metropolitan Detective Police are using new methods of criminal investigation, based on scientific thinking. Their efforts are an essential in England's march toward the modern age. Over all her citizens, young Queen Victoria reigns as a wife, a sovereign, and a new mother. Her first child is a tiny princess, whose smile of innocence shines like a beam of light over troubled seas....

Chapter One
A Dark Blue Line

"Hold still, Mr. Endersby!"

Inspector Owen Endersby pulled in his stomach. His wife Harriet gave him another gentle punch. "Breathe in," she scolded, and pushed the final button of his waistcoat into its hole.

"Now, hurry, dear one, and take this tin of chestnuts with you."

The inspector kissed his wife on her cheek. He pulled on his canvas coat and clumped down the stairs from their three-room flat at Number Six Cursitor Street, flung open the street door, and balked at the shrouded buildings before him. A chill morning mist muffled London's parish church bells, striking seven times to remind the city that its' workday was about to begin.

Along the glistening cobbles of Drury Lane, Inspector Endersby's hired hansom cab rushed its way toward the St. Giles Workhouse. Endersby huddled under the hansom's half roof to avoid the drizzle, his rotund figure of fifty-one years sporting his favorite plum- coloured waistcoat, his broad hat, and suede gloves.

"Faster, cabby," he shouted. Beside him Mr. Thomas Caldwell, his sergeant-at-hand, pulled down his cap of wool and shivered. He wondered if his superior felt as uncomfortable as he did. They had been called to duty one hour before six o'clock, the reason being a dead body found strangled in the St. Giles Workhouse — discovered cold and staring — in full view of forty very frightened workhouse orphans.

"Ugly news, sir," said Mr. Caldwell, flinching. A toothache, which had plagued Caldwell for a fortnight, sent a jolt of pain through his lower jaw. Chewed clove wasn't helping; its scent made his superior wrinkle his nose.

"Indeed," answered Inspector Endersby, "most wicked, Mr. Caldwell. Surely there is enough suffering in St. Giles and in all the wretched workhouses of this city without the addition of murder. And a female at that."

"Most brutal, sir."

"I imagine, Sergeant, the clove is helping?"

"Not as yet, sir."

"How unfortunate."

Inspector Endersby lapsed into silence, allowing dark thoughts to crowd his mind. Trepidation always preceded his observation of a corpse. Any mention to him of workhouses and their cruelty toward children roused a deep anger in his heart. Many times he had passed the filthy courtyards of the city's eight workhouses and seen their young inmates marching around them in circles, their faces wan, their eyes sad like those of inmates he'd seen in the yard of Fleet Prison. What was worse, an animal urge tempted him to use his fists to mete out preliminary punishment. In his twenties, as a Bow Street Runner, Endersby once had license to use hard force. He had resorted to punches and kicks to subdue his villains. To his later chagrin, he would admit how he enjoyed the sport of cracking bones. "My demon familiar," he named the urge. Now, daily, he was afraid of its potential, fearing this morning he might strike out at the bullies running the wards in St. Giles.

"Was anything else uncovered — besides the found corpse, Sergeant?"

"The policeman also discovered one of the child inmates outside the workhouse gate at a very early hour. The found waif, it seemed, was in a state of some mental agitation."

"Outside the gate? Was the waif harmed?"

"Apparently not."

Endersby leaned back as the hansom cab continued on. The thoroughfare bustled with figures rushing off to shops and work yards, heads bent to avoid the gentle rain. London had grown larger since the end of the Napoleonic Wars. Endersby often remarked how the streets never presented anything less than a moving mass of human souls. Two million living in the greater city; one child out of six lived poor and abandoned.

"I assume, Sergeant, that you find your new marital life bliss-ful?" Endersby said to break the silence. It was a courtesy question. Over the past year his feelings toward Sergeant Thomas Caldwell had changed. At one time he had disliked his sergeant, finding him abrupt and presumptuous. But when he had saved Endersby's life in the summer of last year, stepping in front of him to block an attacker's knife, his respect grew. They had become friends. Endersby thought of himself as a scientific man — a policeman in a new age where rank took second place to consideration.

"Yes, sir. Most comforting," Caldwell replied, smiling quickly at his superior's question.

"You've been wedded three months now?"

"Four and half, sir, to be precise," Caldwell answered.

"Plans for the future?" Endersby lowered his voice. The mat-ter of children, of babies in particular, brought out a tenderness of feeling in the inspector, one mixed with deep sorrow. He and his dear Harriet had suffered the death of a son early in their marriage and had been unable to have another.

"My Alice wishes to have one right away."

"And you, sir?" asked Endersby.

"Of two minds I am, Inspector. Money. Alice's health."

"These are difficult decisions, indeed."

Endersby opened his mouth to speak again but changed his mind. The task at hand was brutal. A murder of an innocent woman. He noticed Caldwell's lips held tight with anticipation. "Stir your horse, sir," Endersby commanded the coachman. Time was pressing. A crime site had to be viewed early on before the blood and the clues were mopped up and hidden forever from the detective's eye.

In less than ten minutes, the inspector and his sergeant were delivered down a narrow passage that led to the gate of the St. Giles Workhouse.

"Shall I draw up procedure, Sergeant?" Endersby asked.

Endersby and Caldwell planned what each would do just before the body and murder scene were examined. *What satisfaction there was in working in this fashion,* Endersby thought. During his first years as a junior policeman, the inspector had worked alone, obeying the dictates of the magistrate's court in Bow Street. Then, arrests were swift, too often based on hasty conclusions, class distinction, and malice. Now his role as a detective inspector was based on principles of impartiality and judicial equity, as laid down by the founder of the Metropolitan Police, Sir Robert Peel.

"This morning, Sergeant," Endersby began, "stand close. If you observe anything amiss, as I am sure both of us shall, take a note. If you see a need for a different tack, do not hesitate to speak."

"Thank you, sir. I shall."

"Remember, Caldwell, you and I are the first arm of a fairer form of justice."

"We are indeed, sir."

Caldwell now pointed toward the scene before them. Small barred windows in tight rows — each no more than a slit — dominated the facade of the workhouse. "A prison, no question," Endersby said. With his hat straight on, his right hand clenched as if to rein in his "demon familiar," the inspector climbed from the hansom and paid the driver. Sergeant Caldwell pulled the bell chain. The massive portal squeaked open to reveal a sour-faced man in a greasy frock coat. To Endersby he had a mean and hungry look.

"Good morning, sir. We are Inspector Endersby and Sergeant Caldwell, under the jurisdiction of Borne at Fleet Lane Station House."

The sour-faced master signalled to the two men to step into the large front hall. A high-ceilinged space, it led off into various small corridors. At one end, on the left, an archway opened onto a long ward lined with beds on which sat a host of young girls, rigid, upright, as if an edict had stilled their tongues and feet. What struck Endersby was the eerie silence. A workhouse clatters and clangs with industry. At the entrance to the ward stood a small hearth where a boy was scrubbing the floor in front of a grate of cold ash.

"It is here the wretch was found dead," explained the sour master.

"Did you see the body in its unfortunate state this morning?" asked Endersby.

"Briefly, sir, so briefly. It was very dark," replied the master.

"Were you, in fact, the man who *found* the body, sir?"

"Me, Inspector? Why would you assume such a thing on my part?"

"Perhaps, you came upon it merely by accident?" Endersby squeezed his right hand to remind himself to remain even-tempered.

"It is not my place, sir, to be questioned thus. I would have little or no occasion to come down into this ward unless ordered to do so." The master crooked his finger and the two policemen followed him up a shallow staircase to a bare room, where a woman in a duff-coloured bonnet was standing.

"Matron Agnes," the master said. "These two gentlemen are the detective officers from the Metropolitan Police."

On observing the reaction of the matron, Endersby immediately anticipated an adversary. He removed his hat in salute. "I beg your pardon, Matron," Endersby said with feigned deference. "Inspector Endersby is my name. My sergeant-at-hand, Mr. Caldwell." The matron let out a nervous breath. "Much *too* much confusion, here," she said.

"Most pitiful, the murder of an innocent woman," Endersby replied. "I believe there is also a child."

"Don't you be *so* certain, Inspector, of learning anything from little Catherine, sir."

"If you have no objection, Matron, it is necessary for me and my sergeant to learn as much as I can from her and from others in this place about your matron's demise," cautioned Endersby.

"Well, that is *your* business," she replied, her voice held in close. "The female child is *but* nine. Do not think young Catherine is stupid. She *can* be persuaded. You may meet with her at *our* convenience, sir."

Taking note of the strange emphasis the matron placed on words, Inspector Endersby decided to waylay his sudden impatience with a command: "My present concern is the matter of the dead body. Master, I require of you smart assistance." The sour-faced man turned to Endersby. "Gather all of the staff who work here. I mean by this, matrons, other masters, cooks, scullery maids, coal carriers. And have them meet me and Sergeant Caldwell within the quarter hour in the entrance hall."

The matron stepped forward: "What *you* want, Inspector, is not —"

Endersby cut her off, his voice full of steel: "Second, and most important, send a runner immediately to fetch a surgeon and then another to notify the local coroner." Sergeant Caldwell supported the inspector's order by clearing his throat.

"Doubtless, this is of some necessity?" the peevish master queried.

"Dire necessity, sir," responded Sergeant Caldwell.

"Look here, Officer," the matron began. "I mind informing you that as far as I am *concerned*, the workhouse must *continue* with its duties."

"Matron," Endersby countered: "I cannot draw off into a corner to do my professional duties. A murder has been committed. A life taken. That fact, above all, takes precedence. I am sure you will agree that my investigation will have as much open time and space as it needs."

Reluctantly, the matron begged pardon. She assented to Enderby's request to inspect the body of the victim who, in her words, was attacked "in the *blackest hours* of the night before." The inspector and his sergeant followed the matron to a chamber where the dead woman lay on a table. Her feet were laced into shoddy boots, the kind worn by coster women in the Covent Garden markets. Her hands were blue and a muslin cloth covered her head. Sergeant Caldwell took a lit candle and, bracing himself, lifted off the cloth. The light revealed a face twisted and swollen, the eyes open and bulging, the nose smudged with a dark substance.

"Who was it that found her?" asked Inspector Endersby.

"The *two* scullery maids. They are first up."

"The area around the hearth was washed down this morning," Endersby noted.

"I had her hearth chair removed as well. It was *very* plain, sir: I could not have the children see *any more* of this terrible crime than they had already *witnessed* on waking."

"The children saw the body then? After the scullery maids had discovered its state?" The thought made Endersby shudder slightly.

"You, as a man of the law, Mr. Endersby, can plainly see what *confusion* we have endured."

Ignoring the comment, Endersby turned to the matron. "This woman was in her forties, Matron?"

"The ledger of the parish notes the day of her birth but not the year. Matty was an orphan, brought here from the care of a Dame School near the sea at Brighton."

"If I may be so bold, sir," Sergeant Caldwell said, his voice lowered. "The servants and staff, I reckon, must be questioned promptly in case they talk amongst themselves and confuse their stories."

Endersby nodded. "I can study this sad creature well enough on my own while you cajole witnesses and ply questions." Sergeant Caldwell immediately relaxed his stiff posture: "Thank you, sir."

"Mind you, talk alone with the scullery maids. I want their eyes to speak first, since they found the corpse. Also, check entrances — side, back, cellar — for signs of break-in, broken latches, and locks."

"Thank you, Inspector."

"'For this relief much thanks,'" quipped Endersby, remembering the production of Hamlet that he had attended three nights prior at Covent Garden Theatre. As Sergeant Caldwell left the chamber, Endersby took off his hat and suede gloves. From his shoulder, he shrugged off a leather satchel with a thick strap. "This is my handy carry-all," he explained to the matron. "Purchased years ago, when I worked my districts as a Bow Street Runner." He shuffled the objects inside: handcuffs and a cosh, used to subdue resistant felons. Onto the table he piled a leather-bound notebook, a clutch of lead-tipped pencils, a turban cloth for disguises, a scarf, and an ear trumpet for checking heartbeats. "Ah, here it is," he said. "My latest acquisition." The inspector held up a square of thick magnifying glass. Leaning closer to the corpse, Endersby passed the glass over the face, then concentrated on the dead woman's sunken cheeks. Black smudges reached halfway to her temples. He dabbed a wet finger and rubbed. *Coal dust.* He peered at the victim's neck, its stiffness of muscle raising the chin to show a combination of marks.

"Did you know Miss Matty well?" asked Endersby, straightening.

"Little enough, Inspector. She was a *bitter* woman."

Nodding, he continued. "I see here, Matron, just under the jaw line and across the centre of the neck, a thin blue-black bruise dotted with orange-coloured specks. I think this is the result of a hanging." The line of injury marked the skin like a blue cord. It did not extend far beyond the front surface of the neck. "So not a true noose," Endersby concluded out loud.

"These specks are bits of metal rust," he continued. Matron Agnes watched him pull out a paper envelope. With the tips of his thumb and forefinger he lifted off a number of the tiny scales of metal from the surface of the neck and placed them inside the envelope. Endersby deduced, tentatively, that the murderer had pressed a hand, encrusted with coal dust, across the victim's face and strangled the woman with a tool of some kind. But what had been the prime motive? Revenge? Vicious pleasure?

"Inspector, there is one item I have set *aside*," said Matron Agnes. From a drawer in the table she handed Endersby a six-inch piece of mouldy, coarse lace. "This cloth," she explained, "I pulled from Matty's mouth *and* throat." Endersby examined the lace close to the candle. He turned it over in his hands. "But why lace?" he suddenly asked. "And why, indeed, compound the method of murder with such a cruel gesture?" Endersby raised his head to see Matron Agnes wipe tears from her eyes. "Most peculiar, Matron. I am indeed sorry," the inspector said. He pulled out another envelope and placed the bit of lace inside. "The magistrate," he said, "demands proof of any items found near or on the body."

"Why has this happened?" Matron Agnes cried.

"I cannot say as yet what *I* believe," Endersby answered. "Items speak of their own accord and can help form a picture, if you wish. I apply logic as best I can. I presuppose this is murder, and this lace, which you have most wisely guarded, is strong evidence of a merciless killer."

The two stood for a moment in the gloom of the flickering candle before walking back upstairs.

"Have we finished, Inspector?"

"One last request, Matron. I would like to see Miss Matty's room."

***

As he stepped quickly down the stairs into the vast cellar of the workhouse, Sergeant Caldwell winced from his tooth pain. He popped two cloves into his mouth and settled them on his throbbing molar. He couldn't help wondering about all the poor thin girls he'd seen huddling in the wards. What a horror to think a parent could abandon a child.

"Good morning, sir," he said to the scrub boy.

The boy nodded his head.

"Take me around, boy, to all the doors in the cellar and then on the upper floor."

"To check locks, sir?" the boy asked.

"Yes, lad, to see if and where the killer broke in."

"You won't find any, sir," the boy said leading Sergeant Caldwell up a back staircase.

"Won't find what?"

"No signs, sir. First thing I did before I scrubbed the hearth was to check doors. The intruder never come in here by them." The boy pointed to a door leading to an upper room. The lock was still on and there was no sign of any forced entry. Throughout the walk the same situation occurred. The workhouse had been sealed tight. Sergeant Caldwell wondered if the boy had performed some mischief, but as he watched him he saw he was clever, quick, and obedient.

"You were born in here, lad?"

"In'ere? Two floors up in the women's ward. Never set eyes on me mammy."

The boy's bright voice cut into Caldwell's heart. He did not think of himself as sentimental. How had this lad become so strong? So used to a lonely life? After inspecting all the doors and entrances, Sergeant Caldwell made a few notes in his notebook.

"Now, lad," Caldwell said, his voice more cheerful, "gather all the workers here. Lead them to the hearth room. Fast as you can, young boy. I have questions to ask!"

Chapter Two
Tales of Woe

Matron Agnes led Endersby into Miss Matty's small room, its only furniture a simple bed and a cupboard with two drawers. The cupboard contained a cloak, a pair of shoes, and an outdoor bonnet. *A meagre life,* the inspector thought.

"Can you recall if any other woman or man complained against her?"

"The scullery maids liked to tease her a little. *Such* was their way. Matty never complained, nor did they. Perhaps they saw in each other a similar misery."

"Or loneliness?" the inspector added.

"We are a place full of much loneliness, sir," Matron Agnes replied, a melancholy in her words.

"Did Miss Matty have any friends or acquaintances outside of the workhouse? People she met or spoke about?"

"She rarely talked to me. Her acquaintances were *few* — if any — that *I* could perceive."

Endersby thanked the matron. On his way down to the

entrance of the workhouse he peeked into a ward full of destitute women with small babies. *What sorrow pervades the morning light,* he thought. *What thin hands and thin bodies are arrayed on the rows of beds. Why does our time treat women so cruelly? Why was Miss Matty murdered? What kind of person would wish her dead?* Endersby knew how fear and hatred in some people's minds took time to grow. Like seeds, they lay dormant until a gesture, a cruel word, made them burst out of the heart and force the hand to take a life. But who had Miss Matty wronged?

On reaching the entrance hall, Endersby felt relieved to see Sergeant Caldwell standing by the hearth where the body had been found. Endersby hoped his sergeant had found a clue. A cook in a white apron, the sour haughty master, a tall, pinched-looking younger gentleman, and two other stern women were arranged in a wide circle about the sergeant. Closer to Caldwell stood two very haggard women.

"These are the scullery maids, sir," Caldwell explained. The two reminded Inspector Endersby of the oyster-sellers he frequently visited in the dock streets near Limehouse: shabby in dress, smelling of dirty bare feet. "I tried to scream, I did," said the first of the two. Endersby listened as the two interrupted each other with their tale of finding the body on the floor. "Did you notice anything in Miss Matty's mouth when you found her?" Endersby asked. The two quickly glanced at each other: "Naught, sir, but her cheeks were fat out, like she had taken too much porridge from her bowl."

"Was there anything lying on the floor? Other than the tipped chair?"

The two scullery maids shook their heads. Endersby thanked them and stepped aside to think for a moment. His gouty left foot started to pang. *A bad omen,* he thought, for he relied on his left foot to alert him to the swell of obscurity which often dogged an investigation. This morning he suffered a peculiar confusion from what seemed to be, so far, a murder with scant clues: the lace, the coal dust, the bruise and the bits of rusted metal. He looked at Sergeant Caldwell, who was finishing up the testimonies of the other workers. After they were dismissed, Caldwell gave a summary of his findings: the cook arrived at a later hour and was unaware of the killing; the masters had all been in bed, as had the two other matrons. None except the two scullery maids had acquaintance with Miss Matty. The two masters knew her by sight only. No sign of the coal carrier.

"No adult witnesses it seems, so far. And the doors and entrances, Sergeant?"

Mr. Caldwell grinned and spoke with clove on his breath. "Sir, the scrub boy took me around to the back and front entrances. Both showed no signs of forced entry from the outside. The locks were large and opened by a number of key turns. A villain, sir, would have needed a strong arm and a metal jackbar to open either one of them. Both were locked all night. The windows here, as we have observed, are barred and high up. However, sir, there is a wooden side door. Near the stairs leading up from the laundry rooms. It has a latch, but only on the inside. On the outside, it is without hardware."

"I wonder why?" queried Endersby. "Certainly to keep outsiders from entering via the yard. Dare we assume, Sergeant, that this door was the exit afforded to the culprit?"

"Possibly, sir, since the young child was found close to it by the workhouse gate."

"Ah, indeed. The waif named Catherine. Do we know anything about her?"

"Not as yet, sir."

"But, Caldwell, why was this particular child out in the cold?

I wonder if there are many who try to escape from this dreadful place?"

"If I may suggest, sir, a child wishing to escape would surely have run far away from the workhouse gate."

"Most surely, Sergeant."

Endersby blinked his eyes; on raising his head only a fraction, he dispelled a number of swirling questions and returned his attention to the present situation.

"And the scrub boy, Sergeant?"

"Sir?"

"Did you question him at all?"

"Most efficiently, sir. He said he was asleep upstairs with the other boys. Seems the male wards and the family wing are all locked at night, so no passage between them and this female ward is possible until the morning when the masters unlock the doors and herd the inmates to their breakfasts."

"Curious," replied Endersby. "But with all these locked doors, how did the culprit move so freely? It would depend on where he entered, surely. Caldwell, I have a sense that this person knows well the layout of a workhouse. Knows of locked passages and open ones. How else could such a brutal act be committed if the man were stumbling about getting lost or at worst, being caught by a master and thrashed?"

"I shall keep this in mind, sir. The scrub lad also told me how difficult it was to mop up the coal dust."

"Coal dust! Do we know where the coal chute is for the kitchen?"

"In the cellar, sir."

"Kindly investigate it. See if there are signs of a forced entry, if the chute itself looks brushed or mussed in any way."

"Mussed, sir?"

"The victim was heavily smudged with coal dust. We could

presume it was a coal carrier who decided to end Miss Matty's life. Or, in fact, we might discover that the culprit, whose profession remains, as yet, unknown to us, entered the building via the chute."

"Indeed, sir."

"By the by, find out the name of the coal carrier. Where is the chap? In the meantime, I will go to the young girls before me in the ward. Perhaps one of them can enlighten me. If we have some luck, perhaps one can remember witnessing the villain — although fear of the dark can create monsters."

⁂

Endersby stood alone for a moment, his ears alert to the murmuring of the young girls in the ward. What human flotsam stood before him. The ever-present spectre of young Robert Endersby, his only child, now dead these twelve years, drifted into his conscious mind. Not unlike one or two of the children in this ward, his son Robert had been a weak three-year-old, eventually felled by a lung infection. Seeing so many young girls before him, Endersby felt pity, as each of them might be dead within a week or a month. "For their own safety," Endersby grumbled, thinking back to a statement once made by a politician who supported workhouses for the poor as a way of teaching them to become "self-sufficient."

Honing his mind as best he could, Inspector Endersby now looked with clear eyes. By each bed stood a young girl dressed in blue muslin. Heads lowered in obedience, bare feet, and a smell of sickly skin engulfed the space. When he approached one girl, she raised her face to him and showed a set of drawn features, the eyes ringed with mauve circles.

"Good morning, girls. My name is Endersby. I am a policeman."

A muted round of "g'morning" greeted the inspector's introduction. He asked the children to approach him and stand in a circle. The girls moved quickly, some stumbling. "Have you had your porridge, yet?" he asked. A cry of "No, sir," flew up to the high ceiling. "Then I shall be quick," Endersby said, looking into the homely faces of the unfortunate of his own society. Could any one of these young females tell a story recounting the events of last night? Would they be reliable as witnesses? Given the hardship in their young lives, how well could these storm-tossed children reveal the differences between phantom and flesh? With a gracious severity, he asked the oldest girl to step forward.

"Now, why don't you tell me a story? You tell stories to each other, don't you?"

A few of the girls blushed and responded in the affirmative.

"Blest, sir," the girl said excitedly. Endersby saw spirit in her; he looked at the other girls who held their eyes on her as if they were her acolytes. All stories have a beginning so the inspector asked her to begin. The girl swept her eyes around the circle of her ward sisters. She began with ghosts and goblins. "Ah, wondrous," Endersby said. Then he prompted her to tell a true story. "Go back in time," he suggested. "Imagine yourself in the dark last night, in this very room." The others began to shuffle. One child coughed. The girl began. "Last night, oh, last night." Endersby sat forward. The girl told of a dark figure moving down the beds holding a candle and whispering.

"Indeed," replied the inspector. "Why do you think he went about so?"

"Nothin', sir … only wos 'ere to look … passed close by me, he did."

"Did you see his face, by chance?"

"I dustn't 'cause he was stinking so." The others giggled. The girl blushed and pulled nervously at her sleeve. Endersby gave

25

her a nod as if to say, "good work," and the child came close again, cupping her chilly hand around Endersby's ear.

"Ah," replied Endersby, exaggerating his astonishment at her whispered words. "Are you certain?" The girl pressed closer.

"A broken limb, you say. A limp," said Endersby.

The girl stepped back, proudly smiling. "Well done," Endersby said.

Endersby waited a little longer, gazing in the faces of those around him. No other child stepped forward. Catching a nod from Matron Agnes at the door, he told the girls their porridge was waiting, to which announcement they shouted like a horde of fun-seekers at a seaside fair and dashed off to the eating hall. Pushing through the rush came Sergeant Caldwell, his notebook held in his right hand. Endersby stood up from the bed where he had relaxed his painful foot. Yet another gouty pang made him consider the details he had just heard.

"Sir," said the sergeant next, "best, I reckon, if you walk around with me to see what I have seen."

"…More things in heaven and earth?" quipped Endersby.

"Sir?"

"Mr. Hamlet, Sergeant. He has been stuck in my mind these last few days. At Covent Garden Theatre this past Friday I had the delight to see Mr. Macready play the lead role. Walk on. Let us see together. A few details were gained from talking to the little girls. One said she saw a limping man looking at the faces of the children."

"And yet, sir, the child was left behind."

"The wrong child, may we surmise?"

26

Chapter Three
Clues in the Coal

Caldwell led his superior down two staircases, through a kitchen, and into a cramped room containing the blackened coal chute. Thomas knew the case was already causing the inspector doubts. He knew Endersby's gout would soon slow him down as much as his own toothache was draining his energy.

Standing in the doorway of the coal room, Endersby gazed first at the space, his way of pondering and examining a room before drawing a conclusion.

"Enter carefully, sir," Caldwell cautioned, holding up a lit candle. "Stay to the right, sir. I shall explain."

"I see it has been left open. This bottom flap," Endersby said at the coal chute. He poked his head up the chute, which came down from the yard at a steep slant. The chute was mussed. Caldwell imagined a body had slid down it, kicked open the bottom flap and landed on the floor. The usual coal pile from a delivery had already been cleared into bins and into smaller buckets for haulage up to various hearths. Endersby noted immediately even a light brush of an elbow procured a sooty, oily stain. "Notice, sir," said Caldwell, "a faint boot mark on the inside of the chute's flap."

"May we assume, Caldwell, the intruder pressed his boot to open the flap as well as to break the velocity of his slide?"

"Likely, sir. And see, we can make out even in this light at least six pairs of distinct boot marks leading from the chute toward the door over there."

Endersby turned up one of his own boots; there was black dust on the sole and a shadowy print left behind on the floor. Caldwell did the same and when the two made their way to the door, they were careful to walk beside the other foot prints, comparing their own boot marks to them. "A telltale sign of some import," Endersby said. "Note, the left boot has a worn heel — see the shape. And look at the right. The print is smudged and indistinct." Caldwell bent down and slipped on his wire-rimmed spectacles.

"Most certain, Inspector, the left heel is not truly rounded on the outside. It seems as if the right boot were dragged on the floor as the culprit walked." Endersby examined the boot mark from another angle. "The young girl I spoke to in the ward told me she saw a figure late in the night and he walked about as if he had a broken limb." The two men closely examined the other prints. Outside the door to the coal room, the floor had already been washed, the footprints mopped away. "I question, Sergeant, the manner in which the culprit *left* the building. He did not return here and climb back out; the chute slant is too steep."

"It is, sir."

"And when did all of this skulking about take place? Shall we retrace the route the culprit may have taken from this coal chute to the upper ward?"

Endersby fell in behind his sergeant, who carried the candle aloft. "Sergeant. A partial sooty handprint," said the inspector, joining him on a step. "A narrow palm, sir," Caldwell replied. The inspector looked hard and said: "This little blotch of dried blood is, in fact, a scab left stuck to the brick." Sergeant Caldwell slipped on his eyeglasses again.

A sudden slapping sound made the two men turn. Before them stood a round-faced man in a leather apron, his face and hands blackened by coal dust. He scowled and beat a thick leather strap against his apron.

"Who's the cove that thinks I am a murderer?"

"Who are you, sir?" Caldwell said in a loud voice.

"Andrew Potter, sir. Coal carrier and devout Christian. I do not like my character slandered, sir, by the likes of you."

Endersby stepped from behind Caldwell and introduced himself and his sergeant-at-hand. "Mr. Potter, there has been a mistake. We do not think nor do we accuse you of murder. We are in St. Giles to investigate.... You speak with a good tongue, sir."

"For a coal carrier, sir? Yes. I take no offence at your observation. Mam was a teacher. Gave me a good tongue, a head for reading. Fell ill to the pox. Left me in this place, this St. Giles. Sent out to work at fourteen in the coal works, sir."

"A body of one of the matrons has been found in the front foyer, near the hearth. I assume, Mr. Potter, you have been informed of this terrible discovery."

Potter nodded. "Some here thinks I am the culprit, that I killed poor Miss Matty. Me, who works seven days hard labour a week — all night, rain or snow."

"Are you innocent, sir?" Endersby asked outright.

The coal carrier drew back. "Never hurt a soul. Usual for me to come here Tuesdays and Fridays, to St. Giles," he said, "just before dawn, load four sacks in the chute out yonder. Matron Agnes pays with ready money."

"Do the children recognize you, Mr. Potter?" Endersby asked.

"I imagine so, sir," the coal carrier answered. "I hail them in the mornings, the young ones outside at least."

"Given the days you deliver here — it being Wednesday today — were you by chance delivering coal anywhere near St. Giles Workhouse early this morning? Let us say close to three or even half past three o'clock?"

"Matter of fact, yes, sir. I was at Holborn, not ten minutes north. Haberdasher. Nine sacks."

"Mr. Potter," Endersby said. "I shall be brief. Do you in your night hours of delivery ever make note of the creatures on the streets which you traverse?" Endersby asked. "I mean other than the boy gangs, or the women of the night. Any unusual figures you might see and remember?"

"Man in a lady's gown two early mornings ago, sir. Kimbawed by rum and beer. Hailed me, he did."

"And anyone this past night, or near three or half three o'clock?"

"Near three or twenty past the hour, yes. While on delivery on Holborn. A chap came along, an odd one limping. Right bent, beard."

"Did he speak to you, at all?"

"The cove! Head-on into the flank of my dray. Come up from Drury Lane. Like he was chased by a pack of dogs."

"Did the gentleman reply in any way, perhaps curse or apologize for colliding with you, Mr. Potter?"

"*Struck* my wagon, he did, with a gaff! Said nothing. Stank like a dead horse. Went on his way along Holborn, toward Gray's Inn."

"A gaff. What do you mean?"

"Like what the dredgermen use, sir. The river scavengers. Long handle with a hook. For haulin' in bodies, sir," Potter said.

"Metal?" asked Endersby.

"Like the flounder fishers once used when I was a lad," answered the coal carrier. "I see plenty men using them round the docks. Mind, the dredgers are a closed lot. A guild. No one works for'em unless for pittance."

" Did you by chance see the cove's face?"

"A flash sir. Like he was cut. Or with a mark from birth."

"You will be called upon by the parish clerk and the coroner today — later this morning, in fact — to tell your story again," replied Endersby. "Alert the coal works of your whereabouts."

"Thank you, sir." Potter said. The inspector and Caldwell bid him goodbye. Then, without delay, Endersby asked Caldwell to write down the details of the coal carrier's description: A MAN WITH A BEARD, A LIMP, A STINK, A DREDGERMAN'S METAL GAFF, AND A FACIAL MARK. Outside in the yard, as the two examined the side door's lack of outer hardware they discovered a broken latch on the coal chute. "So far, Sergeant, scant proof provides us a logical connection. Entry of villain here — down the chute; exit of villain by the wooden side door. All of our conclusions based on coal dust."

"Remarkable, sir," answered Caldwell.

"And your professional opinion of the coal carrier, Sergeant?"

"Innocent seeming, sir. To be bold, I cannot conjure a motive for murder in a chap like him."

"I stand beside you on that count, Sergeant. A man with brains cramped into the body of a labourer." The two men stood close, their breaths visible in the crisp air.

"My first question, Caldwell."

"Certainly, sir."

"How did our culprit know about the side door and its particular latch?"

"Perhaps he played scout at first. Or was well acquainted

with St. Giles. Perhaps he was once an inmate, like Potter, the coal carrier."

"Certainly possible," Endersby said. "Or a former master, perhaps? Disgraced and sent into the world without a reference?" Endersby walked a few paces toward the front portal. "Second question: a man brutally kills a matron in a workhouse, a place he *may* know in familiar terms. It *seems* he kills at random. Miss Matty was a shut-in creature without friends. Unless, of course, he did know her and hated her. He murders in a cruel manner, using *a piece of lace,* in order to search for a particular child. But to what end? We can discount the motive to take advantage in a way only the most disgusting of men find pleasing. For revenge? To recover a lost offspring? But then the villain leaves this child behind, unharmed. And what of the waif, herself? The child called Catherine?"

"You do love your ramblings, sir," Caldwell said.

"The highways and byways of the criminal world, Sergeant, make up a most intricate topography."

Standing by the front entrance of the workhouse, Endersby relaxed his shoulders. "Shall we walk a little?" he suggested. Caldwell agreed and he offered the idea they go to a coffee house close by and drink a pot to revive their spirits. "The coroner will soon arrive, sir. We have time," Caldwell said, imagining members of the parish board descending on St. Giles Workhouse like avenging angels, fingers ready to point. "It is time, indeed, for reflection," said Endersby. "Time to wonder about a child named Catherine."

Chapter Four
Double Trouble

Endersby reluctantly stepped once more into the clammy dimness of the workhouse and was shown to a chamber on the second floor. A tin clock on the corridor wall banged out the hour of nine. The workhouse had begun to function again, noise and shouting filling the air. *An inferno, indeed,* thought Endersby. *What a cat's cradle of facts and suppositions.* These thoughts ceased abruptly when the inspector saw, in the chamber before him, Matron Agnes bent over a thin, blonde girl. The child held a pencil. On a piece of foolscap she was diligently drawing out a large oval shape. When the child turned and looked up at him, Endersby noticed the deformity of her upper lip.

"Inspector," said Matron Agnes, "this is young Catherine. She is the girl who was *found* outside the workhouse gate very early *this* morning. Do not mind that she is dumb, sir. She is a *bright* child."

Catherine continued to decorate the oval shape in front of her.

"Can she read and write her letters?" asked Endersby.

"Better than many here," answered Matron Agnes.

Stepping away from the child, Matron Agnes lowered her voice. "How fortunate, Inspector, that Catherine was not harmed in any way."

"Indeed, Matron," Endersby answered. "Have you posed any questions and received any answers?"

"With Catherine, one must always *ask* for a 'yes' or 'no.' Or to have her draw. She is *clever* with her pencil. The intruder carried her *outside into the street* and then left her, *untouched.* I have requested Catherine to draw me a *picture* of the man's face. For she nodded when I asked if she *had seen* the fellow's features."

Endersby approached the table and looked over the shoulder of the young girl. She had drawn a large oval into which she had placed near the top two smaller ovals, side by side. Then below the small ovals, close to the bottom, a straight bold line. A man's face as seen by a child. With much energy, little Catherine now drew a series of circles and lines that with some allowance for exaggeration could be interpreted as a man's beard.

"Well done, young girl," Endersby said.

Catherine looked up at him. She had no fear in her eyes. "This is the man you saw last night, did you?" asked Endersby. The girl nodded vigorously. Her left hand reached up and pulled at Endersby's sleeve. Catherine then stood and pulled again until Endersby's face was at the same height as hers. She blinked hard and widened her eyes and then clasped her right hand over her mouth.

"What is it Catherine?" Matron Agnes asked. "Be quick, child."

Catherine slowly moved her right hand from her mouth and guided it with her pointer finger held up. She pressed the finger on Endersby's right jaw. The tip was icy to the touch but

Endersby stood as still as a tree. The finger began to move up and across his right cheek. It climbed, then dragged itself over his nose. The girl took in a breath and concentrated her gaze. Without lifting her finger from Endersby's face, she continued her cold trail upwards across his left cheek, stopping under his eye. Catherine then turned back to her drawing and picking up the pencil she drew a similar line across the oval face.

"A scar, perhaps, Catherine?" asked Endersby. The girl took her pencil and doubled the line; afterward, she smudged it with the tip of her finger.

"I see, I see. Very clear," said Endersby. "Catherine," he then said, "did you know this man?" The girl shook her head. "Did he speak to you?" The girl seemed to freeze in her place. Her eyes looked into the distance and she frowned and fussed and finally bent her head toward the table. "Catherine?" said Matron Agnes. The child sat still and did not respond. "Do not be *too* hasty to judge her, Inspector. She has tried *her* best."

"Thank you Matron. Thank you Catherine, you have been a good girl."

Matron Agnes subsequently made a small gesture that struck Endersby straight to his heart. Amidst this place of stone and gloom, Matron Agnes put her hand on Catherine's head and patted it softly. "I thank you for your cooperation and attention, Matron," Endersby said. As he turned to leave, young Catherine reached out and caught his sleeve a second time. She picked up her pencil and on the other side of the oval portrait, on the clean side, she began to write out a series of letters in an awkward hand. When she was done, she looked into the inspector's face and pointed to the word.

UNKELBOW.

"Unkelbow?" Endersby asked, pronouncing the last three letters as if they described the limb of a tree.

The girl shook her head. "Do not fool us, Catherine," said Matron Agnes. "This is a *nonsense* word."

The girl stood and opened her little mouth and closed it in imitation of a person talking. She placed her hands on each side of her face, leaned forward, and again mimed the talking mouth. Catherine picked up the paper and shoved it at Endersby's stomach. He read out the word again. "Unkelbow." This time he said the word bow as in Bow Street, or as the twist in a ribbon. "What do you make of this, Matron?" Matron Agnes folded her hands in front of her and stilled her face. "I *cannot* imagine, sir. Children love to *make up* names and fantastical friends to keep them company. Do not forget the realms of fancy, Inspector."

"Indeed."

The child stamped her foot. The inspector obliged and said the word again. "Unkelbow. Unkelbo." The girl nodded furiously. "Uncle Bow?"

Again, a hearty nod from the girl. The inspector looked up into the matron's face. "Uncle Bow. A family name?"

Endersby examined both sides of the sheet and as he did so a light knocking at the door of the chamber commenced and within a few seconds a young constable from the Metropolitan Police was standing by Endersby's right elbow. The constable's hat and his white gloves caused young Catherine to stare.

"I beg your pardon, Inspector Endersby," said the constable.

"Come Catherine," said Matron Agnes, a cold tone returning to her voice.

"Thank you Matron," Endersby said, still pondering the cryptic letters on the page before him.

"Sir, if I may?" enquired the constable.

"And a good morning to you, young Catherine," said Endersby as she was led out through the door and into the corridor.

"Inspector Endersby?"

"Ah, Constable."

The young man stood at attention. Endersby recognized a new recruit from the eager look in his eye.

"Forgive me, Constable. My mind was engrossed in a puzzle," said Endersby, folding the child's drawing and putting it in his pocket.

Sergeant Caldwell rushed in, his wool cap slightly askew and his eyes full of concern.

"Sir," Caldwell began.

"Gentlemen, take your ease," Endersby said. "One at a time."

Caldwell, of higher rank, spoke first.

"Most dire, sir. Another body has been found, a body of one of the matrons at the House of Correction in Shoe Lane."

The constable's words hit Endersby like a kick from a horse. His gouty limb twanged with such sudden pain he had to lift it from the floor to give relief. Another matron? In a workhouse? The building around him seemed to darken and Endersby wanted to light torches, as if to burn out the plague. Some contagion was spreading through the streets of his beloved city. He dared not raise his eyes for a moment in case he saw a monster in front of him. A smiling creature with bloodied hands. Taking a breath, putting his foot down, Endersby gathered himself, holding the rein tight on his rumbling anger, his hands closing into fists by his side.

"Thank you, Caldwell." Endersby was surprised at how calm his voice sounded. "Now, Constable, what have you to say?"

"Beg your pardon, sir. Most urgent, Inspector. Fleet Lane has instructed me to accompany you to the site described by your sergeant-at-hand. A matron murdered. And a child, sir, who I found by chance by the workhouse gate."

"Another child?" Endersby shivered. He was haunted by the

loss of children. His mind flew to the little grave where his son, Robert, lay. *A child once again, abandoned, left as good as dead,* he thought. *Time and tide wait for no man.* Evil was gaining the upper hand. Endersby took but one instant to contract his brow, to concentrate on the sordid information he had been given. He turned to address Sergeant Caldwell.

"Sergeant, the coroner will soon convene his jury and ask for witnesses. This workhouse will be topsy-turvy for a time but the magistrate will want as many clues as we have." Endersby hunted in his satchel, pulled out the envelope holding the piece of lace and handed it to Sergeant Caldwell. "As befits your rank, sir, as Detective Sergeant of Capital Crime for the Metropolitan, I charge you to stand as my representative before the coroner."

"Yes, sir." Caldwell immediately jumped to attention as if he were about to lead a charge of men into battle.

"Be wary, sir," Endersby then said, pulling Caldwell aside. "Listen carefully to all witnesses. Copy down any wavering from the truth — such as it is — that the staff here might indulge in. Present the lace. The surgeon will pronounce strangulation. If commanded, tell of the entry by coal chute. That should be sufficient to have a verdict for us to continue. I will tell you later what other clues — such as they are — have been afforded me by my interview with the child. The coroner, most likely, will have no need or show any interest *as yet* in her words."

"I shall be diligent," answered Caldwell.

"This bodes some strange eruption to our state," mumbled Endersby.

"Sir?" said Caldwell, his shoulders held back.

"At ease, Sergeant. *Hamlet* once again. To your duty. We shall meet again today at Fleet Lane Station House. Let us say past noon or one o'clock."

"Certainly, sir," Caldwell said, and headed toward the staircase.

"Now, young constable, we have dire duties before us," Endersby said, closing his satchel, straightening his hat, and indicating to the young recruit to lead on. The young man went forward and led Endersby out to the yard of St. Giles. Presently, in a rushing hansom cab, Endersby's confusion lay somewhat abated even if his mind kept conflating clues and fears. With a second murder to be investigated, he reminded himself of Peel's Sixth Principle to "exercise persuasion, advice, and warning." As a professional detective he knew he must find proof rather than issue arrests on mere hearsay. And yet, how might he confront two such similar crimes happening in one night? He had to act quickly. He must not hesitate. He felt he was being chased by an ugly troll about to strangle him, an old memory from his boyhood that rose in his imagination as he pitied the second matron lying dead in Shoe Lane. He asked the constable to explain who he was and what had happened.

"I'm a night watch constable, Colby, sir, responsible for Shoe Lane to Fleet Street and eastward to St. Paul's. Early this morning, just before dawn, a gentleman from the Shoe Lane House of Correction approached me and requested I come to view a most unfortunate sight. A matron strangled in her parlour, a bit of cloth choked in her mouth."

"Recall the cloth, Constable. Anything peculiar about it — shape, colour?"

"Sir, not to put too fine a point upon it, I reckon on inspection it seemed to be but a snag of old lace."

"Indeed," Endersby replied.

"And, sir, if I have your permission, I must recall, as well, a most horrific detail."

"Granted," Endersby said, curtly.

"The victim's neck, sir, was bruised: a dark thick bruise. Given the toppled state of the victim — in her chair, sir, lying back on the floor — I had the opportunity to imagine that she may have been strangled, sir, with a rope or some such item."

"Most astute, Constable."

The hansom pulled into a narrow yard in which there was a building of dark stone so similar to St. .Giles that one could conclude they were of the same lineage."Before we descend, Constable, one final preliminary," Endersby said. "Tell me of the child."

"Little to tell, sir. In my view, a most peculiar happenstance. On my way to alert constables and a surgeon at Fleet Lane Station House, I saw crouched in a doorway a young female dressed in the muslin worn by the wards of Shoe Lane. To be precise, she appeared unharmed. She had fallen asleep and was cold. On closer inspection, I noted she was light-haired, no more than ten years old. I brought her back to Shoe Lane whereupon the head Matron took her away."

"Most curious," replied Endersby. Under his professional politeness Endersby felt a deep fear. A copy cat incident? One man trawling the workhouses of London to kill at random? And the abandoned girls?

"Anything else, sir?"

"Let us both keep our eyes open and our ears cocked, Constable. I will treat you, if I may, as a second set of my own senses. To verify what I see and hear. Are you agreed, sir?"

"Most respectfully, sir. I am agreed," the constable replied. While the recruit helped the inspector climb down from the hansom, Endersby's gouty foot pinched him hard. Entering the grand portal, the inspector noted immediately a different atmosphere from St. Giles. Doors were slamming, voices shouting, people rushing by. "Pandemonium, Constable," Endersby exclaimed, walking toward a large door that had just opened. In a room full of chairs, a cluster of men and women stood huddled like cattle in the rain. "Holla!" the inspector shouted. The fumbling crowd froze. A master approached, his hands shaking. Endersby quickly introduced himself and the constable. Like hungry dogs to a tossed bone, the others scrambled up to the inspector and began barking out their stories. Questions flew: who did this? Why our matron? Is the child dead or alive? "Ladies and gentlemen, I ask you to *sit down*," Endersby commanded.

The inspector began his questioning. After a time, he sent the young constable to inspect the coal chute. He then singled out the head master and ordered the others to return to their duties. Endersby viewed the victim, who had been placed conveniently on a pallet next to the female ward. What astonished Endersby were the similarities between this murder and the one he had just investigated not seven streets away in St. Giles. The magnifying glass revealed a bruise. And there were tiny bits of metal rust and a length of the same lace.

Why lace? Endersby asked himself again. He took the sample, opened his satchel and placed the lace in an envelope. While doing so, he listened as the master confirmed that no one had witnessed nor heard the crime being committed. "It was I who found her," he explained, describing his discovery of the body during his morning round. Tracing the footsteps of sooty coal dust that led from the parlour into the corridor, Endersby remarked on their shape and state of preservation.

"Master," Endersby then said. "Will you allow me to speak to any of the children? Those who are calm enough to tell me stories?" The master hesitated. He appeared so distracted it was as if the inspector's words had been uttered in a foreign tongue. A woman appeared and asked the master to come upstairs, so

Endersby decided he could no longer wait for permission. He would have to act before pertinent evidence was destroyed. The girls of the only open ward, the one next to the parlour where the body lay, were restless and agitated as he questioned them — some claiming to have heard a man whispering in the night, one certain it was her dead father come to rescue her. He asked if any one of their rank was missing. On asking once again about the intruder, most heads shook.

"He surely stinks," one child said, her voice hoarse from shouting.

"Did you see him?" Endersby asked, hoping for a description.

"No, sir," came the reply. "My head was under my pillow."

All the girls said they had hidden their faces. *Dark figures are the bane of childhood*, thought Endersby as he thanked the crowd. Here in Shoe Lane there were fewer than twenty females, the oldest perhaps eleven years, skeletal reminders of the injustice of the metropolis. Endersby clenched his fists. These shadows of children had become targets of a roving killer.

A round, squat woman appeared in a white bonnet. "A most horrible deed; I am struck to the marrow with fear." The matron curtsied.

"The found child, Matron. I wish to see her, if I may."

Endersby followed her out the front portal while she explained that the child was being tended in the kitchen at the back of the House of Correction. Sudden spring rain fell lightly. As Endersby adjusted his broad-brimmed hat and his suede gloves, his mind took on the task of preparing questions. Up to this point, no one had mentioned the child's name. He tapped the matron on her shoulder to ask but, as he reached out, she sprinted ahead through the kitchen door and announced the presence of a detective policeman.

An older woman stood up and turned to Endersby. "I am

Matron Bickerstaff. We thank you, Detective, for your attention this morning." Without further hesitation, this matron clapped her hands. A door leading to a second chamber opened to show a large fireplace with a roaring fire. Beside it was positioned a large copper tub. Through the doorway, Endersby watched as two women took hold of a child and led her before the hearth. A dripping bed sheet was held up before the flames. Matron Bickerstaff entered the room, undressed the shaking child and wrapped the now steaming bed sheet around the child's skeletal body. Endersby stood amazed at this spectacle of charity. Once the child was dried, she sat in a chair by the fire where she was joined by Endersby and Matron Bickerstaff. "I am Inspector Owen Endersby of the Metropolitan Detective Police. Allow me, Matron, to speak with the child."

The girl held her arms tight to her sides. Endersby sensed the child might be too exhausted, too shaken, to speak freely. Children in workhouses, he knew, were so often brutalized that they cowered into silence. Feeling her discomfort, Endersby dipped his hand into his pocket and brought out the tin of his wife's candied chestnuts. "Would you care for one, Miss?" he said, politely offering the tin as if the girl were a woman of his social rank. He flipped open the top. The child's eyes widened. "These confections were made by my wife. They are very sugary. My favourites." Without hesitation, the child took one, bit into it, and then took another in her other hand. Endersby offered one to Matron Bickerstaff who chose a large glistening chestnut the size of a sovereign coin. She then cautioned the child to speak honestly to all the questions the inspector might ask.

"Good morning, child," Inspector Endersby began, chewing. The child bowed her head: "Good morning, sir."

"Have you ever stepped out of Shoe Lane before, on your own, where you found yourself in the street?"

The girl raised her eyes toward the matron who in turn lifted her eyebrows.

"Once before, sir. Only once with Annie, sir."

"And what did you and Annie find on your outing in the street?"

The child's face brightened.

"A hurdy-gurdy man, sir," she said, her voice bursting forth from her sunken little chest. "'Twas the only time, sir," she whispered. Endersby leaned forward: "Did you see a hurdy-gurdy man last night, then?"

The child shivered a little and said, "No, sir."

"Then tell me, young one ..."

"My name be Catherine, sir," the girl proclaimed with sudden pride. "My dead mammy gives me that name. And not Cath-er-INE, but Cath-er-IN!"

"Indeed," replied Endersby, his gaze taking on a more serious aspect. Young Catherine had blue eyes, her blonde hair was cut short. "Then, Miss Catherine, tell me how you got out of your bed and onto the street last night?"

"I didn't 'got,' sir. I was taken." The matron quickly looked toward Inspector Endersby. "Taken?"

"A ghost, sir."

"Astonishing, Miss Catherine. You have acquaintance with ghosts?"

"Oh, no sir. But one. He came in last night. I knows about ghosts 'cause me and Annie always tells the stories."

"Did you *see* him, Miss Catherine? What did he look like?"

"I hears him. He tiptoes up and down. He has a stink like a ghost — all dead smell."

"Catherine," the Matron interrupted. "The plain truth."

The girl bowed her head. The inspector waited, but she seemed hesitant now to continue. Endersby took out his handkerchief, folded it in half and handed it to the sullen child. She took it but did not look at it. "If he were here now, Miss Catherine," Endersby whispered, "put my handkerchief over your nose. He must smell if you say he did."

Catherine slapped the handkerchief to her face. She pulled it off quickly and smiled. "He did so stinks, sir." The inspector then learned how Miss Catherine was whispered to in the dark — just her name.

"He called you Catherine?" Endersby asked, to make sure. The girl bowed her head. "Sweet, he calls me, too," she said. "Catherine," the inspector asked, leaning in close as if he were about to share a secret. "Did your ghost tell you his name?" The girl blinked. She blushed: "Knuckle Toe." The sound of these two words were broken by her embarrassed laughter. Endersby said: "Knuckle Toe?" The child responded with a quick nod. Endersby reminded himself that both Catherines had been wakened in the dark. What they heard was so unfamiliar they perhaps confused dream and reality.

"You are very helpful, Catherine." Endersby then asked if she'd seen the man's face.

"Wot a terrible face he has. A big worm runs across it."

"Show me, Miss Catherine. Draw out with your finger," said Endersby, intrigued.

The girl puckered her face in disgust and then reluctantly drew a line across her right cheek, over her nose and up under her left eye.

"Did the man say anything else to you? Did he give you anything?"

"No, sir. He said me name again. 'Catherine, Catherine,' over and over like he forgets it."

"Did he take you anywhere?"

"In the courtyard. Then he runs off, like he's a scaredy scaredy."

The inspector opened his candy tin and offered another to Catherine. "One fer Annie, too?" she asked.

"Most certainly."

Moments later the girl was led from the chamber and Matron Bickerstaff invited Endersby to view the body once again. "The coroner and surgeon will have to inspect this sad woman, as you may know," the inspector explained. "It is common procedure before a verdict on cause of death is announced." The matron could not look long at the corpse's contorted face. She told Endersby she knew the woman well enough, that she was partly blind, but that she had a gentle hand, much like her own, and did not punish her wards like the masters did the boys. Endersby asked about the victim's friends and enemies, but like Miss Matty in St. Giles, the victim had preferred her own company. After looking again at the bruised neck, Endersby pulled out the envelope containing the found piece of lace.

"Curious, Matron, this lace. It appears to be of the same cloth as the fragment found on the victim at St. Giles, where a similar incident occurred last night."

"May I look at it closely, sir?"

Endersby spread the lace on a table. Matron Bickerstaff examined it, holding her hands to her sides so as not to touch a weapon of death.

"If I may, I could be of some assistance, Inspector."

The woman proceeded to tell him that as head matron she had the responsibility to provide clothing and shoes for the female inmates. Her parish stipend was small and so she frequented the second-hand clothing and cloth markets in Rosemary Lane. "In the Lane there is a seller of second-hand lace. All types and shapes. Some old, many well kept and affordable. I believe there may be other lace sellers in Monmouth Street but since lace does not sell readily to the poor, it is not a popular item for profit."

"This segment here is lace for curtains or drapes," Endersby guessed. "It seems too coarse for dress trimming."

Matron Bickerstaff bent and looked at the thick patterns and the unrefined cotton stitches. "I agree, sir, that this is border lace for curtain windows. The man in Rosemary Lane has a stall right near the south entrance. I have seen him often. Although he looks unfortunate, having little exchange of coin for his goods, he is cheerful enough." Endersby thanked the matron for her information. "I have one other query, Matron"

Matron Bickerstaff held her gaze on Endersby's face. "I surmise that this man-*cum*-murderer is desperately looking for a child. One named specifically Catherine."

"Frightening prospect, Inspector. A damning name to have if that is the case."

"If I am correct, I ask you why this culprit does his searching at night. Could he not simply come to the front door of any workhouse and ask for a Catherine, to see her in broad daylight?"

"Only, Inspector, if he has a licence. The Poor Laws and the parish do not allow children out of our protection unless the caller be *bona fide*. This is to prevent exploitation, as you can imagine. We have frequently turned away merchants and factory owners who seem suspect to us. And we rarely, nowadays, let our children out to chimney sweeps for the work is too dangerous. I pity those who are forced into such terrible labour."

"But if one were a relative, a repentant parent searching for a child?"

"The same rule applies. A man in particular must have a reference or an affidavit as to his identity and his ability to nourish and protect a child. Females have often, in the past, been stolen — yes, from workbenches in factories or elsewhere — and taken into brothels and nanny houses to service wretches of all manner."

Endersby pondered the matron's words, then offered his thanks and bid her goodbye. What should be his first foray, he wondered? To locate a lace seller — and perhaps find a lead to the murderer's whereabouts? It was feasible the killer planned his crime and bought lace for a reason. Or, just as likely, he might have stolen or taken lace simply because it was at hand. Endersby had few clues to lead him forth. And he was not comfortable with the observations of the children, for doubt coaxed him to believe their words contained more fantasy than truth. What of the name: Uncle Bow? Knuckle Toe? And the scar, the *worm*? A frightening mark to young eyes. These thoughts bullied Endersby even as Wanton Time, as he liked to call it, pressed upon him to wait for the surgeon and the coroner.

Just before noon, the coroner arrived at Shoe Lane House of Correction and began his session. The parish officer presented summonses to a jury of peers — coal carriers, drivers, a coffee-stall keeper, two dustmen, and two cabmen, halted on their way to a fare. The coroner instructed his jury to study well the evidence: Endersby was called to display the lace, to tell of the matter of the coal chute and to draw a comparison to the murder at St. Giles. The makeshift jury, standing around the coroner in the workhouse dining room, listened to the child and adult witnesses, learned of the gaff, and then heard the surgeon's conclusions. After deliberation, a fair-minded verdict was announced and the coroner demanded Endersby to take the found items to the magistrate for recording and then proceed to seek out the responsible villain.

Out in the air after the proceedings, Endersby decided to walk the short distance from Shoe Lane across Farringdon Street into Fleet Lane Station House. What mist and damp! The streets were astir: cabs, pedestrians, ragged children running. Fleet Prison itself loomed as the inspector limped along, mindful of his gouty foot. Endersby protested his deep fear that a madman was running loose in the streets. *Why lace? What drives a man to such means? Such beasts we are as men,* he thought, reprimanding himself on his own illicit love of punching jaws.

Chapter Five
A Bit of Onion

Ten-year-old Catherine Smeets drew in a quick breath. She kept her head down. Next to her, and on both sides of the long scuffed table, girls her age frantically licked thin gruel from wooden bowls. Here, in St. Pancras Workhouse, the food was scant. In the other workhouses of London, like St. Giles two miles south, pots of porridge with a shred of meat were standard fare for the midday meal. This was not the case in St. Pancras, where a small bowl of gruel was all that was served at each meal. This moment of rest would soon be finished; all children at the tables would rise shortly at the clap of the matron's hands and march off to start the toil of the afternoon after a morning of scrubbing floors.

Catherine Smeets put down her wooden bowl. Her right hand shot out; she grabbed a second half onion from the serving platter — a treat only on Wednesdays in St. Pancras — and glanced up at Nell sitting kitty-corner on the opposite side. Nell jammed her eyes right, then left and blinked twice. Catherine slipped the bit of onion under the hem of her blue muslin shift. *For later,* she thought. *For our plan.*

Matron Pickens approached on her inspection walk. Nell tapped her right hand once. Catherine bent again over her bowl and felt Matron Pickens brush by her back, the *whish* of her birch rod cutting through the cold air.

"Girls," Matron Pickens announced, "extra for those who get all windows washed before supper. Whippings for those who dawdle or whine." Matron Pickens spoke with a scratchy throat, as if she had swallowed broken pebbles for her midday meal. Nell once said Matron Pickens was a puppet and not a human, like the Judy in the Tom Fool shows.

Now the final prayer was intoned by Master Jenkins, who was standing by the iron stove with his hat on, his hands raised up before his face. He had a ringing voice, his thanks to the parish elders and to Jesus echoing off the high stone walls of the dining ward. This afternoon the boys of St. Pancras were to be sent to chop wood for the parish. "A good day's labour, boys, meant to show you the joys of honest work," shouted Master Jenkins. Catherine never could understand how blistered hands were rewards. This same afternoon she and Nell and Little Mag were to be sent down below into the laundry to mend sheets.

Catherine Smeets slowly stood up with her mates. She still had a trace of rose in her cheeks even though she had been in St. Pancras three months, ever since her father, Sergeant Peter Smeets, had abandoned her at the front door in late December and gone off to Scotland to join his regiment. Oh, how she missed him and her mother, dead these past two years of the fever. But mostly her uncle, her mother's only brother. How brutally he was treated. How good he *tried to be* in fighting against her drunken father. But all of that life was gone. *Forever,* thought Catherine.

51

The line of girls marched to the archway and split into sections, then into groups of three and four. Matron Pickens clapped her hands. Nell, Little Mag, and Catherine scampered down the damp stone stairs into a basement of low ceilings and grimy walls. "Skip along," whispered Nell, always the boldest one. Little Mag had a shrunken left foot but she could keep up with the other two. After a moment, all three stopped and panted. Catherine's head ached. The dark corridor drew Catherine's mind back to her mother's bed, back when her uncle looked after her. He often folded her in his arms and told Catherine the story of a brave peasant girl who had rescued a child princess from a witch.

"Hurry with it," Nell now said, shaking Catherine's arm. "We'll wait by the sheet bin. If the puppet comes we'll give out a loud coughin."

From Nell's hand and from Little Mag's, Catherine took their bits of stolen onion. She pulled out the bit she had hidden at table and cupped all in her left hand. She ran swiftly to the far end of the corridor, knowing she must not dawdle. Time was always measured in seconds in the workhouse. From under one of the floor stones, Catherine pulled out a thick bundle of rags — two layers to protect and keep cool the onions, bits of hardened lard, cooked potato skins and dried apple peels.

"There, there," she whispered to the rags, folding them carefully. "You shall have good use soon enough," she said. Fearful of delay, she shoved the wad under the stone, tamped the stone down with her bare foot. She scurried back against the slimy wall into the laundry room where, to her relief, only Nell and Little Mag were sitting, their needles already threaded. Long worn sheets lay over their laps and spread onto the floor.

"Done then?" asked Nell.

"Not even a goblin could find them," whispered Catherine.

Little Mag shivered. "Me, I hate the likes of goblins. Too many of 'em for my needs."

Catherine smiled, reached over and patted Little Mag on her shoulder.

"If Matron comes, let us sit so still only our arms move," Nell said.

"She'll fart at us," Little Mag giggled.

"Dog farts," squealed all three.

Nell and Little Mag began to mend. Catherine threaded her needle and thought back to her village near Frogmore. She pictured again the bright carriage of the old princess riding up the main street and on toward her grand house. She pictured the slim figure of her dear uncle, his nose and chin so like his sister's, Catherine's sweet mother. How Catherine had loved Uncle's jokes and especially his nicknames. Her childhood nickname for him was just a simple sound and she began to whisper it to herself in time to her stitching hand.

"You dreamin'?" asked Little Mag.

"Remembering. 'Tis nothing," said Catherine. "About my darling uncle."

"Tell us the story again," asked Little Mag. Catherine put down her needle and the sheet.

"He was my mother's brother. So kind, so gentle. He told me once he had been brought up in a workhouse. A cruel place."

"No worse than this," grumped Nell, pulling at her thread.

"He found a trade, loved to read books from the village lending library. When my Poppa went off to serve in his regiment, Uncle always came to live with us. He would clean our house, cook. And always buy me things."

"He bought you a pony, didn't he?" marvelled Little Mag.

"Oh, yes. A sad little thing. He reminded me of Uncle."

"Don't be daft," sniffed Nell.

"I mean, he was gentle and quiet. Uncle liked to read by himself. One time I caught him weeping at a story he had read."

"Sounds like a soft head to me," Nell scowled, lifting up her sheet to check her stitching.

"I like the part about your mother and him," whispered Little Mag.

Catherine had to wipe her eyes before going on. "Yes, Momma always said he suffered so much, especially *inside* his head. He was too tender of feeling, she always said. He could break so easily. She saw how Uncle felt pained when Poppa teased him too much."

Matron Pickens stomped so suddenly into the laundry room the three girls jumped. She was dragging a small weeping boy behind her. "This be a weaklin'," she explained. "Master says he has the cough so cannot go choppin'. You filth here, you tend 'im. Mind, no tweakin' no gigglin'," she said, her slash of a mouth breaking into a dry chuckle. Matron Pickens marched off. The boy fell to the floor. He coughed and coughed until Catherine raised him up, dried his forehead with the hem of her shift and sat him down on a basket of soiled sheets. Nell, meantime, found a bucket and pumped it full of water. She hauled it over to the boy where Little Mag washed down his face and made him take a drink. The boy caught his breath.

"I shall always thank you," the boy said, his voice soft like the feeble blowing of a whistle. "My mother and father died in a fire," he said. Then without pause he slumped over and fell asleep on the mound of sheets.

"He'll be carried out soon," Nell said, her voice without sentiment.

"Nell, sssh," Catherine said. "He may hear you."

"Yes," said Little Mag. "Like a goblin hears you from under the floor."

"*Mend*," Nell said, hitting the other two on their wrists. "Mend, and think of our path. The open fields."

Catherine and Little Mag nodded. "I love your story," Little Mag then said in a low voice.

"Me, too," replied Catherine. "I hope Uncle is alive and well."

"To be sure," said Little Mag.

"Work on, you two," snapped Nell. The three girls bent over their sheets. The little boy moaned in his sleep as Catherine quickly pulled her thread into a steady rhythm. She let thoughts of her uncle fade as she concentrated on the day ahead.

"We got little time left in here," she then said to Nell and Little Mag.

"So we do, Catherine," Nell said, her voice full of determination. "Little time before we are free!"

On Tuesday night past, Catherine Smeets had sat alone very late, a quill in her right hand. There'd been enough fire from the hearth in the ward for her to see. Her chilly legs were spread out on the cold floor beside an inkwell and a piece of soiled paper, items allowed her by the head matron. Catherine read and wrote well for a girl of ten years: her uncle had taught her when she was four. Every Tuesday, she would write a letter. Not a real one. Not one she could actually post. It was one she composed even though she had no pennies for stamps and no address. It was always to her dear uncle, a pretend letter to him to tell him about herself, as if he were still with her, as if he were alive. Catherine remembered the terrible things done to him. The constable dragging him to the public prison cell in the village square, the bruises around his eyes from the fists and truncheons. She remembered running out in the night and handing him through the prison bars a letter she had carefully written herself. He had read it and held it to his heart and thanked her. He had put it in his pocket. "I will guard it forever," he had said. Catherine hoped one day he would read all the letters she had written to him.

Matron Pickens had once said her uncle was a convicted felon, words Catherine did not quite understand. Matron Pickens once said he had been hanged and quartered, but Catherine did not believe such nonsense. He was her only hope. She recalled seeing him in the village's courtroom standing before the man in the long grey wig. She was told her uncle was to sail away on a ship. Perhaps the ship sank, but Catherine would never allow that idea into her head. All her pretend letters she kept under her pallet mattress, wrapped in brown paper. No one touched them. Not even Matron Pickens. On this Tuesday night she wrote a short letter since she was very tired:

Dearest Uncle,

Such cold winds today. I have not much to tell! I worked in the latrines all the morning. I don't mind. Dear Mama would hate the smell. Nell says I am very strong. She is my best friend. I miss you so much, dear Uncle. You are on the sea now? Will you see elephants? Will you see strange beasts under the world? I pray for you. God will be kind! I must to bed.

Your Catherine

Chapter Six
Lardle and Co.

At this same hour in fashionable Bedford Square, a distin-
guished-looking gentleman opened up the back door to Number
Sixteen. The house was a three-storey brick affair with an iron
gate and silk curtains at the windows. Number Sixteen lay a
world away from Drury Lane, where the St. Giles Workhouse
stood in early afternoon gloom. The gentleman's name was
Josiah Benton, a physician and regular church-goer. He had not
slept the whole night. He looked again at the clock in the hall
behind him. "Where in blazes is the filthy man?" he mumured
to himself. He felt a constriction in his throat. He brushed down
his velvet waistcoat, his front pocket stuffed with coins ready to
pay his hireling, Mr. Lardle, if the wretch would ever return from
his search.

Dr. Josiah Benton was a proud man, highly respected for his
accurate diagnoses of his patients' symptoms. Today, like all others in his work week, he had to ready himself for the exigencies
of his surgery. No doubt, given his restless night, he would have

to fill his stomach with coffee to keep his mind alert. A solitary gentleman one year short of forty, he had enjoyed being the son of a wealthy father and had learned much from his fine education; he had taken full advantage of his youthful travels, relishing the pleasures of drink and rich food. Fortunate he had been, but he was plagued these days by a pervading loneliness ever since his wife had decided to leave him two years before. Dear Dorothea. She had accused him of unnatural appetites, a phrase which frequently had amused Dr. Benton. For without doubt, Josiah Benton was a man of peculiar passions. He frequently gave in to his penchant for secret games — behaviour which his wife argued had undermined *her* notions of a proper marriage.

The one true tragedy in Dr. Benton's life was his lack of children. Dorothea had been barren. The absence of offspring had been another motive in the dissolution of their marriage.

"Ah, dear little ones," Dr. Benton now sighed, the chilly air catching his breath. Pushing thoughts of his wife from his mind, Dr. Benton stepped back inside Number Sixteen. He went downstairs to the area kitchen in the basement where his cook was preparing his lunch. This sudden change of venue lifted his spirits. He nodded to Mrs. Wells, then walked up the servants' stairs into his surgery and looked through the list of patients he was to greet within the hour. His was a thin, well-formed body, carefully nourished except for the occasional glass of sherry and a monthly visit, incognito, to one of the opium houses in Soho. He brushed his waistcoat again, then with sudden delight marched out of his panelled office. He had heard, at last, the light tapping on the back door.

"No need," he said to his eager butler who was rushing to raise the latch. "I shall attend," Dr. Benton said. In fact, he *must* attend, given the business at hand. Of course, the hour was too late now for him to take advantage. If in fact the scum man had been able to do his duty. Often, the man arrived empty-handed. All Dr. Benton knew of him was that he was poor, and was once an orphan brought up in a workhouse. Pulling open the back door, the doctor viewed his hireling.

"The hour, Mr. Lardle," scolded Dr. Benton. "I have been up all the night. I must to my surgery soon."

The bedraggled fellow bowed his head in reply. He wore long unwashed hair; his face was masked by a poorly kept beard; a large black hat — a dredgerman's hat, the doctor surmised — covered much of his face, and if truth be told, he so often arrived in the dark that Dr. Benton had never had opportunity to look long or close enough at the man's rough features. This morning his hands were smudged. To the doctor's eye they suggested Lardle had been washing in coal dust. As always, the man had a stink; more likely his rotten teeth or his unwashed torso, Dr. Benton concluded.

"Nought to yer taste, Doctor Benton." Lardle's head hung low, his face shadowed by his hat.

"What in blazes do you mean? None on the streets, by the bridges?"

" Fled, sir. Dashed away when I comes close."

"Donkey," the doctor retorted. "You've smashed your knuckles?"

"Yes, sir. All night I been up and down, in and out. Searched every which ways, I did. Found two but not right they were, sir. Not for you. Scarred one of 'em was, not right. Not a fit, sir."

"And the nanny houses?"

"As I been tellin' you, sir, they keep 'em indoors. Up the stairs. *You* must go to 'em."

"How many times have I told you, Lardle, that is impossible."

"Yes, sir," said the man in a hoarse whisper.

"I suppose you want coin for your trouble tonight?"

"If it be no bother, sir," replied the man, trembling in the afternoon drizzle. "And if yer wishes it, I found one last minute, near Covent Garden." The dirty man raised his left hand and pointed to the brick archway leading into the courtyard of Dr. Benton's private lot. A woman in a bonnet, a face soured by poverty and illness. Damp feathers in her bonnet, hands gloved in shredded muslin.

"You are a mad dog," snapped Dr. Benton. "Why bring me a scull, sir?"

Mr. Lardle signalled to the woman with his hand. She stepped forward and pulled with her a short, light-haired girl, no older than thirteen, thin, rouged, her tattered dress made of blue cotton. "Says her daughter is a good 'un, sir. Makes her mum a few coin a day for food. Been at it a couple o' years now."

"Good God, Lardle."

Dr. Benton stepped into the courtyard, waving the two figures to go back under the arch. He surveyed the upper and lower windows of his house to be sure there were no gawking house maids peering down at his doings. In the dimness of the archway, Dr. Benton examined the face of the young girl. She had been pretty but life had already hardened her face and taken two of her front teeth. The girl's mother stretched out her hand. "For my trouble, guvnor, if you'd be so pleased."

"Come here," Dr. Benton called to Mr. Lardle, who came hobbling over to the archway.

"Never humiliate me nor women of this ilk ever again, Lardle, and never at this daylight hour. You know what I want. You have done it before. When you search, you must put effort into it. Pay these pathetic creatures and then get yourself off to home."

"But sir," Lardle said, "I ain't got but tuppence."

Dr. Josiah Benton grasped the coins in his pocket and tossed them toward the man. "Take these and go away," he commanded before turning and moving back toward his back door. As he entered the house, Dr. Benton could hear the two street females giggling in a mocking fashion as they bent down to grasp the coins. "Come away, come away," Mr. Lardle growled at the two of them. From the kitchen window, Dr. Benton watched them go and gave out a sigh of relief. He despised the tone his voice had taken, but it was the only way to deal with such people. Mr. Lardle most times could be trusted to be discrete. As long as he was paid.

"Sir?" said a female voice behind him. Dr. Benton turned to see his cook holding a wooden spoon.

"Your luncheon, sir, is ready," she said.

"Good," snapped Dr. Benton.

The woman gave a quick curtsey as Dr. Josiah Benton made his way toward the dining room. Sitting down alone, he said grace. An ache of despair filled his chest; such disappointment after his night vigil. "Now what to do?" he asked himself. "How desperate must I become? What must I do to find another?" he whispered, his mind full of doubt.

Chapter Seven
A Coincidence of Catherines

Inspector Owen Endersby's first words on meeting Sergeant Caldwell at Fleet Lane Station House were precise. "We have before us, sir, a coincidence of Catherines."

The two men shook hands as professional gentlemen and stepped inside the arched portal of the station. From within came the sounds of men's voices. Doors were opened and shut, but the sense of calm that pervaded the halls relieved Endersby after the panic and clamour in Shoe Lane. Caldwell had arrived at five minutes past one with the look of a man who needed a mug of beer. However, the business of the investigation was of greater importance for the moment and so his sergeant listened, eyes wide with disbelief, to what Endersby told of the murder in Shoe Lane, the coroner's session, and the frightening comparisons to the crime in St. Giles.

"There is a pattern, I fear, Caldwell, which presages a repetition of this foul act."

"So it seems, sir," Caldwell replied, his face showing

concern. Endersby ruminated for a second then turned again to his sergeant-at-hand.

"We must assume both our Catherines were carried out of the workhouse to afford the villain time to look more closely into their faces. What he found was not suitable to his purpose."

Caldwell then said: "But how can we alert all of London? Workhouses abound, as do the houses of correction."

"Sergeant, 'this sore task will not divide the Sunday from the week.' Mr. Hamlet, once again, Caldwell. There is much we must do! We shall set a strategy. First, we need to convince Superintendent Borne of its necessity."

"Can we conclude a motive, sir?"

"Well, Sergeant, I have come to think the villain not only wants to find a singular child, but that his two murders — so far — may be a sign, a signature act, in the same manner as a name written on paper. These two murders show us a planning mind."

Sergeant Caldwell pondered these words in silence while around him and his superior the halls of the station house continued to echo.

"To protect the innocent, Caldwell, I suggest we first mark out the locations of all the workhouses within walking distance of St. Giles and Shoe Lane and give them warning. I assume our villain is poor, lacking the means to travel too far, and he appears to have a halting limp. If he uses logic and if he has such intimate acquaintance with institutions of this kind, he might strike others in the most convenient fashion."

"It does seem likely, sir."

"Therefore, let us anticipate the monster. Sergeant, go into our registry of addresses within southern Finsbury district. We can draw out a circle of possible next 'hits.' Visit each institution and check the ledgers! The workhouses are required by law to record births and deaths and other pertinent business. Most certain, the first names of the males and females will be noted down. We cannot eliminate, however, a workhouse where the name of Catherine is *not* recorded. But we can warn matrons to be vigilant. When and if we find more Catherines, we must speak with each child as soon as possible."

"It is, sir, an uncommon name for the times. I have a question."

"Certainly, Sergeant." By this time, Endersby and Caldwell had strolled into the inner courtyard of Fleet Lane Station House. It was a narrow enclosure inside what was centuries ago a medieval fortress. "Might our villain," Caldwell asked, "become desperate enough to strike during daylight hours?"

"Might he, indeed, Sergeant? Which would mean he may still be out in the streets, gaff in hand. With the workhouses opening their doors for deliveries of coal and food — it may be possible. We need to act with great speed." Endersby's mind began constructing mental bridges going here and there. Walking farther on, their hands held behind their backs, the two men circled in unison the perimeter of the courtyard. The smell of London wafted into the courtyard — sewer stink and the usual pungent odour of the Thames.

"Caldwell," said Endersby after a moment of meditation. "One final thought: have the workhouse masters lock down the coal chutes — no matter what exception may be raised. I will ask Superintendent Borne to allow us two constables to go around with you to warn other houses of the danger. Needless to say we must alert station houses and our seven other detective branches in all constabularies. A description of the murderer most certainly will be helpful."

"And capture, sir? How will untrained workhouse employees tackle the villain if the occasion arises?"

"Ah, Sergeant, what a question. Will these parish folk believe us enough to gather men, station them, arm them?" Endersby stopped then started again.

"You and the other constables must use strong persuasion. Describe the manner of death. Go to the parish offices and demand cooperation. I shall instruct the other detective branches to alert their night constables and have each check workhouse yards more frequently on the assigned routes." Inspector Endersby wiped his brow with a handkerchief. The pitiful memory of the two dead matrons had returned to his mind for the moment. But he felt sure he and Caldwell had begun a valid search.

"Let us hope, Caldwell, our detection methods will bear fruit," Endersby said at last.

"Indeed, sir."

"Any peculiarities at the coroner's session in St. Giles?"

"No, sir. The jury was most efficient in declaring murder. With your permission, I shall inspect the holding chambers here in this station. Street arrests from last night. Perhaps we have been fortunate with a capture."

"What a wish," Endersby said, raising his eyebrows. "I suggest you do so, Sergeant. And with haste. I, in the meantime, shall permit myself the pleasure of requesting the impossible from Superintendent Borne. As Prince Hamlet might utter, I shall endeavour to prove 'the pith and marrow of our attribute.'"

Endersby straightened his hat and took in a deep breath. "Onward, Sergeant." The two men shook hands and parted. Climbing a cramped staircase, Endersby came into the central rooms of the station house. Moving on, he crossed a hallway and stopped in front of a door on which brass letters spelling SUPERINTENDENT were attached by small nails. From under the door came the delicious smell of cooked food. Borne was taking lunch. In spite of the resistance his superintendent would present, the matter of murder must take priority. Endersby clenched his fist and knocked.

***

"Yes, no doubt. Just so," responded Superintendent Borne.

A scrawny man dressed in poorly tailored wool and affecting a vain-glorious gaze, Borne displayed his usual impatience during Endersby's report on the workhouse murders. "A gaff and lace? Yes, yes." Borne had worked his way up diligently from constable to appointed bureaucrat. He was efficient, mindful of his rank, often cantankerous. Endersby believed he was a man who paid scant attention to daily police work except when his budgets ran over limit. Endersby also knew Borne to be arrogant and unreasonable. He was an old-fashioned authoritarian trained by the Bow Street Runners. He showed little respect for the "new" detective branch, which in his mind wasted too much time searching rather than questioning miscreants. Justice, he always argued, must be hard, immediate, to strike fear in the public and thus deter the criminal mentality. "Sir Robert Peel," he said once to Endersby, "is too much the reformer and not enough the law enforcer."

With this knowledge of Borne in mind, Endersby decided to try a less aggressive approach in the hopes that his superintendent would be moved. Endersby explained his strategy. He asked Borne to grant him the time, the funds, and manpower to investigate the murders.

"This is a simple matter, Inspector. Install better locks. No further attacks can occur. The villain will disappear." Borne sat down at his desk and shot a disgruntled glance at the plate of cooling food he'd barely started.

"Our victims are blameless women and children, sir," said

Endersby, a plea under each breath. "This devil will do anything."

"Supposition, Inspector. We are discussing the problem of a
coal chute. Nothing more."

Endersby felt a tremor. His "demon familiar" stirred and
he knew he must suppress it. Shifting his feet, taking in a
breath, he removed any hint of a scowl from his face. In reaction, Superintendent Borne pinched his mouth. Borne stood up
and slid his right hand into the front of his frock coat as if he
were Napoleon Bonaparte about to give a command: "Inspector
Endersby, may I remind you that these people — the children
and their female guardians — are of the lower orders. The irre-
sponsible laggards of our society. We place them in workhouses
for their own good. The poor kill their own kind, sir; they breed
and abandon their offspring. We can show pity, but to devote a
man of your rank to an investigation of this kind is a waste of
time and coin."

Inspector Endersby clenched both his gloved fists. His hat
dropped to the floor. Borne stepped from the behind the desk.
He was about to speak when Endersby interrupted:

"With due respect, sir, the members of the lower orders are
Christians, as are you and I. We cannot relinquish our bonds
of human brotherhood when the killing of innocent women —
women with souls, sir — has taken place. Our noble sovereign
has but recently given birth to her first child and she has stated,
in her joy, that *all* her subjects are equally beloved of her as is her
infant, the Princess Royal, Victoria. Likewise, we men of the law
must extend our protection to all. We cannot allow prejudice to
rule our conduct."

Endersby had countered Borne's obstinacy on several occasions with allusions to persons of higher social standing, be they
the Queen or an admiral of the imperial navy. Borne removed

his hand from his frock coat. He sniffed, looked down at his shoes, then stared Inspector Endersby straight in the eye:

"Inspector, I find your remarks impertinent. Perhaps you have misunderstood the meaning of my words. Our prime minister and founder of our detective police, Sir Robert Peel, has wisely stated our mission is to *prevent* crime and disorder. By finding the simplest way to do this shall result in greater trust and safety for *all*."

Not to be out-maneuvered, Inspector Endersby formed a quick reply: "With due respect to you and to Sir Robert, our founder also stated that to preserve public favour we police must demonstrate absolute impartial service to the law. A murder has been committed; the law requires action. It is for this reason alone..."

"Inspector, please," Borne said, his face reddening. "I am quite capable of quoting Sir Robert's nine principles. And I can see that if we continue in this manner, I shall not have the luxury of finishing my meal."

Endersby did not move. Superintendent Borne sat down again. He picked up his fork and took hold of his cloth napkin. Endersby folded his hands together. He spoke in a flat manner as if he were defeated and was willing to succumb to Borne's dismissive manner: "What, then, sir, might be your suggestion in handling this matter?"

"Surely, Inspector, that is what your keen mind must conjure on its own. I have given my opinion. Do you wish me to issue an order? Please be advised, sir, our city has over eight hundred constables and at least twenty well-paid detective inspectors like you. We have a roster of crimes to investigate. I suggest you consider delegating duties and, if you wish, you may appoint two constables at most to give you aid. I can see no other recourse. But once better locks are secured in workhouse institutions, I reckon the murders will cease."

"Most just of you, sir," was Endersby's quiet response. Somehow without losing face, Borne had managed to recognize the severity of the situation Endersby had presented to him not minutes before.

"We have your permission, then, to proceed, sir?"

"Search and capture, Inspector." Borne's voice was without enthusiasm. He then pronounced: "You have much to do, sir. I want facts, conclusions and arrests."

"Thank you, sir. We already have some clues to lead us."

"You make your duties sound like a child's game, Inspector. How clever. I grant a three day subsidy only for the workhouse matter. If, as you say, you have clues, follow them with speed. And warn the houses of the need to lock their coal chutes." These last few words of Borne's were accompanied by a mocking chuckle.

"Report Monday next, Inspector," Borne added. "Haste and dispatch."

With simultaneous gestures, Endersby retrieved his hat from the floor while Borne snatched up his dinner knife and began to slice his pork cutlet. In the corridor outside of Borne's office, Endersby tapped his large stomach and then wrung his gloved hands: "Ledgers and new locks!" he said with some glee. Endersby pulled down his hat and when he stepped into the courtyard, Sergeant Caldwell was waiting.

"Any culprits in the cells, Sergeant?" Endersby asked.

"Only two women, sir, a lad, and a drunken man. No scar, no fearful faces, sir."

"Come then, follow me, Sergeant."

Hobbling a little with his gouty foot, the inspector mounted the steps to the first floor and entered a large window-bright room. A gathering of constables and other sergeants stood at attention.

"Gentlemen of the law, I wish you a good afternoon," said Inspector Endersby as he lifted off his hat and pulled off his suede gloves. "Before I begin, may I remind you all as members of the Metropolitan Police Force what our purpose is as public servants. We have before us an unusual crime. We are to perform our duties dependent upon the public approval of our actions. Unlike our French compatriots abroad, we do not use fear or the ways of the military to mete out justice. You and I are not judges or hangmen; we are instead guardians of the peace." The men stomped their boots in agreement.

"I desire, gentlemen, your strict attention to my proposal." One of the desk sergeants took up pen and paper. Endersby instructed Caldwell to take a stand in the middle of the room. "Kindly describe the murderer, Sergeant," commanded Endersby. "Use only the details based on what has been learned from the witnesses." Caldwell began his profile, starting with a description of the culprit's overall appearance, elaborating afterward the remarkable facets which had impressed the young Catherines.

"A singular villain," added Endersby. "Now, gentlemen. Write out copies of this verbal picture of the murderer-suspect and have a copy delivered to each of the station houses in quadrants north and south of St. Paul's. The villain, we surmise, will most likely strike again in the area near St. Giles, but have all detective branches alerted and warn constables to keep sharp eyes on anyone who resembles the man — his limp, beard, scar, and the weapons he carries."

"Yes, sir," was the resounding response, spoken in unison. Endersby thanked them; he subsequently commanded the station sergeant to release two constables on day duties to accompany Mr. Caldwell on this most demanding mission. Within moments, two young men appeared in full constable wear — black stovepipe hats, white leather gloves and navy blue jackets.

"Mr. Rance, sir," said the first one, tall, lean, dark-haired.

"Mr. Tibald, sir," said the other, equally as tall, sloped-shouldered and light-haired.

"We can forestall the cruel murder of another unfortunate. If our logic is correct," Endersby concluded after explaining to his new recruits the strategy for the afternoon. The men had adjourned to a vacant office where on the wall attached, by tacks, was a large map of London. "Look gentlemen," Endersby began. "Do you see the circle?" The inspector's right hand drew a line from St.Giles, along Holborn, to Shoe Lane. "In this quadrant of London," he explained, "the city has erected six workhouses built to a standard with wards, some for children or prostitutes, others for destitute families and bachelors. I believe our searcher has begun his hunt in this area first — and that he will follow this circle, if he can, from Shoe Lane over to Wych Street, north again toward St. Giles and the Seven Dials, then again along Holborn where he may end at the Foundling Hospital. This is a poor, hobbled man," Endersby reminded his three law men. "He must travel by foot — and slowly — given a noticeable limp described by one of our witnesses. I conjecture he will investigate any one of these places tonight and the next, if he has not done so already. He may murder as well as search for his Catherine if last night's crimes are an indication of his method."

The two constables studied the map and turned to Sergeant Caldwell for instruction as to which one of the three of them would tackle the various workhouses. Caldwell outlined his agenda before Endersby stepped in to give his final words. "And, gentleman, be sure to ask questions. Ask of the masters and matrons if any similar action has taken place within the last month — in terms of break-ins. Enquire as to the appearance of any man or woman who has deposited a female child at any one of these workhouses in the past six months. Do not forget the

Foundling Hospital near Mecklenburg Square. Young girls are often left there, despite the lack of funds needed to secure them a bed."

Sergeant Caldwell, Constable Rance, and Constable Tibald followed the inspector through the courtyards and out into the street.

"Until nine o'clock this coming evening, then, sir?" Caldwell asked.

"At the coffee house across the way. All three of you. Sharp."

Endersby's gaze subsequently turned eastward. Sound sleep would evade his next few nights as it was his habit to ponder as much as he could, given the clues he had gathered. "A tight puzzle," he said to himself. He walked a few paces remembering the word, UNKELBOW, written out by the mute Catherine; if this clue meant the culprit had called out "Uncle Bow" then it followed that the child could have recognized him as *familiar*. This explained one peculiarity in the case: the two Catherines — so far — had been abandoned because neither child had *known* the intruder. With this thought in mind, Inspector Endersby immediately hailed a passing hansom cab.

"To Rosemary Lane."

Chapter Eight
A Burden Indeed

It is not unusual in the great city of London to find, in a respectable family, one offspring who has somehow ignored the blessings of a good upbringing. This certainly was the case between Mr. Richard Grimsby, undertaker, and his youngest child — his only son — Geoffrey. In many particulars, father and son mirrored each other. The father had black hair (still), a large nose, high cheekbones and pinched eyes; likewise the son, with the exception that his younger eyes were pinched out of spite rather than age and experience. Mr. Richard Grimsby was proud of his accomplishments; Master Geoffrey was simply proud.

In their greater differences, chief among them lay in movement and appearance. Old Grimsby, as he was often called by his neighbours, skipped when he walked, his calves strong and well-exercised from years of morning walks. At sixty-three, his face brimmed with colour, his skin remained smooth from daily scrubbing, his chin, in particular, held firm against any fashionable addition of hair. Young Grimsby, on the other hand, sauntered; although only twenty-seven years old, his gait was hampered by a weak ankle obtained from a fall down the stairs of a gin house. Indeed, he limped. Most mornings, and lately most afternoons as well, his cheeks and forehead took on the colour of soured milk; and not two months ago, in defiance of his father's wishes, young Geoffrey permitted his chin to sport a bushy beard, often left untrimmed.

And, of course, there was the younger Grimsby's scar.

"An accident," explained Old Grimsby when anyone enquired. "A boy's game at school — a rapier, I believe — Geoffrey's lack of attention to the sport at the moment of his playing."

"A broken branch catching the face out riding" were the words young Geoffrey used. The scar drew great attention because of its length. It looked very much as if the sharpened point of a Toledo blade had cut across the right cheek, run over the nose and halted just under the left eye. Some women of Geoffrey's age — much to his delight — claimed they found the scar attractive. Frequently, they asked to run their fingers over it, their eyes bright with delighted horror at its shape and colour. Curiously enough, young Geoffrey Grimsby was well known in Marylebone for his scar, if not for much else. And without doubt he told its story to gain female sympathy and free glasses of gin.

Now on this damp March morning in Marylebone, one street west of Bedford Square, the older Grimsby sat at his dining room table. He blew on his tea in a saucer while Mrs. Grimsby, his wife and opponent for thirty-five years, clashed the hearth irons, mumbling to herself as to where the younger Grimsby had disappeared on this most busy, upcoming day.

"All the night and now all the morning," Mrs. Grimsby repeated. "Gone, flown away like last January's snow. What shall we do, Mr. Grimsby? Two funerals, at half three, then at half four, and no bill set out, and our mute boy ill and absent from duty. We are too old to manage all of this ourselves, too old, too much in need of a thoughtful child to lift our burden."

"*Lift*, my good wife? I fear that occasion will never come to pass."

Below the dining parlour, in the entrance hall, there was sudden noise. A banging, a bumping. A door slamming, a voice snarling a profanity. Mrs. Grimsby went to the head of the stairs. The undertaker and his family lived above the shop, where coffins were made to order, shrouds sewn, and funerals orchestrated. Four black geldings were housed in the inner courtyard stable next to an ebony hearse.

"That you?" Mrs. Grimbsy hollered down the stairwell.

"No, Missus. 'Tis the 'Lord of Flies' himself."

"Where have you been, son? Your poor father and I have —"

"Father is not poor, Mammy. Not a farthing gets past his tight fist."

"Come up for your tea, son. There is much to do."

"To do? Toodle do?" A slumping sound, another profanity and a chair toppled.

"Shall I come down, Geoffrey? Shall I?"

"Mammy, leave me be." Feet stumbling up the stairs, then an appearance. Mrs. Grimsby recoiled: her only son's trousers were torn and splotched with street grime; his boots mud-speckled; his frock coat — a new purchase only last week — wrinkled with blotches of grease.

"What is this? What has happened, son?"

"Fisticuffs."

Geoffrey Grimsby's knuckles were bleeding. His beard was wild, uncombed. His ankles purpled with bruises on top of scratches. Worse, the younger Grimsby's eyes were half-shut, his breath smelled of gin, and his entire body stank of the stable.

"Where have you been, young Geoffrey?" the elder Grimsby

now asked, standing beside his wife at the top of the stairs. "He's been in a fight," Mrs. Grimsby said. "So he says."

"Young Geoffrey, clean yourself now. Get into the crepe and dark gloves. We have business to attend." The father reached out to take the son by the shoulder, but the son pulled back and started to laugh loudly, a laugh not completely dependent on the looseness of alcohol but one, instead, of a darker variety, a laugh of consequence betraying bitterness and defeat.

"Father," the son said, trying to stand at attention. "I shall take myself to my dressing chamber and not delay you nor the dead any longer." He patted his frock coat. "Milord," grunted the younger Grimsby, "I have waylaid my purse — money, cards 'n all. Dear, dear."

With these words the young Grimsby made a valiant attempt to walk forward but then, with no warning, fell flat to the floor and began to snore. Mrs. Grimsby, having leapt to her feet when her son collapsed, wiped a tear from her eye. Such continuing behaviour often inspired her to fits of weeping. But it had not always been thus. Young Geoffrey had once been such a kind and gentle man. Yes, she could admit, he'd been spoiled as a child; but once he had attained responsible adulthood he had, for the most part, been a cooperative and agreeable man to have living as a bachelor under the family roof. *What was it now,* she wondered. *Had it been only three years since he had begun to change?* He refused to confide in her after that long-ago evening when he had come home elated, filled with a joy she suspected was caused by his having met and wooed a woman of his age. He had carried the look of a smitten man in love then, the gleam in his eye, the subsequent careful attention to his dress and his hair. But then, somehow rather slowly, he had soured. He had begun to curse. He acted as if he had been cheated of something — not just money in a card game. Had he discovered the pain as well as the pleasure of love and his disappointment had darkened every corner of his young life?

Mrs. Grimsby bent down to stroke her son's hair when she spotted something in his hand; gently pulling it open she found a small piece of fine blonde hair. "Mr. Grimsby, whatever do you imagine this to be?"

She stood and placed her find into the hand of her husband.

Old Richard Grimsby looked closely through his costly spectacles.

"It looks like a lock. A wisp of child's hair, perhaps. None of our affair. Come. We shall have the footman give Geoffrey a good wash and a few cups of tea so that we can proceed. And we must urge him to find us a mute-boy. No funeral is complete without the sorrowful sight of a child in black."

"But Mr. Grimsby," his wife said with some alarm. "Wherever could he find such a child on short notice?" Old Grimsby sighed: "The workhouse, madam. Children abound in workhouses. And can be for ready hire." Fingering the lock, Old Grimsby handed it back to his wife and said: "I imagine you may toss this curl away."

With that, Mr. Grimsby returned to his tea table. Standing alone by the stairs, her sleeping son at her feet, Mrs. Grimsby could not help but examine the lock further; she wondered if her son had been up to some mischief. *But what could that possibly be,* she asked herself. *Why a lock of hair?*

My sweet lost boy, she thought, slipping the blonde curl into her apron pocket before taking hold of Geoffrey's limp arm and, gently shaking him awake, helping him to stand.

⁕᎙᎙᎙᎙⁕

Under sunnier skies west of London, not more than six miles distant, there lay a small tree-shaded village. One resident, whose cottage sat under a spreading oak tree, Mrs. Bolton by name, had tended her dying husband and now was helping her sickly sister. The invalid had for years lived a hardscrabble life, working for mere shillings a month. In truth, Mrs. Bolton rarely spoke of her sister's occupation although she accepted it as respectable to be a matron in the county workhouse.

Now as the village clock struck the hour for the midday meal, Mrs. Bolton spooned two ladles of broth into a bowl, placed the bowl on a tray and walked from her large kitchen toward a snug room at the rear of her cottage. She stepped lightly while at the same time calling out:

"Coming, Jemima. I'm coming. Be patient."

Kicking the door open, Mrs. Bolton entered her sister's sick room. A window guarded the light with a thin curtain; a tiny hearth and a narrow bed soothed the aching body of Jemima Pettiworth, who opened her eyes at this moment and from under her covers, pulled herself up to reveal her soiled cap, night dress, and pale yellow complexion.

"Not this. Not this," Jemima said, a low whine in her voice.

"Simple broth, Jemima. Sit forward. That's it."

"You are *too* kind, sister," Jemima said, a cruel edge to her words.

"Shall I or shall you?" asked Mrs. Bolton, holding up the spoon. Jemima snatched it and began to sip her broth with no further complaint. Mrs. Bolton sat in a chair next to the bed and waited. She ignored her sister's manner. After all, it came from her years of living in the workhouse. The old stone building lay beyond the village, isolated on a low hill, a mud road leading up to its gate. Its bell was placed in a tower to sound over the fields. The wards housed villagers, farmers, children, and the poor and needy of the parish that had lost the ability to survive independently, through injury or poor harvests. The children had been deposited in the workhouse from many venues around the countryside: some were orphans, some unwanted babies. All had suffered equally under the dominion of the impatient Jemima Pettiworth.

Now it is true that even in the meanest of breasts there hides a tenderness that must somehow express itself. In the case of Matron Jemima, now jaundiced and fading, this expression once took the form of lace making. Mrs. Bolton needed only to gaze around her sister's sick room to see framed samples of Jemima's fine handiwork. Beside these, there was on the mantel a runner of delicate lace flowers; on the back of the other chair, a draped net of cotton lace once used as a tea table cover. Jemima had an eye back then; even now on some afternoons, as she sat alone in her fetid chamber, she would rummage for her needle and hook and calmly pass an hour spinning out patterns.

"Enough," Jemima said curtly, her spoon sinking into the bowl.

"Very well," sighed Mrs. Bolton. She rose and took the tray. But she turned back to gaze at her sister who had in an instant changed from a cranky invalid into a wet-cheeked, weeping penitent. "Oh, oh," Jemima cried, hands wringing, her hollow face staring ahead into the fire.

"But what is it, sister?" said Mrs. Bolton, setting down the tray.

"I cannot *speak* the words," her distraught sister moaned. "I cannot hear them anymore or I shall go ..."

"There, there. Such remorse. What may I —"

"Nothing!" Jemima howled. Then letting her voice crouch into a hoarse whisper, she said: "Nothing can be done now. I must hear them. They will never leave me." With this pronouncement, Jemima Pettiworth fell back against her thin pillow.

"I see. Well," said Mrs. Bolton. "I shall be in the kitchen,

Jemima." The tray was lifted, the door nudged open again. "You must climb from your bed today, Jemima. Move your legs. You are wasting away."

"This bed shall be my coffin," Jemima whispered. Mrs. Bolton muttered under her breath and returned to her hearth. Washing up, she heard rustling and lifted her eyes to see her sister, her yellow face like a mask, standing in the doorway of her sick room.

"Come along then," said Mrs. Bolton, her voice encouraging. "Step by step."

Jemima Pettiworth stepped into the parlour, opened the desk by the window and took out a sheet of writing paper. She held it to her chest as if it were a needy child; she then lifted it up to the light as if there was writing for her to read. Then she slowly crept back into her sick room. Once there, she let her spoken words float toward her sister in the kitchen:

"Sister, I beg of you," Jemima said. "Bring me pen and ink. I have words I must write down before they burn away all of my strength."

"Oh, dear," said Mrs. Bolton. "Whatever are you planning to pen, sister?"

"A confession."

Chapter Nine
Fish and Foul

Stepping down onto the cobblestones in East London, Inspector Endersby reminded himself that he was in the business of executing the law. Thus, he ducked into a narrow doorway, pulled out a multi-coloured scarf from his satchel and wound it around his neck as if he had a cold. He folded his hat inside his pocket, giving himself a curious bulge on his right side. He mussed his grey-lined hair to seem eccentric —"mad north-north-west," quoting his beloved *Hamlet*. Finally, he lifted from an inner pocket a pair of round spectacles he'd had made by a glass grinder in the Burlington Arcade, the lenses plain glass.

Rosemary Lane opened before him as he gazed through his spectacles at the buyers and sellers gathered this afternoon. The lane held tall leaning houses, home to dredgers, coal-whippers, watermen, tradesmen connected with the commerce of the Thames. Down the side streets sat rows of lodging houses, while on either side of the lane proper, merchants displayed their goods on pieces of carpet and mounds of straw. All about were dogs and dirt-blackened children, vegetable baskets, and fresh fish tables humming with flies. Near the south entrance, just as the matron from Shoe Lane had said, sat a man under a canvas umbrella, three chairs lined up beside him on which were piled and hung samples of lace. Next to the man sat a huge woman selling slabs of fresh eel and mounds of dried pulled pork. She had a booming laugh and she jostled the lace seller, knocking his elbow with her wide left hand.

"Afternoon, captin," bellowed the woman. Endersby drew his mouth into a thin smile and wandered over to the lace samples. *Keep in mind,* he warned himself, *that the murderer may not have purchased lace but in fact stolen it, or brought it from where he was living.*

"It don't matter, sir, touch 'em," said the lace seller. "That's the ticket. Good quality." The lace seller had rum-slurred speech, but his eyes were sharp when Endersby inspected his samples. "You here on a lark, captin?" asked the woman with a merry bounce in her voice. "I've fine eel for your supper. You don't strike me as a cove," she said. "You're a genl'eman, here to purchase."

"Most likely," Endersby said, his voice pitched high to squeak a little.

The lace seller reached into his pocket and drank from a small jug. Endersby said: "I search for a particular old form of lace to replace a border on a drape."

"Take your pick, sir. The stained bolts are a penny a foot. The white and the coloureds, three pence a foot. All handmade, sir, by the Belg'ums."

Endersby searched in his satchel for the lace samples found on the victims in St. Giles and Shoe Lane. He held up one piece, leaned into the lace seller to afford him a closer look, and requested if the merchant had any more of the same pattern and kind.

"Poor seller that one, a fact," the lace seller mumbled. "A bolt or two … under the chair." The lace seller rose with great effort. He pulled out a soiled bolt of coarse lace of the same pattern as the one found on the bodies. "Ah, I believe this is the particular I search for," squeaked Endersby. The lace seller lifted out a pair of large scissors from one of his pockets. "Any length, sir, you wish. Give it you for ha'penny a foot." Reeling from the jolt of coincidence, Endersby refused to believe his good luck. Was this, perhaps, Fate mocking his effort? The inspector rummaged in his trouser pocket for coins. "A peculiar run of lace, sir," slurred the lace seller, "not pop'lar any more 'mongst those around here."

"On second thought," Endersby began, playing the charade. "This swag of lace I carry was given me by my brother. For his house down in Kent. He bade me be sure it was a *perfect* match."

"No trouble, sir," the lace seller said, putting up his scissors. "Let's put our 'eads together. Lookee, your swag next to the bolt; you're in luck, that's the tickle. The two are the same."

Endersby stuttered: "You see, my good fellow, my brother claims he sent *his man* some time ago to buy from you. He has sent *me* today in *his* place and bid me buy more of the same lace since he tallied the length wrong. So I must be absolute."

"His man, sir?" asked the lace seller. "No sir. No man-servant in the past few days purchased this bit of lace. We serve women; that's the sum."

"Then indeed I have made an error, good merchant," answered Endersby. "Yours may not be the place of his purchase."

"I knows of no other who sells this particular lace stuff, captin," said the woman, who looked vexed. The lace seller pushed back his hat and his eyes widened as he lifted his head: "Now, waits. A man you says. Yes, dear wife, cast your mind back to a few days past. That chap — sore-lookin' lot he was — with a dirty beard and a fine frock coat."

"Ugly man, beg your pardon, captin, a red cut 'cross his face. He wore a dredgerman's hat over his brow. Peculiar smell, now that I recalls," the woman added. "Like he had been sleeping in a stable."

"Most astonishing," squeaked Endersby, searching now for a way to find out more about the man. "Tragic," he added: "My brother's manservant is a sad fellow, indeed. He cleans the stables and does light chores. I reckon my brother keeps him out of pity. He goes by … oh, the name escapes me at the instant. Was he in any way impertinent, sir?"

"He said not a word," the lace seller pointed out. "Saw these very bolts, bought a shilling's worth of this same lace. Peculiar, I thought. Made me wonder, that's the brush. Why such a cove would wish for lace."

"Did he purchase anything else?" said Endersby.

"Ow, captain, only lace. He looked hungry for a working man. And peculiar, for he had on a fresh frock coat of quality." explained the woman.

"A frock coat. New, you say?" asked the inspector.

"Will you purchase, then sir?" asked the lace seller. "Seems your brother has need."

"Two yards is all," Endersby said, his eyes alert to any changes in tone of voice in the two figures before him. The heavy woman held out the lace while her husband used his scissors to cut off the required length. Once Endersby had paid and graciously thanked the couple, he ventured one last ruse: "I was not at liberty to tell you of one concern I still have," he said.

The woman leaned forward. "A concern, captin?"

"My brother's man has run away to London once again. Yesterday evening, I was told. My brother is troubled by the matter and requested I search around. Have you by chance seen this same chap in his frock coat again?"

"Not at all," replied the huge woman. "The day we sold him the lace he went off to the gin shop yonder at Hairbrine-court. Last I sees of him."

"You are certain as well?" Endersby asked the lace seller.

"You be concerned about' im, I can see," says the merchant. "He likes his drink."

"So I feared," said Endersby.

"An odd gen'leman, captin," said the woman. "Enquire at the lodging houses near Hairbrine Court. Low places, sir, full of thieves and sickly men. But cheap and a place to sleep."

Endersby considered the woman's words: "I thankee both once again."

The couple went back to their chatter and Endersby tucked the recent purchase of lace into his satchel, along with the two samples he'd brought, and walked up the lane into the gin shop where a crowd of men and women sat in the gloom, drinking. The sweet smell of juniper and sugared water filled the air. The barkeep was a young lad of no more than twenty; a pipe lounged in the corner of his mouth; his left hand flashed cheap tin rings from every finger.

"Tuppence," the lad spat out and slammed down a mug before the inspector. Endersby paid and then, by design, tipped out his change purse, allowing a couple of shillings to roll onto the serving board in front of the lad. "Careful, git," the lad said. "You a fool boy, old man? Lose those you will." The lad picked up the two shillings and stuck his hand out to Endersby as he poured out a mug for another customer. Endersby leaned into the lad and crooked his finger: "Keep 'em, lad, I'm on the lookout."

The bar lad squinted, showed a mouth of few teeth, and bent closer. "Your wife run away, then, git. Turned slattern on you?" Endersby frowned and gave out a theatrical sigh of regret. "No lad, worse. My brother's gone missing," he said, changing his story for the sake of variety. "Loves the gin. Comes up to London often. We're from Kent, yonder. Been looking for him now for two days."

The lad held his face as if to say he found the whole story a fraud.

"A chap, you say?" said the lad.

"A stranger to you, I wager," said Endersby. "I'd give a pound to know if you've seen him. A man with a beard, not old, a new frock coat, secretive in his manner."

"You are certain, git?" mocked the barkeep. He puffed on his pipe. His face then wrinkled with thought. "Anything peculiar about 'im?" asked the barkeep. Endersby sat forward. Would he be in luck yet again? Although he did not want to put words or ideas into the barkeep's mind, he let slip that his brother had once been in a bad fight. "His face," Endersby lamented, "was no match for his assailant and so came out the worst."

"Stinks like a sewer?" asked the barkeep. "I reckoned that mark on his cheeks was from a tumble."

"That be my poor Will," said Endersby.

"He's hiding from you, git. Comes in here in the last few days, drinks a mug or three. If he be your kin, he stumbles off each time down toward Irish Bay, there."

"Irish Bay, sir?" pleaded Endersby.

"Rotten Row, Irish Bay, all the same. Blue Anchor Court, just off the corner. No place for a coun'ry genleman like yourself." The lad laughed. As Endersby was about to leave, the barkeep called out to him. "Come 'ere, git. Best you find this brother of yours. Summat happened to him besides his face. Bad legs, like he was beaten up in the docks. You knows, maybe he's been a week or more in Fleet Prison? Secured, I warrant. Got high old boots but they don't hide the 'duck walk,' like he's still in leg irons." Endersby shook his head as if he were in grief. The lad then poked him in the chest: his palm lay open.

"I'll appreciate another shilling, guv'nor, if you does have no objection."

Endersby opened his purse and handed the lad the shilling.

Outside in the lane, he asked an oyster seller to point him to Blue Anchor Court. She nodded her chin toward a grimy half street with murky water running down the cobbles and groups of haggard men sitting on stools. *A new frock coat? Legs in irons? A dredgerman's cap? How many men could fit that description,* Endersby wondered. And was any one of them the workhouse killer? *An innocent man may buy lace as easily as a guilty one,* he reminded himself. Was Luck guiding him or leading him astray? *Just follow your leads,* Endersby thought. *They are all you have. Leave supposition behind for the moment.* He shook out the cramp in his foot and began to walk slowly toward Blue Anchor Court.

"Careful, dearie," warned the oyster woman. "There be thieves and murderers down there."

⁂

"We'll all be killed."

"Quiet!" the master shouted at the three trembling women. He turned his bony head toward Sergeant Caldwell. "Do you see, sir, what trouble you have brought?"

Sergeant Caldwell stood at attention, his shoulders pressed back. It was his way of showing resistance to the five-foot bully facing him. The master of the Theobald's Road Workhouse reminded Caldwell of a scrappy street dog: his set of yellowed teeth, his growl full of threat. "Sir," Caldwell said, "It is my duty to inform you to lock down your coal chute for the safety of these matrons and their female wards. This is a measure of caution that the Metropolitan Police are demanding of every institution since the two murders were discovered."

The three matrons pleaded. The master took them aside. While the master tried to calm his staff, Caldwell examined the ledgers of recent arrivals of children, their names and ages. There were no Catherines. There were, on the present list, only seven girls of twelve years old. The rest were young women with small babies. Dread overtook Caldwell's mind. Forcing the master to secure the workhouse had been difficult. Caldwell thought about his wife, Alice, safe at home in her bed. Surely to be safe is what every man, woman, and child needs in life. Caldwell flipped through the records. Very few female children had been registered in Theobald's Road over the past year.

He said goodbye to the staff and decided to walk around the yard of the workhouse. The building was jammed into a dark alley, its yard no larger than three horse-stalls. Sergeant Caldwell valued the training he'd received from Endersby. He'd learned to sharpen his eye for details, for unusual signs that might provide a clue. Finding one always brought him an immediate sense of accomplishment. Ducking under the roof of an old shed, Caldwell cocked his head and noticed a small wooden door, almost invisible in the gloom. It was makeshift and when he pulled it open he found it led to a smelly hut. A sudden movement inside the hut made Caldwell jump back. He reached for his leather cosh that hung inside his blue police jacket and his breath caught. The figure was bent, black with dirt. He had a beard, a large black hat. "Git away," he yelled.

"Stand still, sir!" Caldwell cried. The figure dashed at him, swinging a metal hook. His body reeked of filth. He rammed Caldwell to the ground. It was impossible to see the full face as it was covered by strings of hair and the rim of the hat. A heavy punch slammed into Caldwell's right shoulder. He rolled on his side; another punch by his ear. Grunts and curses bounced off the walls of the hut as Caldwell turned to see the hook fly again.

Caldwell's left foot cracked the attacker's ankle. Howling in pain, the man tumbled forward. Grabbing his assailant's coat sleeve, Caldwell held tight. But the fellow kicked back, broke free, and clambered to his full height. Then he turned and fled. Out of the shed and between the buildings he stumbled, huffing, his boots dragging as if stuffed with bricks.

"Halt," Caldwell yelled. He chased the man into the broader street. A carriage blocked his way. He dodged around its back end and saw the man push aside two teenage boys. *What strength he had, what speed for a man with bad legs,* Caldwell thought. A woman screamed from a doorway. The filthy man pushed her down, ran into her shop and out its back door into a maze of alleys. Caldwell gave chase but his assailant seemed to evaporate like steam from a kettle.

Panting, Caldwell picked up speed. *A stink, a limp, a beard, a hook.* The eight words had become like a child's rhyme in his brain. He headed down one of the alleys, looked for broken doors, swinging gates. Back again down two more lanes, but there were no more indications of a man passing through. As he stood to write in his leather notebook, noting the time, the details of the incident, a dog barked inside a walled-up yard. Caldwell ran to its gate.

"You!" he shouted to a young boy playing with the dog. "Did you see a man pass through here, lad? I am a policeman." The boy turned to him and Caldwell saw that the child was blind. Caldwell pulled down his cap. Where had the figure gone? Was he, in fact, the culprit? *It's no use,* Caldwell thought. *There's no profit in wondering about a fled rabbit.* He popped a fresh clove into his cheek, checked the address of London Wall Workhouse and headed northeast, the Tower of London visible in the distance.

Chapter Ten

Friends in Need

Chin up, back held rigid, Inspector Endersby did not dare move an inch farther. He had no desire to suffer the knife point currently tickling his throat. Three minutes walk through Blue Anchor Court and into the first lodging house, where he now was looking up, much against his will, at a low ceiling streaked with water stains. *Sudden good fortune too frequently turns bad,* Endersby reflected.

"Clean'im," said a rough voice behind Endersby's back. Two young boys in large coats and broken top hats thrust their hands into Endersby's coat pockets. They whistled as their hands dove in and out, their movements so quick Endersby could barely notice their touch.

"Wot's this great lump, d'ye see?" One of the boys pulled Endersby's folded hat from his coat pocket. "Oh, Lor', a fine piece."

"Oh d'ye see, a box a sweets," said the other. "These'll fetch four pence."

The rough voice at Endersby's back said: "Hand'em here, rum boys, quick, quick."

The man holding the knife at Endersby's throat wore an old shooting jacket with wooden buttons. His eyes followed the artful hands of the boys. "Three shillings," cried one, as he slid his hand from underneath Endersby's coat. The contents of the inspector's trouser pockets were now on display in two sets of dirty hands: the shillings, a change purse, a clean handkerchief. "Giv'em," said the rough voice. There was a shuffle of feet; from the corner of his eye Endersby saw a short fellow move slowly around him. The fellow wore a red plush waistcoat and a long military coat reaching to his boot tops. When he stopped in front of Endersby, the man holding the knife stepped back and Endersby lowered his chin. To his surprise, the fellow facing him whose voice had been so deep was a mere boy; his face was stubbled with light beard; his hat had a drooping feather in its crown.

"Welcome, Master," the boy-fellow said, his rough voice incongruous with his thin body. Endersby nodded: in a flash he knew he must play the charade to guard his disguise as best he could. His satchel at his feet had yet to be pilfered. And when it was, there would arise a dangerous situation between him and the lodgers — especially the boy-fellow with the rough voice.

"You've a full purse for today? You a *gonaff*, then?" asked the boy-fellow.

The two young boy-thieves snickered.

Pitching his voice high and stuttering, Endersby said: "I beg pardon, sir. What is a *gonaff*? I am up from Kent, yonder, just this morning."

"Chumps, we 'ave a country squire come to visit. Lookee right smart," said the boy-fellow. The two boy-thieves and the man holding the knife laughed. Endersby glanced around at figures clustered at the far end of the lodging house's central room.

On arrival, he had entered this room, a kitchen, long and smoke-filled. Tables and benches lined up in front of the hearth. The other figures did not show any concern or interest in what was happening to Endersby. He was ignored in his predicament.

"Welcome, Master, my name be Hawkins, Nicholas Hawkins, sir," said the rough voiced boy-fellow.

"How do you do," Endersby said, thrusting out his right hand. In an instant, Nicholas Hawkins jumped back, his left hand clasping a short wooden cudgel. "Shall I crack your skull, Squire?" Nicholas Hawkins mocked, grinning before slapping the little club against his thigh. Endersby felt sweat gathering on his forehead. "Call me Nick the Hand," said Nicholas Hawkins. The features of Nick the Hand held no threat — despite the draw of his brutal weapon. It was as if he were performing for Endersby, showing off his fighting skill; what was evident in his stance was a natural authority; he was the kingpin of this particular lodging house gang — small as it was. "I do beg your pardon, sir," Endersby sputtered, taking off his round spectacles and wiping them on his sleeve.

"A *gonaff*, my master, is a boy-thief," explained Nick the Hand. "A picker of pockets. We, here, are all gen'lemen thieves," explained the boy-fellow. "No harm done: handkerchiefs, coins, small purses — that be what makes us our livin'."

"I see. Well, well," said Endersby. Before another second could pass, Endersby had to make sure he could grab and hold his satchel which lay at his feet. He conjectured that if he asked after his 'lost brother,' he might be able to distract his captors and find out more about the scarred man in the frock coat. Endersby began: "My wayward brother has come to the city and wasted our money on gin. He must return to Kent. That is the sole reason I am in London, to find him."

"Lookee, sir," said Nick the Hand. "We are honest men 'elping each other. No burglars or smashers. So, why does you start here, to this particular house?" As Nick the Hand spoke, one of the boy-thieves bent down, stretched out his hand, and grabbed Endersby's satchel. "The gin seller pointed me here," Endersby replied, suddenly nervous. "Said he'd seen Will. A man with a long scar across his face, a beard and a frock coat." The two boy-thieves began to fumble and search in the satchel.

"Wot 'ave we, my rum boys?" said Nick the Hand.

The roll of lace recently purchased by Endersby fell to the floor. Down banged the brass ear trumpet, pencils and note-books amidst *oohs* from the two boys.

"You a scrivener, then, Master, a sensible letter composer?" asked Nick the Hand. He had walked closer to the boys and his words carried a hard note of suspicion. "Metal cuffs, Master? A cosh, 'ere, too." Endersby stepped forward. Nick the Hand shoved him back, held his two lapels and shouted to the knife man to come forward. Like a trapped stag, Endersby was immediately surrounded while Nick the Hand slowly raised his short wooden club and pressed it against Endersby's nose. "A Bow Street man, my rum boys. A Bobby? Or a spy. Where's his policeman's rattle?" A flurry of hands into pockets, boot tops, waistcoat lining. These fellows were not murderers, Endersby reasoned, but they might prove injurious; worse, they would not trust Endersby, nor grant him any information he was seeking. Thoughts stumbled about the inspector's mind even as his canvas long-coat fell to the floor and his waistcoat became unbuttoned. "This be your notebook, Master?" asked Nick the Hand, holding high Endersby's leather-bound note pad. "Your spyin' words come to peach us out?"

"Nick. There be no Bobby's rattle," whispered one of the boy thieves.

"Walk 'im, Jack," commanded Nick the Hand. Jack the Knife stuck his blade close to Endersby's right ear as the two boy-thieves shunted Endersby into a corner. There, their collective fists pushed him onto a bench while Nick the Hand closely inspected the satchel, spreading its contents out on the table. In particular, the magnifying glass took his attention.

"Yer a clever cove," said Nick the Hand. "A good weasel. Wot you think, rumsters, we send our squire out with a beating? Let him hop the twig? Or do we take him to the Thames, to the waterboys, and see wheres they can take him?" The two boy thieves pulled on the rims of their hats: "Why not a beating and a visit to the Thames? He's out to nab us, Nick, out to peach on us straight to the gallows." Nick the Hand listened; he picked up the cosh and put it down. With some caution, he lifted up one of the soiled lace samples Endersby had carried from the crime scene to the market.

"Wot's this then?" he asked, his fingers dropping the fouled lace to the table.

"A murder weapon," Endersby answered quietly.

"Ow, that's a good'un, eh Jocko," said one of the boy thieves to the man holding the knife. "Must'a used it on a canary?"

"You, Mr. Bobby," said Nick the Hand, "I reckon you be a detective policeman, a spy, too."

"Inspector Owen Endersby, Fleet Lane Station House. Not a spy, however, Mr. Hawkins. Rather I am a searcher. I am paid to solve murders."

The two boy-thieves looked at Endersby with rapt attention. One of Endersby's methods in situations where he knew he was in danger was to soften his voice and speak his words slowly, carefully, without menace or anger. Nick the Hand looked at the soiled lace. He glared at Endersby.

"Once, I was in Fleet Lane prison, Master," Nick the Hand said. "As a boy. Caught for stealing a penny muffin from a muffin seller. Ten lashes, forty days of water and gruel."

Endersby now took a chance. Most likely, he figured, Nick the Hand or the knife man or the two boy thieves had been in workhouses. They had the forlorn look of those raised without affection.

"You a St.Giles boy, or a Bethnal Green inmate, by chance, Mr. Hawkins?" Endersby asked.

"Close enough. A charity boy out of Bow Parish, me mammy sick with the cough. She died. I buried 'er. I entered the workhouse, but I gave it up, true to speak, and took up the profession of thieving. Right good I was, till I found I could manage a crew. These boys and Jack my knife, we does very good, we do. Meat on the table every Sunday supper."

"That piece of lace," said Endersby, "was found in the throat of a workhouse matron, Mr. Hawkins."

"Was she deservin'?" Nick asked.

"She was a quiet weak woman, Mr. Hawkins. She had no defence. The villain strangled her, hard and slow, her breath viciously choked by that innocent slag of lace."

Nick the Hand lifted up Endersby's police cuffs and dropped them with a clunk onto the bare floor. He kicked the table, looked over to Jack holding the knife, and stared at him for no more than an instant. At this point, Endersby's years of confronting the criminal mind convinced him Nick the Hand was not about to do grave harm. Likely he wanted to avoid losing face with his crew.

"Mr. Hawkins," Endersby said. "Do you know the punishment for beating or harming an officer of the law?"

"A beating, a cell in Fleet Prison?" said Nick with a flippant air.

"Worse," said Endersby.

Jack the Knife spat at Endersby's feet and said: "I knows it entails floggin'. And somethin' evil beyond what we knows here."

"The hulks," said Endersby. "Pits of hell. You may die in

the hold of those prison ships before you reach the shores of Australia."

Silent terror fell over the crew. These men were poor and hungry — but free. The hulks were every felon's nightmare: re-fitted ships made into prisons, anchored in the mouth of the Thames, three hundred men chained below deck in quarters designed for cannons and gunners, at best a space for a hundred fighting sailors. More cholera and lung cough than in any slum or coal mine. And the long voyage to a desert continent on the underside of the earth.

Nick the Hand stood up. "All of you, scat away. I wishes to talk to this Squire Policeman alone." Jack the Knife rose and confronted Nick the Hand: "Wot you mean? Cut a scam with 'im and leave us out. No, lookee here, Nick." The two boy-thieves also stood, but they scuttled behind the big frame of Jack.

"Rum boys, I loves you," said Nick the Hand, his voice now gentle and without irony. "But don't get me hot. I say, trust your Nick, he won't peach on you. Scat, dash!"

The dejected members of his crew withdrew, but stood close by the kitchen entrance within earshot. Nick the Hand picked up Endersby's metal cuffs, his magnifying glass, and other items and stuffed them back into the inspector's satchel. He tossed the shillings across the floor toward his crew, who scrambled to secure the coins. Endersby decided to waylay Hawkins, to play into his pride: "I need your help," he said, his voice low. Nick the Hand raised his chin.

"I am willing to pay you and your crew," Endersby said. "You are men of honour despite your profession. I admit, I too am often reviled by members of the public who disdain the police. But I *must* find this murderer. He has killed two women, kidnapped young girls, and may continue his devilry if I do not find him."

"How will you pay?" Nick the Hand asked.

"A reward? Shillings and perhaps —"

"Not for us a one-time purse, Squire. We's business folk."

Endersby rubbed his chin. Could he propose a bribe and not insult or silence Nick the Hand? Endersby knew it could be a prickly arrangement. Making bargains with felons was not unheard of among police detectives. To hunt truly dangerous criminals — murderers, rapists — a detective had to rely on finding a reliable spy, a paid voice to give up names.

Nick the Hand grinned. "Saleables, sir. Pay me in those."

"'Saleables?' Please, Mr. Hawkins, explain."

"Simple fare, Mr. Inspector. A leg or two of cooked mutton; a tin of cigars; a box of cheese. My rumsters and I, we can make much profit sellin' these stuffs, bit by bit. You see? We gets to eat part of it, but sell the rest and find ourselves easy for a time, if you catch my wind."

"A handshake between honourable men, then, Mr. Hawkins."

"You understand me, Squire? I don't take to two-faced dealing."

"Nor do I," said Endersby, his voice firm, his eyes held on Nick the Hand's serious face.

Nick the Hand spit into the palm of his right hand. Endersby removed a suede glove from his. The two men shook. "And when can I deliver this fare?" asked the inspector.

"Well, Squire, we have a delicate problem first to hash."

Endersby held still, unsure of what to expect. Nick the Hand signalled to his crew to cross the room. Once they had surrounded him and Endersby, Nick the Hand said: "Rumsters, our Bobby spy here is needy of us. No, do not mock. We have shook on a fare. But tell me and 'im honestly if you've seen this cove he is searchin' for."

"A bearded man," Endersby said. "He limps, has a scar across his face — right cheek over to left eye. Witnesses tell me he wears a new frock coat and a dredgerman's black hat. At times, he may carry a gaff."

"Let me ponder. No, no I don't conjure such a man in these parts," said Jack the Knife.

"The barkeep in Rosemary Lane said such a man came in to drink over the past few days," said Endersby. "He was seen walking into Blue Anchor Court."

"There be lodgings about only for them who pay," said Nick the Hand.

One of the boy-thieves stepped forward: "I *thinks* I saw such a cow-hearted chappy, sir," he said. "But two nights gone. At the gin shop, then later. Came he into this court, silent-like, not a word, a scar on his face to make the dogs bark. Pompin' about in his shiny frock coat. And movin' his legs like he wos in the chains."

"Did you see where he rested, lad?" asked Endersby.

"He scampered, sir, once he'd paid a penny for some tobacco. Scat away down one'f 'em alleys nearby." Nick the Hand then said: "I know a jim-cull who knows *all* hereabouts."

"Fitz?" cried one of the boy-thieves. "Old Fitz?"

"He won't budge, Nick. Tongue-tied he'll be," warned Jack the Knife.

Nick the Hand scratched his nose. "No, I thinks with a bit of fare he'll crow. Fitz bears a hard weight on 'imself, yet he's no scag. He knows *all*."

"As soon as possible, Mr. Hawkins," said Endersby. "Time affords men the chance to flee if they need to, especially under cover of darkness."

Nick the Hand did not hesitate. He pushed Endersby toward the kitchen door and barked at his crew to hurry up. "Mind you, Squire," Nick the Hand said, pulling Endersby along by his sleeve, "you needs to charm Old Fitz with yer wit and yer coin if you want any favours. He owns a lot of houses round here, makes profit from beds as well as whores. So he deserves for respect, he does." Endersby, ignoring the hot pangs of his gout, slapped on his hat. *Now,* he thought, *I must be diligent.* The streets wound out before him, lanes, alleys, arched passages, a feeling of apprehension at every turn as the gang pushed through mist and the sharp stink of rotting timber. Here indeed was a half-acre of Hades. *Might this Fitz fellow divulge more substantial clues and information?* The afternoon was passing. Clues were appearing. If only Fitz proved reliable. If only he and his men would tell their secrets. What a help he might be if, at least, this kingpin of the underworld was open to helping the police.

Chapter Eleven
My Brother's Keeper

Ten-year-old Catherine Smeets felt the bee kiss her ear. How happy she was: she had flown up the chimney of St. Pancras Workhouse and was now sitting at a grand table with the old Princess eating roast beef, boiled trout, and a great potato pie full of thick gravy and —

"Wake up," the voice said, Nell's fingertip in her ear giving her one more little scratch.

Catherine sat up with her needle and thread still in her hand. Nell pointed toward Catherine's bare feet. Below her, folded on the floor, were ten huge linen sheets. Each had been mended and stitched by her aching fingers. Her stomach tightened; early supper was being served. The St. Pancras Workhouse rang with a bell and clanking pots. Matron Pickens' footsteps came down the stairs. Opening wide her sleepy eyes, Catherine could see Little Mag and the sickly boy leaning against a laundry basket.

"Well, well, girls," Matron Pickens said, entering the room. She stood tall, her hand holding up her birch rod. All three girls sat at attention, pulling their needles in unison and humming. "Come, boy," Matron Pickens said, shaking the pale child. He stood on wobbly legs and followed her out into the corridor. "Soup in one quarter of an hour, girls," Matron said. "Do not come late unless you wish to feel this." She shook her birch rod. "Tea will be at eight this evening so do not expect bread at this hour." Matron Pickens then marched off with the boy dragging behind her.

"Now!" Nell whispered.

"But what of our poor boy, Nell?" Catherine asked. "He will not survive the day in here if Matron does not tend him."

Nell took hold of Catherine Smeets and shook her hard: "You are not his keeper. You can only fend for yourself. Like all of us. Now come or stay behind." Catherine put down her needle and thread and with Little Mag followed Nell into the damp stone hall. "Hurry," Nell whispered, grabbing the hands of both Catherine and Little Mag. Down the corridor, round the corner they scampered, mouths shut tight; they stopped, pulled up the floor stone and lifted out the bundle of rags — their cache of lard, potato skins, apple peels, and onions. "Stuff 'em," ordered Nell. Catherine and Little Mag lifted their smocks and hid the bundles inside the tops of their ragged undergarments. "Done then," said Nell, pulling down her own smock. "Separate. You, Catherine, run to the kitchen, past the coal bin and up to the side door. You, Mag, come with me as far as the shed. We meet at the back gate by the washing tubs."

The girls parted. Catherine leaped up, raced by the coal bin and scaled the empty staircase to the side door, which she slowly pushed so as not to set the hinges creaking. Out into afternoon light she crept, clenching her fists twice to relieve her cramped fingers; her bare feet splashed through mud puddles until they reached the washing hut at the back of the workhouse. Under the eave, by the stone tubs, she knelt and waited in the shade.

The bell rang. The workhouse doors closed. Voices full of eager shouts filled staircases and then disappeared into the cold breadth of the huge dining hall. The clunk of bowls and the mumble of prayer and then silence as broth was ladled out. Catherine held her aching stomach. She wondered about her father, Sergeant Smeets, if he'd ever felt hunger like this as a soldier. *How could he have left me here?* Sighing, Catherine peeked around the edge of the washing hut. A horse stood tethered by the blacksmith shed. Close to it, Little Mag and Nell were crouching. Nell straightened up, still holding tight to Little Mag's hand, then looked both ways and darted out into the open ground between the blacksmith shed and the washing hut. Catherine watched them quicken their legs, two thin bodies galloping across the mud of the yard.

A voice rang out from a high window:

"You two, stop at once!" A spoon clanged against a pot. Catherine's hand covered her mouth to stifle a scream.

The sharp voice shouted again, the raspy hard cry of Matron Pickens. "That you, naughty Nell? And you, cripple Mag? Get back in here. Get now."

A thick-shouldered boy ran out from the blacksmith shed in pursuit of Nell and Little Mag. "Help," Little Mag cried as she tripped and fell hard against the dirt of the yard. Nell let her go and ran like a frightened pony toward the washing hut. The thick-shouldered boy stuck his hand into his mouth and blew a shrill whistle. He came upon the struggling Little Mag and with a brusque hand pulled her up by her hair. Catherine, now breathless with fear, stood, ran toward the open gate at the back of the yard. Nell bumped into her and knocked her down and kept on running ahead, not looking back, until she reached the gate. She stopped, turned and called out: "Catherine, *run.*"

Catherine Smeets stood but her shoulder shot with cold pain. Her breath escaped; she fell again and raised her eyes to see Nell flee into the street, dash between a carriage and four, and head into the push of pedestrians crowding the pavement.

Marching footsteps came upon her: "You! Get up."

Matron Pickens grabbed Catherine's panging shoulder. The birch rod stung the back of her legs. From out of Catherine's undergarments tumbled the rags, the onions rolling, the lard bits dropping like baby's tears onto the earth at her feet.

"The latrines for you and the cripple child," snarled Matron Pickens. "Naughty scum you two are," as she pulled Catherine by her elbow toward the back archway. Inside, the two shivering girls grabbed each other's hands and stood facing Matron Pickens.

"You foolish savages," Matron Pickens said. "Prodigals, you are. We must make sure you do not try this again. Never again shall you two be 'fugitive and vagabond.' Off to the cellar without your broth or tea. Expect a hard beating when I come down to discipline you. And no snivelling, cripple child." As the two girls turned to walk down into the forbidding stairwell, Matron Pickens said one last thing: "Little Mag and Catherine. You two have done with your adventures."

Oh, how like an angel he is, thought Mrs. Grimsby as she stood in the doorway of her son Geoffrey's bedroom and looked upon his sleeping body. Boots kicked off, new frock coat tossed onto a chair, his beard and his lovely pink scar. *What a mark of his bravery*, Mrs. Grimsby thought. She placed the tray with its bowl of soup and slice of buttered toast down on the table beside her son's bed. Afternoon light seeped through the dusty curtains and made the room feel gentle, a cradling light for Mrs. Grimsby's favourite child.

I should not wake him as yet, Mrs. Grimsby thought to herself. *Dear Geoffrey must soon rise, set up the horses for the funeral at half three. Then another at half four. And he must hire a mute boy to lead the procession. Yes, my most precious one must be clean and ready.* Mrs. Grimsby had already commanded her kitchen maid to start boiling water for Geoffrey's bath. She herself would tend to combing his hair, making sure his unruly beard was trimmed. But what was this? What could this be? Mrs. Grimsby frowned on looking more closely at Geoffrey's hands. Under the nails lay black thick soot as if her beloved boy had been playing in the bin with coal chunks. Mrs. Grimsby took up a letter opener from the desk facing her son's mussed bed. She sat next to him and ran the tip of the opener under each nail and deposited the oily black dust onto a handkerchief she had taken from her pocket.

The clock struck the hour. No doubt Old Grimsby would soon come barging in with demands and reprimands and calling his only son a lazy good-for-nothing. *Oh, what injustice,* Mrs. Grimsby thought. *But time flies,* she reminded herself, rising carefuly and walking toward her son's clothes closet. She opened its door and pulled out his long black suit and top hat with the crepe band and laid all on his dressing table, his hat perched on the seat of a chair. With a secret smile, Mrs. Grimsby bent down and drew out one of the drawers of the standing closet. What memories! There they lay as she had stored them. Ten years ago, maybe more — jackets of black velvet she had sewn for her young Geoffrey. Smart buttoned jackets for her blessed ten-year-old's small body. And of course, the lace. *What lovely flowing collars of white lace, suitable for the son of a king,* she thought, *a bonny King Charley of old. Lace collars and lace cuffs.*

Mrs. Grimsby held one of the little jackets up to her face and stroked her cheek with the velvet sleeve. *My, oh, my,* how her Geoffrey had once fought her; "no, no," he had cried. He did not want to wear lace; but she had insisted until he gave in and stood — his cheeks red with shame — glaring at his father and mocking older sister. *But then, lace is so becoming on a lad,* Mrs. Grimsby thought, placing the jacket back into the drawer as she heard her jewel of a son begin to wake up.

"Mammy?" Geoffrey mumbled. He sat up. Mrs. Grimsby went to him, led by her motherly instincts. Geoffrey rolled over and with eyes shut hugged her, his breathing heavy. She stroked his dampened hair and spoke soothing words. He fell back; he sighed; he groaned and whispered: "Oh, dear mammy, what have I become?"

"There, there sweet one," Mrs. Grimsby said, her hands holding his.

"Shall I hold the bowl?" Mrs. Grimsby then said pointing to the tray she had brought to him.

"Mammy leave me be," Geoffrey grunted, his tone suddenly abrupt. He sat up and rubbed his eyes. It was as if a dark cloud had blackened out the sun. His foul mood had surfaced again, sudden and sharp. A coughing fit prompted Mrs. Grimsby to pat his back. "There, there," she cooed. Her son's left hand flew at her cheek. The smack sent her backwards. "Keep your hands off," he shouted. Mrs. Grimsby forced a smile, rubbing the sting to cool it. Mrs. Grimsby regained her composure and reminded herself that Geoffrey was a quick, clever boy.

Geoffrey kicked off his bedcover and began to wail. He buried his face in his hands.

"What have I done?" he cried. "What have I *gone and done?*"

"What is it, my precious?" Mrs. Grimsby said, her eyes widened in astonishment.

"Get away, dear Mammy. You must not touch me. I am a cursed man." Geoffrey began to rock back and forth. His hair tumbled over his forehead; his long pink scar reddened as if it had been suddenly inflamed.

"Dear one, whatever is the matter? Tell your mammy, dear," Mrs. Grimsby pleaded. With a brisk thrust of his right arm, Geoffrey pushed his mother away a second time, the violence of this strike knocking her against the dressing chair, sending his top hat tumbling to the floor. "Oh, Lord, my son," she whimpered. "What have you done?" Geoffrey threw himself back against his pillows. "I am nothing, Mammy. Do not dirty your hands on me. I am a lost creature." He kicked the foot board of his bed: "I shall be cursed, Mammy. Vengeance will come against me sevenfold for what I have done. Oh, my poor little one. I shall be *cursed*," Geoffrey cried and fell into louder weeping. Mrs. Grimsby slowly made her way to the bedroom door. The sobs of her dearest one tore at her heart. Into the hall she tiptoed and then, lifting up her long skirt, she ran as fast as she could past the parlour, through the dining room and into Old Grimsby's study where the stalwart man was standing before his looking glass adjusting his black tie.

"What is it?" he snapped. "Where is *your* son?" he said, contempt frosting his words.

"Oh, Mr. Grimsby. Our dear Geoffrey has gone mad. He has taken to weeping and remorse." Mrs. Grimsby pulled out her handkerchief, soot-stained as it was, and wiped her moist nose.

"Mad, indeed," grumbled the older Grimsby. "Out of his mind with drink and lassitude, Mrs. Grimsby. And your endless fussing over him." Mrs. Grimsby collapsed into the nearest chair, bent her frame forward and, with much effort, began to weep. "Heavens preserve us, Mrs. Grimsby," chided the older Grimsby. "We have business to attend to, and work to do."

"But Mr. Grimsby," his wife moaned. "Our Geoffrey is ill!"

"Tut," the Old Grimsby said. Then, turning toward the doorway, he shouted "Master Grimsby! Get up. Get out and find me a mute-boy. To a workhouse and quick. Bodies to bury!" The old man's voice travelled down the hall and did not fade as it rushed into young Geoffrey's bedroom. Rising from his damp pillow, the young Geoffrey screamed back: "Find a mute boy yourself, sir. As for me, I shall die here alone and damned!"

Mrs. Grimsby stood up, determined to face her husband. "Sir," she began, her voice quivering. "Your only son and male heir lies sickly. Can you not afford some sympathy for *him*?"

"Damn him," snarled the older Grimsby. He pulled out his watch and gasped at the time. "Labours to perform, madam," he growled. He took her arm and steered her toward the door. "Get down to the horse stalls and alert the groom to hitch the geldings. Get on with you," he commanded. Mrs. Grimsby stumbled forward, her eyes vacant with obedience to her harsh-voiced husband. The older Grimsby grabbed hold of one of his bamboo walking canes. He flexed it in his right hand. The sound was swift, a cutting sound pleasing to the patriarch's ears. Then with purpose he marched from his study. In the hall he shouted down the stairs to his hurrying wife:

"Mrs. Grimsby," he said, cracking the cane. "Ready yourself. For your only son is about to *feel* just how far his sickly madness will serve him."

⁕⁂⁑⁕

Having taken the final forkful of his late luncheon, Dr. Josiah Benton sat back in his chair in what seemed to Mrs. Wells a more pleasant state of mind. His food had been prepared to perfection: a parsley soup followed by chicken in jelly. Mrs. Wells was standing just behind her master by the dining room entrance. His smile brought her joy; it was ample reward for labour well done. Mrs. Wells considered herself a kindly woman and an obedient servant, always at the ready to serve her educated and refined employer. For ten years she had lived as the cook at Number Sixteen Bedford Square. Without hesitation she had sympathized with Josiah when his tight-lipped wife had packed her trunks and moved to the country to be with her brother. How sad, how defeated the estimable doctor had appeared on that grey morning. This abandonment only added to Josiah's daily sufferings: his insomnia, his lonely evenings. Mrs. Wells always wondered how much loss the doctor could bear considering what he had lived through in his childhood.

Reflecting now on an event that he could never forget, Dr. Benton rose from the table and left the dining room. No matter how hard he tried to block out memory, the same dark scene rushed into his inner mind every hour of every day. A drowning, a terrible grief. A year before his twelfth birthday he had been visiting an aunt in the seaside resort of Brighton where the great palace of the king, George IV, had been opened to the public for viewing. The building was a fantasy of domes and Chinese dragons, coloured walls rarely seen outside a sultan's tent. With him that day had been his blonde-haired younger sister, the nine-year-old Katherine Helena. Josiah's afternoon visit to the Brighton seaside allowed him to dip his feet into cold sea water. His dear Katy likewise had followed suit, splashing her hands and bare feet in the waves. She had become so enchanted she ran into deeper water and been caught in an undertow. Young Josiah called to her. Father ran to the edge of the water to catch her bobbing body, hearing her last cries for help. Now there was only the memory and the guilt, a hard knot of sorrow that kept Josiah awake at night.

Mrs. Wells watched her master go upstairs to his rooms. Whenever he became quiet and thoughtful, he went to the second floor of the house to relax. Mrs. Wells gave orders to the parlour maids to clear the table. After these chores, she told the others she would be busy for a time, and then made her way up the servants' stairs to the second floor where she knew her master was spending time in his special room. She meandered down to the door of the small bedroom at the back of the house. She walked on her tiptoes so she would avoid creaks in the floor boards. She had never spent much time inside the doctor's "quiet" room. Still, the hidden aspect of it, its secret nature, got the better of her common sense. No doubt, if Josiah invited her again, she would … but for now, she was pleased simply to be by its shut door. She could hear the doctor walking slowly back and forth as if he were ruminating on a patient's file. Most times, this was all she ever heard and it made her feel happy that this good man was finding some peace from the pressures of his surgery.

Ignoring the kitchen clatter down below, Dr. Josiah Benton looked about carefully at what he always imagined was the interior of a huge meringue cake. Always amazing, always delightful, he thought, checking the door to the small back bedroom was locked. The narrow bed covered by its muslin veil, the two little chairs and the table, all in pink, each one clean and neat. The table remained set as if for a child's afternoon tea party. The walls glowed like summer roses as did the silken curtains. "Ah," Dr. Benton sighed, crossing his hands behind his back. He went and stood alone by the pale window, the room around him casting its fantastic spell.

Today, oddly enough, as she leaned against the door, Mrs. Wells did not hear the usual footsteps pacing. She recognized a sound which brought alarm into her heart. Could it be the sound of a grown man weeping? She ventured to flatten her ear against the keyhole. No doubt of it — sobs and sniffles. And then she heard the anguished questions:

"Oh, where are you my sweet one?" Josiah said. "Where must I go to find you, my quiet child. Where?"

Chapter Twelve
Barrels of Piccadilly

"A hard task, Mr. Sender's Key," said Fitz, using the rhyming slang of Cockney London. "Our vicinity breeds scars and limps." Mr. Patrick Jeremiah Fitz was round: his belly, his nose, his goiter. He reclined in a bishop's chair, wearing multi-coloured rags and a fur collar. Always merry, his toothless mouth formed a perfect "O" when he laughed. "But Malibran can help. We had a scum fellow drop in a while back. Not old, not young, bitten up by Fortune, I'd wager. You can help, Malibran. Can't you, chucky?" A dark man with a waxed moustache and yellow coat stepped away from the wall. In his right hand was a green concertina, common among street singers along the Strand. In this attic in Nightingale Lane late afternoon light revealed other men about the room, each displaying a trade — a penny profile-cutter with his scissors, a juggler and a doll-fixer, his paint brushes and glass eyes displayed in small boxes.

"What'll you pay, Bobby?" said Malibran, his voice hoarse from singing.

Nick the Hand spoke up: "Saleables, Malibran. For profit."

"I've no need of 'em," Malibran said. "For what I know I need a pound note, nothin' less."

Fitz broke into a sharp laugh. "The beak here carries no blunt! All gone to Nick and his crew to buy vittles. You're no covey," he said to Malibran.

"I've nothing," Inspector Enderbsy admitted. "I am at your mercy." Endersby was apprehensive among these street folk. He sensed their distrust of him as a man of the law.

A quick-flying sovereign from the hand of Fitz hit the floor at Malibran's feet. "Speak up. This'n I *will make* pay me back," Fitz said pointing to Endersby. "I take no fork-out from you, Fitz," Malibran growled. He picked up the coin and tossed it back into the wide lap of its donor. "Nought for nought," Malibran said, turning back to his corner. The other street men grumbled; some lit up their pipes and stared at Endersby, standing bewildered before Fitz on his throne. Endersby, stepped toward Malibran. "I will ask you, sir," the inspector said, "to help me. Agreed, you have seen better times. But we live in a dark age. I can promise you food, if you wish, or a warm coat in exchange for words. Words that may save the lives of a number of innocent children. A monster roams about. If you know of him, you can judge best if he should be allowed to continue his deeds. With your aid, I can better navigate the ship of the law."

The assembly of men listened in silence to Endersby's plea. Nick the Hand began to whistle very low, his lips held close to give the sound of a mournful wind. "Wot?" Malibran shouted at the others. Fitz, the profile cutter, and the juggler began to whistle low, joining in a chorus under Nick the Hand. "I ain't no fool-mouth," yelled Malibran. The whistling reached a wave. Malibran paced while looking hard at Endersby. He then pushed the inspector aside, strove up to Fitz, and gave a quick bow of respect.

"No name that I know of, told me nothing of 'imself, no question the git-scag had a jag marking his face, a sword cut, like a soldier's," Malibran confessed. "Fitz and me, we found the scum at the door, a beggin'. I helped him out for seven, eight days, getting scraps, teachin' 'im to beg proper and play the 'pity-man'. He shallowed by puttin' out his hand; his sore legs had bindin's but Fitz said to take 'em off to gather more coin from the passing crowd. He was honest enough, paid me my share. For a week we did it. We worked always by day, searching out the parish churches and some afternoons he'd stand by workhouse gates with me. Two evenings ago he took gin with me and then moved off. Didn't say where."

Fitz said: "We help our wanderin' brothers as long as they pays us back." Endersby suspected Malibran was too wily to divulge more without receiving money. Perhaps this pity-man was but one of many lost men who worked the streets; they found lodgings in all parts of London and lent a hand to others as part of their code of honour. "Mr. Fitz, you and Malibran have told me much. But still I am lost. How could I set up spies to help me track this man — or any like him — in case he be the monster killing innocent women?"

"Monster?" roared Fitz. "Bogey-man? You reckon this 'pity-man' be your culprit?"

"I can only wager, Mr. Fitz. Fate grants me speculation only, not the eye of the prophet."

These words brought out a ripple of laughter from the men. Fitz slapped his knee. Endersby realized that sentiment — heartfelt — and even his own wit had short shrift with these men of hard luck. He decided to appeal to vanity. "All great generals, particularly our grand Duke of Wellington, had to resort to trackers to find out where his prey lay. I need your power, Mr. Fitz, as Duke of the Docks, to do the same." Fitz stood. He asked the company of street men to gather near his throne.

"This heavy-swell here ain't out to nab *us*. Murder is no slam," Fitz said in a grand tone of voice. "Wot's here is blood. You passengers of our streets see all, know all the masters of the lodging houses. And the cribs." Fitz stretched out his right arm and raised his palm toward the others. "We be here to stump this Bobby, and *to nab* the murdering covey," Fitz proclaimed. "He be worse than any. *Killin' women.* Lay on, chuckies, there be vittles and honour for your pains, I wager. *If the pity-man be him.*"

The juggler stepped forward. "I be from Dublin, sir. I went about with the scag a couple of times, down near the river. If you wishes it, I can shows you tonight at where he sometime come and go." Malibran shoved the juggler's shoulder. His face wrinkled with anger: "Wot, Irish, you get in a string with this git-bobby, with a trap for nothing but a boiled chop? I knows best where the scum sleeps. He's come back to Blue Anchor, near the fancy-house."

"With your permission, Mr. Fitz," said Endersby, "I could square this Dubliner, Nick and his crew, you yourself, Mr. Malibran, and any others a roast beef supper with potatoes at the corner of Fenchurch Street and Lark Lane — if I may have the chance to spot the culprit where Mr. Malibran claims he lives. And to have bodies help apprehend him if need arises. I need to question him, take a look at him. I do not wish to arrest him on a false supposition." Fitz reached for his pipe and applied a taper to its bowl. "To put up a sell, nab the scar?" Fitz said, thinking out loud. "I might allow my workin' men to give you help, sir. We needs *income* as much as hot suppers. You in turn must scratch me, and scratch me where I do itch." Endersby waited for the demand. Fitz trained his gaze on the herd of street men: "We 'ave here, my fellows, a Bobby-gull with a conscience. But we are men of few means. Gin is a boon. My men need it to keep 'em warm. I can sell it for profit on the docks. Bring tonight five barrels of finest clear Piccadilly. Scouts and aids then we'll be."

"Agreed, Mr. Fitz," Endersby replied, not knowing where his next words might take him. "Mr. Fitz," Endersby then said. "I have but three days to put an end to this brutality. On orders from my superintendent. I must work on absolute guarantees or the culprit will vanish. If the man in question gets away somehow this night, or if we be mistaken in our search, I will *still insist* on your help."

Fitz lifted up his pipe. His eyes did not waver from looking straight into Endersby's features. "Done," he then said to the inspector. Climbing down from his chair, Fitz walked among the cluster of men who stood slack-jawed in anticipation. "Mr. Bobby-Endersby will give you who want it your instructions as to how to procure your roast beef," Fitz announced. The congregation gathered hats and portables and stood at attention. Endersby gave the address of the chop house again, told the men to bring clubs and rope and ended with the statement: "Gather at ten o'clock."

Inspector Endersby entered the open street a free man once again. Nick the Hand and his crew flew off down an alley with the promise of a reunion later in the evening. Endersby now felt his mind manacled by a new set of problems to solve. And a thorn of doubt pricked: who was this Malibran? Was his resistance a matter of money only? He had spent days and nights with the 'pity-man' on the streets. If this scarred man was *the* murderer, was Malibran an accomplice in stealing girl children to sell to the nanny-brothels where virgin girls were prized for their so-called "healing" powers? All was possible, Endersby thought, given the desperation of street men.

A blur of pedestrians and carriages greeted the pondering

inspector as he slowly walked past the mass of the Tower of London, then north toward Cheapside and St. Paul's Cathedral. At Lark Lane, Endersby entered a chop house run by a cousin of his old friend, Inspector Smallwood of Seven Dials. With an advance of ten shillings, Endersby had the proprietor set aside an upstairs room with tables and chairs and a joint of beef to be served sharp at ten o'clock. Leaving by a side door, Endersby continued on, noting the old women, London's gutter-scroungers, searching for cigar stubs and lost pennies up and down the back lanes. Street-sellers of drink lined the curbs in this far eastern end of the city. Here were food stalls charging a ha'penny for Endersby's favourite, lard-smeared baked potatoes. He hired a hansom just in time to save himself from gluttony and drove off to Covent Garden. He went into a gin merchant's and ordered the barrels of Piccadilly. Once the barrels of gin were marked for delivery, Endersby hired another hansom and drove home to Number Six Cursitor Street to dine with his beloved wife, Harriet, wondering all the while how he'd convince his reluctant superintendent to pay out coin to men of London's underclass.

Chapter Thirteen
Madness for a Penny

The ragged fellow in front of Mr. Henry Lardle hung down his head. Early evening light from the one window spread narrow shadows against the slanted ceiling. What else could Mr. Lardle do? Should he stay angry? No good would come of harsh words. He tossed a glance at the dirty walls. An attic mouldy and pungent as a sewer tunnel. A penny more a week — if he could squeeze such a coin out of Dr. Josiah Benton's fist.

"Luvly?" he called out. He listened. "My Kate? Gone 'ave you, my dear?"

Sadly, Henry Lardle resumed his gaze at the pathetic fellow in front of him who now raised his head and leaned forward as Lardle did himself. *Such a weathered, wind-torn chap to look at,* Henry concluded. His beard was scruffy. His cheek ugly as ever. What a filthy pair of hands! "Look at 'em," he scolded.

"You need a good washin."

The face in the mirror did not smile. Henry did not despise it; he did not pity it, though he knew it so very well. *How cruel the world had become,* he mused. "You still have time. Best to keep on," Henry said to himself. "Doctor Benton pays you; Simple work, really. A young one here and there. No harm done, not really. Better than a dredgerman's wage, or a soldier's, if you thinks about it. Given a coin, a young gal will do almost anything."

With that bit of advice, Henry stood. He walked to the bed and removed his frock coat and sat down to ease the pain in his legs. Carefully, he slid off one boot and then the other. He lay down, wishing he had a plug of tobacco in his pipe. At least he had a couple of farthings for a gin or two. "Never miss out on your gin," he cautioned. Lucky he was to have found cheap, no, cheaper lodging. Tonight he would capture at least one gal to earn his money. Not like last night — ooh, last night, what a ruckus. In and out, up and down. Not Benton's type, they wasn't. *Best to lie low now until night falls,* he cautioned himself. "It ain't my doing in the end," he said aloud, as if Dr. Benton were standing in front of him. "You gets what you pays for," Lardle whispered, wiping the back of his hand over his mouth.

"Best try and rest. No violence tonight," he promised himself. "No need for hurting." And with that, Henry Lardle slipped into calm sleep.

⁂

As evening fell over the tree-filled village five miles west of London, Mrs. Bolton finished her sweeping up and placed her trusty twig broom back into the closet. The two candles near the hearth were extinguished. From the bedroom of her sister, Jemima, came the sounds of sighing, of scratching quill upon paper. "Dear Jemima?" Mrs. Bolton said quietly to the locked door leading to her sister's room. "May I get you anything before I retire?" Silence. Mrs. Bolton let out a breath of relief.

She turned to walk through her kitchen to the far room at the other end of her cottage.

There, in her large canopied bed, the same one she had once shared with Humphrey Bolton, her long-dead husband, she would rest her head and her mind from her long day. She had fetched many sheets of paper for her frantic sister and carried into that same fetid bedroom two hot meals, both of which were refused with her sister's quick brush of a hand.

And there was the lace to fetch. Poor Jemima had demanded to see all her oldest pieces; an assortment of items once made by her in her youth. And now, just as her feet stepped across the threshold of her sleeping chamber, Mrs. Bolton's ears heard a long low groan. Then a scratchy voice called out: "Sister, sister dear." Mrs. Bolton imagined her sickly sibling fallen from bed, her head marked with blood from an injury. Mrs. Bolton turned and rushed through the house until she reached the door of Jemima's bedroom. "What is it, Jemima?" The lock was slipped open. The pale, drawn face of her sister looked into Mrs. Bolton's eyes. "I need a quill, dear sister. A fresh quill."

"At this hour?" Mrs. Bolton replied.

"Yes, I beg of you. I plead," was Jemima's barely audible reply.

"But I have none. I brought you the last two at luncheon. We are clean out, sister, dear."

A cold hand with skin as rough as the bark of a dead tree shot out and took hold of Mrs. Bolton's right wrist. "I shall die, then, sister," was Jemima's response. "My heart shall crack."

"Nonsense, Jemima! Get into bed and to sleep. I will fetch new quills tomorrow morning at Mr. Burleigh's stationery shop."

The hand squeezed harder. "Fetch a quill now, sister! Now, before I fall into darkness."

Never before had Mrs. Bolton heard her sister Jemima speak in such a way. Mrs. Bolton feared the worst: Jemima had collapsed into madness. "Oh, dear, Jemima," Mrs. Bolton said. She yanked her arm free. She found herself in apron and cap, dashing out the side door into the mucky yard, toward her hen house and goose pond. Into the stench of the hen house, past the laying roosts and beyond to a trough full of dried corn and one young white goose all aflutter, from which she pulled and pulled out two tail feathers — hard to manage with such flapping and squawking — and then a journey back, slipping and sliding, Mrs. Bolton's vision fixed only on one spot, the pale loitering face of her mad, clutching sister who, on being handed the fresh quills, said nothing, slammed the door shut, and began to hum a frenetic tune that Mrs. Bolton, hearing it from behind the closed door, could not recognize.

With her breath barely recovered, Mrs. Bolton then found her way to her own room, whereupon she felt the bloody scratches on her arms. "Oh, my," she whispered through a yawn.

Mrs. Bolton subsequently fell onto her mattress in a grand flop, already half asleep before her cheek touched the down-filled pillow. From across her swept floors floated a late-night descant of sounds: the scratch of a newly plucked goose quill and the child-like singing of her desperate sister.

Chapter Fourteen
A Reckoning of Sorts

"Splendid, Mr. Endersby. Most gallant."

The admiring voice belonged to none other than Harriet Endersby, the inspector's wife. Blue-eyed and clever were but two words Endersby used to describe the love of his life. In moments of reverie he often delighted in the phrases that had joined the two of them in holy matrimony twenty-one years before: *to love and to cherish, till death us do part.* At this instant Harriet Endersby was sitting at her round card table across from her neighbour, Mrs. McLaren. The motive for her commending words was the appearance of her husband in an outfit made by Harriet from a pattern she had purchased in Regent Street. "Oh, do turn again, dear one," she said.

On the inspector's head sat a rounded cap, a red tassel hanging down over his left ear. His great chest was enfolded in a long-sleeved gown of satin that was patterned with Madras flowers. A twisted red rope belt hugged his ample waist and thus, his "Persian Gentleman's" smoking outfit was complete.

"It is indeed the latest fashion in Paris," said Mrs. McLaren. "I believe our dear Queen's husband Prince Albert himself wears much the same in private chambers."

"So the fashionable intelligence informs us," said Harriet Endersby. "I was most fortunate. I purchased the cloth from a delightful gentleman in Soho Square, a Mr. Nejad. He claims he is from Persia itself."

"How intriguing," said Mrs. McLaren.

"Persia?" questioned Inspector Endersby. "The family name is foreign, certainly."

"My dear Owen," replied Harriet Endersby. "Do you doubt my powers of observation? The man most certainly had the dark handsome eyes of a gentleman from that region. He said he was from Tabriz. And his charming accent was neither that of an Englishman or a Frenchman."

"My dear, I do beg pardon," said Inspector Endersby. "My objection was not to your superior ability to determine national origin, but rather to express some doubt that a gentleman from so far away would be selling goods in Soho Square."

Harriet answered with a smile of affection: "You are too suspicious by half, sir."

"Good evening to you both," said Mrs. McLaren, rising and heading toward the door. Both Mr. and Mrs. Endersby wished her a good night and thanked her once again for bringing over one of her delicious homemade meat pies for their dinner. "You are too, kind, my dear," said Harriet as the two women bid goodbye.

Later, after their dinner, Endersby helped his wife to clear the table since it was the maid's night out. "My, how wonderfully logical you are, dear husband," Harriet said after having listened to Endersby's strategies of bargaining with Mr. Fitz between bites of pie smothered in chutney.

"We are a new breed, my dearest Harriet," Endersby said, pouring boiling water into the scrub sink. "Caldwell and I attempt to solve crimes *after* they have occurred using deduction, reliable witnesses and proof. The old Bow Street Runners years back used brute force to get confessions. *We* employ science. No more leading of ruffians to the gallows on mere conjecture."

"Yes, dear Owen, I know." Harriet smiled.

"Am I making speeches again, my love?" asked Endersby, his face warm from the steaming basin.

"You are tired, dear one," Harriet replied. "How fortunate we are in London to have men like you to keep us safe." With that, Harriet left the dishes and pots to soak, kissed her husband, and said: "We shall have tea in the parlour in half an hour."

Endersby retreated into his small study to work on a new wooden puzzle he had recently purchased in the Burlington Arcade. Sitting down at a small table, he unwrapped the brown paper, examined the wax seals and the large stamp from the French customs. He read the bill of lading from the English shop and then touched the puzzle itself. Each piece of cherry wood had a bevelled edge and each could fit into three others to make up a larger picture. *Ingenious,* he thought: *how very rational of the French.* He clicked the pieces together for a time, his mind relaxing.

"Tea, dearest," came Harriet's voice. Endersby and his Harriet sat alone by their cosy hearth with a pot of black Indian, Harriet's favourite. It was their nightly custom to take tea and to sample one of the many cheeses the inspector enjoyed. Such culinary indulgence was limited by their household budget. A detective-inspector's salary was low, though adequate — food, taxes, servant's wages and fuel were all accommodated. The French puzzles Endersby purchased, however, were saved up for, a penny

at a time. Best of all, the theatre they both loved was affordable —
if only once every two weeks.

Harriet re-filled his cup: "I suppose you will soon leave to
meet your constables, as you warned me?"

"I must, Mrs. Endersby. In their company, I will also consort
with gentlemen from the criminal classes to help me locate the
villain."

"Gentlemen?" Harriet asked. "You are lenient, Mr. Endersby."

"It is the only recourse I have at the moment."

"Two young girls named 'Catherine,' you said?" Harriet
asked. "Picked out of the crowd as if they had been lost and forgotten." Harriet sighed, sitting back in her chair.

"Sad young things. Soiled cargo on the sweep of the tide."

"How terrible," Harriet said. "And to think of all the labour
you do — you and your constables."

"I thank you for that recognition, Mrs. Endersby," said the
inspector, pulling out his watch and noting the time. "But I must
be off." Endersby rose, kissed Harriet, who in turn embraced
him and smoothed down his mussed hair. She carried a candle and went down the stairs with him to the street, where he
hailed a hansom cab and instructed her, "Do not wait up for
me tonight, my dear one. I shall be very late." Harriet patted his
cheek affectionately and added: "And most certainly hungry!"
The cab from Number Six Cursitor Street clattered through
gas-lit alleys and passages full of roaming people, costermonger
barrows, riders on horses with fine bridles. At Fleet Lane Station
House, the inspector descended and walked briskly across
the lane to a brightly lit coffee house. On entering, he spotted
Sergeant Caldwell, Constables Rance, and Tibald sitting in one
of the wooden booths; set before them were a large pot of coffee
and plates of buttered toast.

"Good evening," Endersby said as the three younger men

stood. "Gentlemen, I asked you to investigate a number of work-houses in the northern district."

Caldwell spoke first and told about the man he had found in the hut — but lost after a chase. In London Wall Workhouse he discovered only old men and boys. Constable Tibald reported on ledgers, entries, the lack of Catherines, and the new locks put on the coal chutes.

"Curious," said Endersby, stirring his coffee.

"Sir," said Constable Rance. "I was sent to the Foundling Hospital. The ledgers were most detailed but no Catherines were written on the lists of the living or the dead. But this Sunday past a man paid the hospital a visit. A gin-smelling, scarred man came to the door and asked to see the ledgers. On demanding his reasons why, the matron was told he was looking for a young female of ten years with the first name of Catherine. The matron refused the man entry and did not divulge the records of the led-gers. By law, she cannot do so. Once he had been told he could not search inside the man walked away. The matron said she felt pity for him as he had a limp."

"May we assume," said Endersby, "that this chap, perhaps, was our culprit? If so, it seems he showed himself first in day-light, attempting a more legitimate form of searching than what we have witnessed in St. Giles and Shoe Lane."

The four men sat momentarily in silence. Mr. Caldwell obliged his superior by noting down the details of each constable's story. "We are facing a desperate man," noted Endersby. "I suppose he shall try at least two workhouses this night, if he is continuing his search. He is compelled to do so, I wager."

"How to proceed then, sir?" asked Caldwell. "Detective branches in all station houses know of our story, here in central London. Constables are on the alert."

"Let us deduct first," smiled Endersby. "We shall cancel out the Foundling Hospital for the moment. St. Giles and Shoe Lane have been visited — with horrific consequences. I have discovered from my own investigation that a fellow survived his first days here in London as a wandering street beggar. He resembles the descriptions of our culprit and to my mind is suspicious. So, we have one or more possible suspects at loose. Let us assume that *he* may choose to continue his nightly search." The men made note of the inspector's words. Endersby stood up.

"Mr. Caldwell, you shall come with me for a roast beef supper."

"In truth, sir?" Caldwell asked, somewhat in surprise.

"Mr. Rance, you shall take your cosh and darkee lantern and return to Baribcan and post guards. You, Mr. Tibald, shall follow Mr. Rance's example, but you shall acquaint yourself more fully with the masters and children at the Theobald's Road. If there be any rattlings, any cries, do your duty." Endersby quickly paid the bill. The golden light of the coffee house gave way to the blue cold of Fleet Lane, where the men agreed to meet next morning at eight o'clock sharp in Fleet Lane Station House. With little else to say, they parted company.

"Are you not well, sir?" asked Caldwell.

"Well enough for an aging man, Sergeant. I fear this night. We are not gaining ground."

"Certainly, sir."

"Sergeant, let us look forward. We have an adventure before us. Kindly be prepared for a supper with thieves and in the meantime, hail us a hansom."

"*Most* certainly, Inspector."

A half moon shone through cloud. Gulls cried out to each other over the river. The night promised rain.

"There it be, sir. Yonder."

The Irish juggler pointed to a three-storey brick building in Blue Anchor with an upper roof built at a steep slant. In it sat a small dormer window, now dark. "I seen the pity-man at that window, sir. Tis the same place Malibran spoke of, the same lodging house."

"I ask you," Endersby said, "why Mr. Malibran has declined to join us this evening?" Fitz grunted at Endersby's elbow, "A wayward man, Inspector. Take no account."

Nick the Hand appeared round the corner of the suspect's building. He ran up to the little group: Endersby, the Irish juggler, Sergeant Caldwell, and Fitz, all huddled in a darkened archway. "Not a peep, Inspector Bobby-git," Nick the Hand said. "A stinkin' rot of a house, fittin' for one killin' women." Fitz spoke up in a hoarse whisper: "Did you put Jack the Knife down at the foyer, lad? And yer two nippers at the back?"

"I did, Fitz. No chance if a bolter be in there hidin'. My two boys can trip 'im."

Endersby stepped forward. He and Caldwell stood ready in ambush, eyes peering into corners. The party of thieves had finished their joint of beef at midnight, meat with roasted Irish spuds washed down with pints of porter. Now it was in whispers the five men spoke. Endersby remained puzzled by the absence of Malibran, but he had to be content to pass the evening hoping for the limping 'pity-man' — the possible killer — to show his face. Silence fell among the men as they waited. An hour passed. What horrors were being committed as they lingered, the inspector wondered. The night grew blacker. *Where was the man? Could one truly trust the word of thieves?* Caldwell began to cough; his jaw was bound in a fresh cloth and he chewed cloves to dull the pain in his molar. Another hour dragged on. The Thames lay quiet; no steamboat wheelers churned upstream.

The night seemed too still for comfort. *Was this becoming a foolish gamble?*

"Look, sir," Caldwell whispered. Out of the dark, a bearded figure slowly hobbled down the alley toward where the five men stood. Thin, bent, head covered by tangled strands of hair. The voice was grumbling. In the figure's right hand was a staff — *a broom handle, or a gaff,* thought Endersby. A few hesitant steps and then the figure stopped. He looked around, checked the street running to the river. He then held his gaze on the men in the archway. Coming closer, he looked directly at the group as if he knew they were there, waiting. A soiled bandage covered up most of the face. The man's trousers did not fit well — inside out they looked — and high military boots ran up to the knees. A limp, a stink, a beard. The bandaged head lifted; the figure tried to peer at Endersby as a mole might from a narrow tunnel.

"Who are you?" asked the figure.

"Endersby," said the inspector.

"Don't you observe the cobbles, *you,*" the figure said. "Move out, *you* move out."

"Your name?" asked Endersby.

"Mr. Bub. Beezle Bub, the Devil take you," the figure answered. From his mouth burst forth a guffaw that ceased abruptly not a second after. Endersby now dared to test the figure by stating the first name of the girls taken from the workhouses.

"Miss Catherine," Endersby began. "She is at home, is she?"

"Very likely," the stranger answered. "Yet, very likely not."

The figure cocked his head toward the inspector. "She asked after you," Endersby said. Nick the Hand and Fitz now stepped forward out of the shadowy archway. Endersby and Caldwell waited for the figure to respond. If he wished to run, he would be blocked by Nick and Fitz.

"By Heaven," the man said. A pain-filled cry rose from the

creature's throat. His right hand pulled out a pistol. Caldwell rushed out to grab the hand. The pistol fired, missed its mark, a puff of smoke trailing out the barrel. Dropping the gun, the man swung the wooden staff and struck Endersby on the forehead. With sudden speed, the bandaged man jabbed the staff into Caldwell's chest, forcing the sergeant to fall back with a moan. The figure swivelled and began to scuttle away. "Grab him," shouted Endersby. The cohorts reeled; the Irish juggler ran into the fray, about to give chase.

But all then halted. A shout cut the air. Endersby turned to see a man. A swirling figure in a broad hat, a bandana over his lower face, a black cloak. He came flying out of a narrow alley hidden in the gloom, a club held high.

"Holla, holla!" the man shouted. From a side pocket in his cloak, the figure also brandished a long knife.

"Gentlemen, stand aware!" yelled Endersby. He and Caldwell stood side-by-side shouting orders to the other three to join them in making a offensive phalanx, an ancient Roman army manoeuvre Endersby had read about in the books of Livy. All five advanced in unison, swinging fists, knocking the limping man in the chest while attempting to elbow the man in the broad hat who backed off a pace, holding up his long knife. Nick the Hand jumped the line and kicked the knife from the man's hand, sending it clattering over the cobblestones. Endersby and Caldwell then strode toward the figure, their arms held wide as if to catch a runaway horse. "Stand, sir," Endersby commanded. The man spat at the inspector, raised his club and charged. The club found its first mark along Nick the Hand's shoulders, who tried to trip the attacker but failed. Endersby's arm subsequently suffered a heavy thunk. In a blink, the club's end shot forward — aiming at the inspector's right eye. Ducking, Endersby struck back with clenched fists, his "demon familiar" filling his eyes with rage. The crack of a jaw bone gladdened him for a moment but his pounding was not strong enough, for he glimpsed the man swing again, his arms flailing like those of a wrestler in the Blackfriar Sporting Ring. Full of fury as wild as a maimed bull's, the man in the broad hat slammed into Fitz, even though Endersby kept smashing his knuckles into the man's nose.

"Caldwell, look sharp," shouted Endersby, catching his breath. His sergeant-at-hand scrambled toward the figure with the bandaged face who shouted in panic and stumped away into a darkened passage. In the meantime, the man in the broad hat tried to strike again but Endersby rushed him, kneed him hard, reaching out to grab his neck. The felon moved fast, much to Endersby's dismay, and slipped out of grasp, escaping in the opposite direction to where the bandaged figure had run.

"After the bandaged man," Endersby shouted. Caldwell started up toward the passage. Endersby wiped blood from his face. His gouty foot was now throbbing from his physical effort. "Irish, follow the other fellow. Watch out for his club." The juggler jogged off, darting in and out of alley entrances. Endersby fell into a halting step behind his sergeant. They stumbled into the murk of the passage. No gaslight shone. Cobblestones wriggled loose and tripped their hurrying feet, but footsteps clumping ahead led the two to push on. Walls and broken barrows kept blocking the policemen's attempts to grab the figure; only a man familiar with this passage could find his way in haste. "Keep on, Caldwell!" A door squealed open, then shut. Onward, further, the cobbles turned into slushy mud and sewage. A stink of mould. Caldwell's voice rang out like a cry in a storm: "Stop, you — hold!"

Inspector Endersby tripped. He fell, hands first, into a puddle of muck. Caldwell stopped and ran back, searching for his superior. "No, sergeant, keep apace. Get on," croaked Endersby. Caldwell set off again, but soon after reappeared, his boots and trousers splattered with slush. "Gone, sir," he mumbled as he reached down his hand to help Endersby stand. "Like a phantom," replied Endersby. Appearing together out of the passage, the two men heard Nick the Hand's voice echo in the street: "The gaffer's leaked out!"

When the four exhausted men gathered together, they looked defeated. "No luck, Bobby," admitted Nick the Hand. Under the archway, Fitz was cursing. "He bobbed us, the ratter. Betrayed us. That was Malibran in the black cloak."

"You sure, Fitz?" asked Endersby.

"Malibran?" said Sergeant Caldwell.

Endersby wiped his face. "Did you know of this, Fitz?"

"You take me for a shit-hole stick? No, sir! The son of a leech, he crossed us, no scratch for no scratch, the buggered fool."

"He was no good cheese," said Nick the Hand, rubbing the back of his neck.

"So how and why did Malibran show up?" the inspector asked.

"Ah, covey," answered Fitz. "The two's in cahoots. If that be yer culprit all bandaged up, then Malibran and him have a gig. The pity-man knew we was on the lookout. That's why he had the pistol. Malibran dressed him up in disguise. Malibran loves coin, Inspector. He needs the cripple git to earn him." Fitz spat out a bit of tobacco after his explanation. "Let's at 'im," said Nick the Hand. Inspector Endersby thought quickly: *if I let the street men fight each other, no good could come.*

"Fitz, you and Nick, retreat for now," commanded Endersby. "Let Caldwell and I move on. When you can, wander back to your attic and let your men know Malibran's 'pity-man' is on the run. No doubt he will go into hiding. Find out, if you can, where the bandaged man has gone. Knock on doors. No saying this chap is our murderer. But he is suspicious, as is Malibran."

"Fitz, too, can knock on any door," Nick the Hand said with pride. "Crack 'im, we will."

"Gather Jack and your mites, Nick," commanded Fitz. "Come morning, Bobby, you shall find yer culprit. Come to Nightingale at your wont. Malibran is hoping you didn't recognize him in his black."

"I was stumped," admitted Endersby, his fatigue now drying his throat. "Listen up, Fitz. If Malibran is bold, might he go back to his digs?"

"Or to a cunny house, Bobby. Then to home," Fitz said.

Fitz and Nick the Hand started to walk off.

"Where does Malibran lodge, Fitz?"

"Planning a short visit are you, git? In Nightingale, Number Six. Up the top." Fitz waved goodbye. Endersby's mind tumbled. Bones and muscles ached. He had to lift his gouty foot a few times to alleviate the hot pangs. He yearned for his bed with every step forward, but he felt driven, his "demon familiar" now riding on his back, ready to jolt him into a fight. Beside him, Caldwell kept pace. His low moans of tooth pain inspired Endersby to imagine a future meeting between his own gloved fists and Malibran's jaw bone. "Sergeant," said Endersby. "Come. We have one last chore before us."

With renewed purpose, the inspector straightened his hat. He commanded Sergeant Caldwell to find a hansom at this late hour. "Onward, Caldwell. We shall walk if need be."

"You are certain, sir?" Caldwell said, the weariness in his voice making Endersby smile. "Sergeant," Endersby said. "Bear't that the opposed may beware of ... us!"

Chapter Fifteen
A Monster in the Night

The night now entered its final hour, the sun still biding its time before dawn. Down a dark alley, a few blocks east of Blue Anchor, there stood a small stone building: the Little Queen Street House of Orphans and Derelicts. A hidden place where, at the chime of the clock, a child rose from her bed, her blonde hair mussed from sleeping with her head ensconced between pillow and mattress. She was no more than nine. The ward held only seven beds, all for girls her age. Next door, a room contained older women who coughed and coughed and always woke the child. She began to wander. Her eyes were half-shut. In her troubled mind, the fire nightmare had come again: her momma, her papa, her brother danced in the flames and called out to her. A man in a black hat pulled her away from them, the smoke catching them all and making them disappear.

"Matron?" the child whispered. "Where are you?" The child had been gently taught. She knew not to yell out, to scream in the night, for the matron was kind and she slept in a little room down the hall from the main ward. The child recalled the matron's instructions: "If you need me, child, come to my door and tap with a soft hand." *She is like Momma*, the child thought as she stepped past the few beds, her arms held out in front of her.

In the hallway ahead there was the staircase and doors to the other parts of the house. The child had never ventured beyond them. She knew the staircase was not to be climbed. She knew the courtyard was open only for one hour a day — a small square of cobblestone surrounded by high grey walls. There, she played hopscotch and dog-chase with her bedmates, most of them tired and unhappy. The child liked to hold hands. She liked it when the matron held hers and walked with her. All she ever wanted was to hold hands and hear the trees rustle far away over the walls.

Stopping, the child stared at the matron's door. She liked the sound of the latch and the lock clicking open when the matron came out in the night with her candle. *But what was that*, the child wondered as she raised her fist to tap. On the staircase. In the corner where the staircase turned. *Was it her Papa there?* She lowered her fist and walked into the hallway. The air felt colder. A window up above the door to the courtyard gave some light to the stairs. "Papa?" the child whispered. The figure hiding in the shadow did not move. The child approached it. *Papa*, she thought; *he has come out of the smoke.* All she could see was a black shadow, a head all fuzzy with hair and long hands that hung down at the sides of the black body. "Papa?" she said again. The child knew her dream had come true. Papa had returned to rescue her. She ran up to him, her bare feet patting the cold stone floor.

"It's me," she said, grabbing hold of the figure's cold hand. She looked up into the face. The hair hid his eyes but the child knew it was her father. He was all black. He smelled like the river where they had once lived together. She pressed her head against his body. The figure's other cold hand moved. It placed itself on the child's head and stroked her hair. "I miss you," the child whispered.

Just then a noise from the top of the staircase. Male voices. A thin band of light under the door at the top, then footsteps. The child lost her grasp. Her Papa let her go, lifted her carefully and set her on the step below, his face close to hers for only a moment, his eyes looking into hers before he rose and began to move away. "No," the child moaned. She stood up. "Papa, stay," she whispered. But the door at the top of the stairs opened. The child ran back into the ward. The shadowy figure limped away, dragging himself toward another door at the end of the ward where he disappeared. The child found her bed. She buried her head under the pillow. Men stomped past her. Shouts and more shouts and a door shut with a bang.

Alone, the child wept. But then she felt a warm shiver run through her body. Her Papa was still alive. He had touched her. She rubbed her hand and felt the oily dirt he had left behind on her skin. "Come back, Papa," she said, her heart content. She fell back to sleep so quickly, she hardly had time to whisper "Papa" once again.

***

Morning light was an hour away. Catherine Smeets and Little Mag had spent the better part of the evening before pacing in St. Pancras Workhouse, trying to stop the stinging from the beating given them by Matron Pickens.

"Give me your hand," Catherine said to Little Mag. "All are still asleep. We can bolt out the side door before light."

Holding her hands behind her, Little Mag shook her head: "I'm too weak, Catherine. I have a terrible ache." Little Mag sank to the floor and Catherine could not make her budge. "Goodbye," Catherine said before sneaking her way to the stairs. To her delight, she found the passage open. Down the hallway and out the side door she raced. *I am like Nell,* she thought, *I can disappear in the streets.* Where might she sleep and remain unharmed? Catherine had left behind everything, even her secret letters to her beloved uncle. There was no time to go back and fetch them. Quietly, she crossed the empty yard. Onto the wash house roof she climbed and balanced herself. Leaning out, she grabbed hold of the top of the wall and pulled herself up, her bare feet pushing her body until it lay across the narrow ridge of the brick. Catherine leaped out to land on the pavement outside the compound.

Hurry! She scampered into the dim gold of the gas-lit street. *How easy to escape,* she thought. But her stomach reminded her she was hungry! Catherine found her legs could run hard. Down one street, through a narrow courtyard, and into a crooked lane leading to shelter under an overhanging partition of an ancient house. She found a dry spot, knelt down and folded her cold legs under her workhouse dress. *Quiet, like a sleeping puppy....*

Up at the corner stood a ramshackle gin shop. At this late hour customers were stumbling out its door. One man pushed out and stood, his body leaning one way then another to find balance. *What a grumbling he uttered,* Catherine thought. She huddled closer to the wall. He was more a creature than a man. He dragged his feet along the cobble stones. Catherine could hear his voice better: "Where, oh, where?" it said. The whisper became a cough. "Where to find *you?*"

Catherine wanted to dash away. This awful man could harm her. Slit her throat. She could now smell him as he drew closer. If she ran, he would chase after her. Catherine shut her eyes to make the creature disappear. The spot where she lay was dim but not so dark she could rest invisible. The man's boots scratched against stone. Catherine took a quick peek. As he passed under a street light, his face caught the gaslight. *Oh, help me*, Catherine's inner voice cried.

"Damn you," the man said. He entered the archway where his boot tip struck against Catherine's bent knee.

"What's this?" slurred the man.

The monster bent down toward her. A scream caught in Catherine's throat. "*You*, there," the man barked. He reached into a pocket. He pulled out a wooden Lucifer match and flicked it with his thumbnail. In the wavering light Catherine saw a hairy chin, a terrible scar; her face grew rigid in terror. "Rest, little one," the man whispered. A finger tilted Catherine's chin. "Ah, *you* will do!" Catherine tried to jump up. She slapped the man's hand away from her face. "You are the one," the hoarse voice said.

"Let me be!" Catherine shouted. Before she could blink, a sweaty palm clasped itself over her mouth. One arm held her close while the other slipped out a bit of rough cloth and covered her head. Blinded now, her nose barely free to breathe, Catherine felt herself being lifted up and carried.

"Have no fear," the man said. "Such a lovely sweet gal you are."

Chapter Sixteen
A Meeting of Fists

Malibran's club thumped to the floor. Stepping back, he collided with a table, knocking down his green concertina.

"Where is the ruffian, sir? Your pity-man!" Inspector Endersby shouted.

Early light seeped in through a patched window. The squalid room in Nightingale Lane stank of wet clothes. Malibran cowered in self-defense, facing the two intruders. Sergeant Caldwell blocked the doorway; Endersby stood in front of him, his face crusted with blood from his wounds. "We meet again *not* by chance, nor for your good fortune, sir," Endersby said. "We shan't leave until you tell us facts!" Endersby's voice had become a deep rasp. His "demon familiar" was clearly on view — fists clenched, feet firmly planted — ready for assault. An old memory of a chase and a beating rushed into his mind. Relishing it, he wiped his mouth; what he desired at this very second was to hear the crack of jawbone against knuckle.

"What'll you pay, Bobby?" snarled the cornered Malibran. "You've lost me my pity-man for makin' profit."

"I was at your mercy, sir, once...." snarled the inspector. "Now I give nor take no quarter. You and your man ambushed us. You no doubt helped him change his pelt and armed him. He may be a killer and you and he have beaten public officers of the law. Your bag of skin will lie in Fleet Lane prison forever!"

"I take no threat from you. I ain't no fool." replied Malibran.

Endersby grabbed hold of Malibran's shoulders and shook them. A surge of power drove the inspector's large belly against Malibran's frail frame. His fist swung out; Malibran dodged the blow and the inspector's knuckles tore into the plaster of the wall; on withdrawing his weapon of flesh, Endersby winced at the cuts splaying his skin.

Malibran picked up his club and raised it over his head: "Get out, scum-Bobby, or this bludgeon will smash your brains."

"Caldwell!" shouted the inspector. The sergeant leaped forward and knocked Malibran off his feet. Endersby rumbled over to him, stomped his boot onto the prostrate man's heaving chest. "Now, sir, it is time to tell a story." He picked up the shaking man and shoved him onto a chair. He signalled to Caldwell who ran behind Malibran and held him fast, pulling his arms back. "You know this man. You have worked with him. What is his name and where does he come from?" Endersby shouted.

"You deaf git," replied Malibran, who struggled unsuccessfully against Caldwell's iron grip. "I know not his name, as I told you. Nor nothing of him but that he came to Fitz for help."

"This evening you gave up a hot supper, Mr. Malibran. Was it to warn your pity-man we were on the chase?"

Malibran shut his mouth. He looked down at his bare feet. Endersby stepped forward and, before Malibran could move, pressed his boot on Malibran's right foot and crushed it down with his whole weight. "I can stand here, sir, quite comfortably if you wish it." Malibran tried in vain to pull his foot free. On command, Caldwell yanked harder so that Malibran's arms looked like two broken wings of a bird. Malibran yelled out: "You scummy policeman! I cannot walk nor earn my livin' if you keep my foot — ahh!" Endersby did not relent. With each breath, he relished the discomfort of the squirming man before him. "I shall be quick, Malibran. You have but a foot to lose; I have children's lives at stake. Tell me. Did you run to your pity man and betray our cause?"

Malibran tried to spit in the inspector's face, but Endersby's hand was too quick — a sharp slap to the jaw sent the man reeling to the floor.

"Yes, yes," Malibran moaned. He began to cough. In less than a second, Malibran was again shoved onto the chair, his torso doubled over in pain. "Speak, man," Endersby ordered.

"I went to his digs, in Blue Anchor," Malibran winced. "I told 'im I'd be his lookout, his protection. He's like me, out to get a penny the best way we can. He brought the pistol on his own. I know no more, Bobby. Can you not leave us in peace?" The pleading voice and the fear in Malibran's eyes touched Endersby. Here was an outcast, a lost soul. What privations had he suffered? And what real proof was there so far of the pity-man's guilt other than his appearance, or rather, his similar characteristics to that of a man described by two frightened girls.

"Caldwell, free the man," Endersby said. A breath filled the inspector's chest. The rabid fury of his demon calmed. Malibran slowly rose. His poorly nourished face reminded Endersby of the faces of the lost girls in the workhouse. *These people are the flotsam of life,* he thought. "You could lose profit, sir," Endersby began. "But two women not unlike yourself in luck have lost their lives. If your 'pity-man' is a murderer, I must find him. He may kidnap an innocent girl. He may lead her and a matron to join the ranks of the dead."

Malibran's eyes held fast the sorrowful gaze of the man who

moments before was prepared to maim him. He reached out his hand: "Pity means nothing to me and my sort." Endersby leaned back, fishing out two shillings from his waistcoat pocket. He knew enough of the wiles of criminal minds to figure he could not exhort any more from this man hardened by the world of London's poor.

"No reckoning where he will wander now," Malibran lamented, fingering the shillings and rubbing his sore stomach. "He rooms here, sometimes, in Nightingale Lane. Other times, he strolls north. To Seven Dials slum, or thereabouts. Claims them lodging houses is cheaper. The man tells no one his name. Fitz and me, we thinks he was a soldier who deserted." Endersby pondered the man's words. Malibran looked up into the inspector's face. "I don't know if I can ever find him now."

"Inspector, sir?" Caldwell asked. "Shall we escort Mr. Malibran to Fleet Lane?"

"Leave him be," came the inspector's response. *London is like the sea and hides its bodies well,* Endersby thought. Letting Malibran go free could prove helpful as he would most likely search out the pity-man for more work on the street. Malibran was worth following. Moving toward the door, Endersby felt a rush of despair. Time was rushing on. Only two days left to procure a conviction. Had the murderer struck again this past night if indeed the pity-man was innocent?

Endersby went out of the room and down the stairs. Alone in the street, he raised his head and relished the first fingers of light emanating from the eastern sky. Caldwell soon stepped up to his side. His sergeant was a good man, always patient with him in spite of the rambles the two of them were forced to make in chasing culprits.

"To your bed, Sergeant. We must let the wicked rest and go free for a time. I thank you for your constancy, sir. I value it much, indeed." The inspector shook his sergeant's hand. "Rest, Sergeant, and then let us meet as arranged to hear news, if any." Caldwell nodded, his face twitching with his tooth pain. "And Caldwell, get yourself to a barber and have that molar pulled out!"

"Goodnight, Inspector."

In a hansom cab that he found near the river, Endersby laid his head against the leather headrest. He began to catalogue his vices. He wondered if he'd ever balance his desire for justice against the fury of his "demon familiar." His wife Harriet would no doubt be dismayed at him arriving home bloodied and injured. The cab rattled along deserted streets. Hungry dogs cowered in doorways alongside ragged children. Endersby's pity went out to them. *How sad a world where children starve and animals hide in fear.* Crossing behind St. Paul's, the sun peeking over the horizon, Endersby looked out at the mass of London, soiled, ramshackle, indifferent and cold. He yearned for his hearth; he wished to fill the hollowness in his heart with cheery, loving voices. He concluded that he was a man of good conscience who must be careful, always, not to allow his disdain for evil men destroy his better self.

"Here it be, sir," the cabby said, his voice tired from his long night. Endersby paid the man a few pennies extra: "For you, cabby, and your labouring horse."

"Harriet, my love?" Endersby called as he entered Number Six Cursitor Street. The inspector washed and bound his smashed fist. Searching in his leather satchel, he pulled out the bits of lace and the envelope of rust bits he'd picked from the two corpses earlier in the day. The pencil drawing made by the mute Catherine he set beside the other objects on a table. He ran his finger across his face, tracing out the line of the scar made by the child's chilly finger. Was this line representing a scar or could the girl have seen only a shadow or a birthmark or a smudge of blood from a fight? To his seasoned eye, the objects seemed even more ambiguous than before. How sure could he be about the "pity-man" as a murderer?

Wishing to soothe his mind, Endersby moved into his flat's little kitchen. He went to the pantry and ran his eyes over the remains of a pork pie. He began to pick. Soon, he was gobbling the pie, grabbing fistfuls of pastry and meat.

"Mr. Endersby?"

It was Harriet. Her voice so startled him he swivelled and dropped the pie platter.

"Good Jesus!"

Harriet stepped back. Her soft white hand rose to cover her mouth in surprise. Endersby immediately burned with embarrassment. "I beg your pardon," he said. Harriet moved swiftly up to him and pressed her hand upon the cut marking Endersby's forehead. "Well, sir," she said. Endersby took hold of Harriet's hand. She pulled it away.

"A fight, sir?" she said "Your 'demon familiar,' Mr. Endersby, has finally got the better of you. And you have conveniently eaten all of our evening meal."

Endersby bent down and picked up the platter. Harriet took it from him. She took water from a jug and bathed his cut. "Come," she said as if speaking to a stubborn child. She took Endersby and led him into their bedroom. "Lie down, please," she said. She took hold of both his hands and simply looked at him.

Endersby began to weep. "Forgive me, dearest one," he said, his voice catching in his throat.

"Forgiveness granted," she said.

"I am a lost man, Mrs. Endersby," the inspector moaned. "I have beaten a man in rage. I have left you to starve."

"You are a man in need of a night's sleep, my dear," Harriet said. "You are a good man, a hardened man at times, but you are not lost."

Endersby slowly sat up. He circled his arms around his Harriet and held her close as if he were a child seeking comfort in a thunderstorm.

"May I suggest, Mr. Endersby, that you retire to your study. Your snoring would keep me awake." Endersby bent forward, kissed Harriet and headed toward the bedroom door.

"And, sir," Harriet said pulling up the counterpane. "Remember we have the theatre later on this day. Shakespeare at Covent Garden."

"Indeed, madam," the inspector replied.

Endersby retreated to the couch in his study. Lying on his side, he gazed at his canvas long-coat drooped over a chair. His hat sagged from early morning rain. "What a sorrowful costume." He grunted, then turned and fell into a restless sleep.

※

Chapter Seventeen
A Rogue and a Waif

What a morning! The sun shone in the eyes of Inspector Owen Endersby as he stood beside his sergeant-at-hand, the two bidding a good day to each other in the entrance foyer to Fleet Lane Station House. Caldwell's face was less swollen this morning. The pungent odour of clove, however, remained on his breath.

"As to our methods, Sergeant. Two witnesses supposed our culprit may have worn leg irons. Do we have an escaped prisoner on our hands? Or is this conjecture?"

"A good point, sir."

"I want you to follow Malibran, this morning. Tail him, if I may use a vulgar term. Up the Strand and along his route. Take along a constable to spell you off if you need time to investigate the area. If Malibran meets up with his 'pity-man' to earn coin, arrest the chap and bring him here. It is in Malibran's interest to search out his pity man for the sake of profit."

"Very good, sir. I shall start at Malibran's lodgings."

"We have only words, sir, to guide us for now. Whether they are telling us truths, we shall soon discover."

"Yes, Inspector."

Caldwell left the Fleet Lane Station House and hired a cab to take him down to Nightingale Lane. Endersby ruminated on the facts he had: if the pity-man is a killer he rooms in Nightingale Lane or sometimes in Seven Dials. If he is *not* the murderer, then only two other clues can be counted as worthwhile. One is that the brute is an escaped prisoner — likely from the prison ships near Greenwich. Or, he may be a dock worker with his dredger-man's gaff.

A moment later, Contables Rance and Tibald entered the courtyard as the clock chimed eight.

"Good morning, Constables," greeted Endersby. "Most punctual."

"Good morning, sir," they replied. Rance and Tibald were wearing black stove-pipe hats, blue uniforms and white leather gloves. *Sir Robert Peel had been accurate in his visionary policy,* Endersby thought. Dress a policeman like a gentleman and not a soldier and the public will respect him as a working member of a civil society.

"Constables, Sergeant Caldwell is off to chase down a Mr. Malibran. Let us hear of last night."

Mr. Rance began: "Sir, as you may recall, I was sent to the Barbican to post guards and aid in a night watch. To my relief and that of the masters, no incident occurred."

"Well spoken, sir," replied Endersby. The constable's words aroused doubt, however. Had Endersby miscalculated? Was his logic not in tune with the criminal impulse, as the inspector once prided himself on being able to predict? Constable Tibald stepped forward: "Sir, in Theobald's Road there was a break-in of sorts."

"Of sorts?" said Endersby.

"The locked coal chute had been tampered with, sir. And some children heard a man's voice yelling in the night."

"Did anyone see the culprit?"

"Everyone said it was too dark. But this was found in the courtyard, by the gate." Constable Tibald handed the inspector a black oilskin hat, a type worn by dredgermen on the Thames.

"This is a fortuitous find, Tibald."

Endersby's mind raced. "Gentlemen, I want you two to explore prison ship records and the roster of hangings and escapees from London's prisons in the last three months. This may occasion you to travel to Newgate as well as searching our archives. The Naval Office will have information to guide you. Meet me back here no later than one in the afternoon. I shall take the air down at Wapping near the Docks."

In a cab, Endersby hoped this latest find would not be a false lead. *But how coincidental,* he thought. The coal carrier met a man carrying a dredgerman's gaff. And now, in the inspector's hand, lay an oilskin hat, one similar to those worn by fishermen and dredgermen. As always Endersby needed to move quickly on any lead — especially considering he had only one day left to investigate these crimes.

At Wapping Street in east London, he stepped down from the cab. He deduced that this part of the river was near Nightingale Lane where the pity man often lodged. Might he work at the docks as well as play for coin with Malibran? "Wait and see, old gander," he said and went into a wooden hut by the entrance to London Docks. Inside, he saw a man sitting in a chair and holding a writing quill.

"Only night help, Inspector. For coal retrieval and moving of bales. Our dredgermen are a proud lot. We don't hire them who was not in the business with their fathers." Endersby told of the gaff and showed the man the oilskin hat. "By a workhouse, you say?" The man rubbed his chin. "Let me glance at our records, sir." He opened a ledger and checked the employment lists laid out in columns. "We have taken on night workers for the past two weeks only. Strong backs needed to lift the tea chests comin' in from China." Endersby scanned two pages. Each showed a column of Xs — marks of illiterate men, beside which were payment sums of one or two pennies up to a shilling. On the third page, the inspector noticed one full signature, that of a Mr. William More.

"Sir, I ask you about this man named More."

"On and off, sir. Comes and goes. Likes his gin. Will work only from ten to one in the morning. Claims he has a sickly daughter."

"Does he lodge here, sir?"

"Here and around. He is tight fisted. Claims he searches out the cheapest lodging houses so he can buys medicines."

"What does he look like?"

The man sat back and blinked. "Ugly fellow. I only sees him in night light. Looks as if he has a wound on his cheek, from soldiering perhaps." Endersby was taking notes with his lead-tipped pencil. "Does he wear anything peculiar?"

"Rags, sir," answered the man.

"How does he walk?"

"Walk? The chap stumbles. Drags his feet like he was a cripple."

"Thank you, sir." Endersby went into the morning sun. *Does this similarity to the pity man add up to anything?* Endersby wondered. The inspector strolled along the dockside, watching the workers unload cargo. Many of the men looked tired; a few of them had scars on their cheeks and arms. Were these but marks of the trade? He asked a couple of men if they knew of William More.

"Yonder, sir," replied one man with a crooked leg.

Endersby went into a chop house. He looked around but saw no one who resembled the culprit. A lone man by the window was smoking a pipe.

"Sir, I am looking for a Mr. William More."

"Fled," was the curt reply.

"You were acquainted with the man?"

"No, sir. But I worked by him. Cripple chap. Could read and write. Wrote letters for us all for a ha'penny."

"Fled, you say?"

"North. I figure Seven Dials. Labour is needed there and lodging is cheap."

"Was he a good looking man?" Endersby asked.

"What you after?"

"Endersby of the Metropolitan Police, sir. I am searching for a man with certain features."

"He done break'ins?"

"He murdered two women."

"Devil," the man muttered. He relit his pipe. "Slice along his face. But I took little notice. A hazard of working with gaffs, sir."

"Why Seven Dials, sir? And not Saffron Hill?" Endersby asked again.

The man pondered: "Has a sickly daughter, in a charity hospital. Best to be near her. So he says."

"Did he ever mention her name?"

"Never to me. But the chap was peculiar. Said he was called More, then one day says he is called Kirkham, or such nonsense. A cracked git, I figured."

Endersby indulged in a coffee and a plate of toast before searching again along the docks, talking to workers, describing the culprit. One or two had heard of a William More and knew he could write letters. "There be plenty with scars, here, sir," one of the dredgermen pointed out. "Best to come by at night. New crews with hour-by-hour workers. You may meet him then."

By now London's clocks were striking eleven, and back at Fleet Lane Station House Endersby ran into an excited Tibald dashing down the staircase. "Sir," Tibald said, "we have a discovery." Endersby followed his sergeant into the archives. Shelves held thousands of papers crammed into cubby holes, each hole bearing a date above it and a span of months. "We have found names, sir. From Newgate and here, Fleet Prison. Rance will soon return from the Naval Office." Endersby perused the list of names and dates telling of executions and the rare escapee. Each name had a crime described beside it. "This one, sir, is from Fleet Prison," said Tibald. *A man in his forties condemned to the hulks for kidnapping children from the street. Two of the females were sold to chimney sweeps in the north.*

"Name of Henry Quick," read Endersby out loud. "Broke free while being transported to Greenwich, last December 5. Tibald, commendable. Keep this file open." Rance appeared and showed a list he'd had copied from the Navel Offices of escapees from the prison ships. "A difficult undertaking to do, gentlemen," Endersby said. On the list of recent escapees were three names: Tobias Jibbs, William More, Elijah Horn.

"Indeed," mumbled Endersby. Rance then showed the inspector a secondary list of the dead. "William More, sir, was murdered — by strangulation — right after his escape," Rance explained. "His body was found near the estuary a mile from the prison ships."

"Do the dead walk, I wonder?" said Endersby. Rance and Tibald looked puzzled until the inspector told of his investigation at the docks earlier in the morning. "Good detective work, Constables. Let us walk in the courtyard and take the sun. We need to strategize." As the three men walked outside, Endersby noticed a tall, gaunt gentleman looking around the foyer. "Yes, sir? Good morning," Endersby said. The gaunt man approached with the caution of a child being summoned before a school head master. "Sir, you are Inspector Owen Endersby?"

"I am he."

"I was told I might speak with you on a troubling matter."

"You are most welcome to do so."

Rance and Tibald stood at attention, eyes attending to the figure before them.

"There has been a ruckus, Inspector Endersby," the gaunt man said. "In St. Pancras Workhouse. North. I was sent by our head mistress to fetch you. As of late yesterday she had heard of the murder incident at St. Giles Workhouse and of your name."

"A body found, sir?" asked Endersby, trepidation and excitement further elevating his spirits.

"Not a dead one, if you mean that, Inspector," the man replied.

"What then? I beg of you," Endersby said, his right fist closing and opening to affect some calm in his restless body.

"A body found, sir, but one living. An intruder," came the gaunt man's description.

"An intruder? Dangerous?" enquired Endersby. Rance and Tibald had taken out their notebooks and were scribbling down each word with their lead-tipped pencils.

"Searching for his daughter, he claims. A dirty fellow and drunk. Fists up most times."

"Where was he found?"

"Hiding in the washhouse shaking with hunger. A soldier, we reckon, from his soiled uniform."

"Curious, indeed," said Endersby, his facial features now posed to show professional concern. It was his habit to take facts and immediately turn them into suppositions. In his younger days as a Bow Street Runner, he would have arranged for an immediate arrest in order to earn his commission as a "felon catcher." An arrest notice was the next official step; instead, Endersby would indulge in a visit to St. Pancras to confront the soldier — the searcher — himself, a method he figured was the most honest way to proceed.

"We shall accompany you, sir, to St. Pancras on the moment. Constables Rance and Tibald are at your service, as am I."

"I thank you, Inspector. We are in a state of some fear."

"Why so?" asked Endersby. "Has the man threatened any-one?"

"The man is desperate mad. He is most concerned he shall die if he does not find his young daughter."

"Did he call out her name, sir, by any chance?" Endersby took in a breath.

"He did. He said nothing after a time but her name. 'Catherine,' she is. To him it is the catechism, I beg pardon. Over and over he said it."

"Then we shall make our visit one that may afford the man some relief," said Endersby.

The gaunt man followed Endersby and the two constables into the street where two hansom cabs were hired. On his way along High Holborn Street, Endersby planned his next strat-egy: a soldier searching at night for a workhouse child named Catherine. Has this evil become a contagion in the city? The desire for young orphaned females a sign of darker times ahead? Or, indeed, is *this* man the villain, trapped by his own despera-tion? Endersby looked ahead at the hansom carrying Tibald and the gaunt man. How slowly they were moving. Old London town had become harried, torn up, torn down. A dog-bite-dog world, the shrill whistles of the new steam-powered trains blasting away the cries of sickly children. One thing remained constant:

fathers yearning for lost children. "Men who would murder to find them," Endersby whispered as St. Pancras Workhouse loomed ahead at the far end of the street.

⁂

Dr. Josiah Benton finished dressing and went downstairs for his morning eggs and tea. He had slept well, if only for a few hours. How wonderful the day appeared to him. How successful he felt, privileged to be a hearty man. As he drank his tea he kept raising his eyes up toward the back end of the house, toward the little bedroom in the upper hall which now had become for him the most lovely of places.

"Good morning, sir," said a bustling Mrs. Wells. "Here, Dr. Benton, are the weekly bills for your audit, sir."

"Thank you, Wells," Dr. Benton replied his voice so merry he imagined he had swallowed a lark with his toast and jam. "I shall not be in surgery today, Wells. I will have Johnston cancel appointments. No one must come upstairs for any reason this morning until after I have taken luncheon. Please inform the butler and upstairs maids."

"Certainly, sir," Mrs. Wells replied, laying down her bundle of household bills before leaving the dining room. Dr. Benton read his pocket watch. He would call Wells into his confidence, as usual, once he had made his first foray into the little back bedroom. He smiled and stood up and wiped his mouth of crumbs. With all this movement and thought, Dr. Benton was precise, holding in his excitement and his eagerness to bound up the stairs and thrust himself into the little back bedroom in all his joy. But no. He must remain decorous. There was time. Mr. Lardle had done well. Mr. Lardle had come through. What was a fistful of shillings when what awaited upstairs was a world of peace, of caring.

Dr. Josiah Benton now climbed the stairs. He reached the second floor and pulled in a breath. He entered his sleeping chamber. Pulling out a small key from his upper pocket, he unlocked a drawer in his bureau. He lifted out a small paper box. The smell rising from it was delicious. Chocolate, sugar, a hint of rose petal. Moving next toward his toilet table, he removed his frock coat. He decided this morning to wear red velvet. He pulled on his smoking jacket, its lapels quilted with a gold fabric that reminded the kind doctor of fields of autumn wheat. He quickly washed his hands. Checking his fingernails, he then sprinkled his finger tips with a touch of French cologne, a bottle he had purchased not four months ago in Paris, in the Palais Royale.

"And so, sir," he exclaimed to himself. A not unpleasant feeling of elation, of being light-headed overtook Dr. Josiah Benton as he whisked himself out of his sleeping chamber, toward the door of the little back bedroom. No time to waste. "No, no," he smiled to himself. He pulled out his second key. He inserted it into the keyhole of the little back bedroom and slowly pushed open the door. *There, there*, he thought, *there she lies.* So endearing, so innocent, so blonde. *I must be gentle at first. I must not frighten the darling thing. She will be obedient,* he thought. *She will so appreciate what I will do.*

"Good morning to you, my lovely. Rest quiet, child," he then said in a kindly voice, before locking the door behind him.

Chapter Eighteen
New Quarters

Catherine Smeets sat up quickly. Her first breath pulled in the coarse cloth that encased her head, its ties in bulky knots too hard to undo.

"Quiet, now. Rest child."

The woman's voice sounded sharp at first, not unlike one of the matron's at St. Pancras Workhouse. The cloth was untied; it rose from over Catherine's head. Her eyes blinked at the morning light, which poured into the window of a small clean room. Catherine felt her stomach churn; she held back her tears; was she really alive or was this a dream? Worse, would she soon die at the hand of this tight-mouthed woman with shiny brushed hair and a golden ring on her finger? The woman stood before Catherine. She spoke again, this time her voice softer, like a mother's: "I know you are neither dumb nor deaf, child. I see your eyes are curious as well. You may be in luck if you are obedient."

Catherine began to shiver. A door opened behind her. She

turned and saw a younger woman in a starched white apron step into the room. In her hands she carried a tray. On it were a cup and saucer with blue birds painted on its surface. A plate covered with a silver dome sat next to a stack of buttered toast. "Put it here, please," said the older woman, her gold ring catching the sunlight as she waved her hand toward a small table. "Come, child," the older woman commanded. She took hold of Catherine's thin hand. "My, you are a stick of a child. No doubt your ghastly frock is the uniform of a charity house." Catherine was breathless. Her guts ached and her mouth watered. "Yes, hurry child. This is for you." The dome was lifted from the plate. Two fried eggs shone yellow and slick. A piece of fried ham curled pink beside them. The woman in the apron poured perfumed tea into the cup and saucer. "Speak something at least, will you?" said the older woman. "I know you are able."

Catherine wiped her eyes. "Yes, Mistress," she whispered.

"There now, I was right. Now do not hold back. Hurry, child. There is much to do with you yet, and I cannot stretch my patience much longer." Catherine gobbled the two eggs, gulped the hot tea, tore into two pieces of toast. Her mind now lost any fear for the moment as her stomach began to feel good. When had she last tasted such sweet, juicy ham? The older woman dismissed the servant. She then stood behind Catherine and watched her eat. "Manners, child, manners. Take your fork. Is this what our money pays for in these institutions? To turn young innocents such as you into ravenous wolves?" Catherine did not listen to the older woman's prattle. It reminded her of the raspy nattering of Matron Pickens. Once she had finished, she wiped her mouth with the back of her hand.

"Oh, no, dear me," the older woman cried. "Take this, take it in your hand. That's it. Now ... oh, I see child, you *can* use a proper napkin. You are not such an urchin after all."

Catherine folded the napkin in spite and laid it beside the plate to show the witch — for now Catherine believed she had somehow ended up in a fairytale house with a witch who no doubt would soon lock her in a cage and feed her sweets until she burst with fat. The woman's hand took hold of Catherine's shoulder. "Stand up, child. You cannot dash away. I have had the servant turn the lock. Hurry, now." The woman led Catherine toward a door. As she passed by the window Catherine spotted a well-kept courtyard. Dashing through it was a young man in a frock coat. He had thick hair. Catherine could not see his full face. "No gawking, child. If you are a bright one, in no time you shall grace the presence of the dead very well."

Catherine pulled back. The woman rushed toward her.

"Leave me be, old hag!" Catherine yelled. The woman folded her hands in front of her. "I see," she said with a cool tone. "You are an ingrate. Your stomach is full now. You have nothing to fear from me. Look ahead through that door. Tell me what you see?" Catherine looked around. She could smell steamy water. She remembered the copper tub she once bathed in at home in her snug village, her dear departed mother squeezing a sponge over her head. *Oh, that this place could be a cottage in a dream,* Catherine wished. The older woman had not budged from her position. A thin smile broke upon her lips. "Look, child. Tell me what you see."

Catherine allowed herself to take one step. There it was, sitting in the centre of the room. Beside it a chair. Hanging on the chair a large white sheet and a clean towel.

"I see a bathtub, Mistress," Catherine replied.

"Yes, child. Ready and waiting for you. Now come along. Young Mary will bathe you and then bring you to me."

Reluctantly, yet eager for the pleasure of a warm bath, Catherine gave in. She entered the far room. The young girl helped Catherine out of her smock. She laughed a little. She whispered "hello" and took hold of Catherine's hand. The water was clear, the copper bottom shiny. Catherine knelt down. Young Mary poured water from a jug. Soon suds filled the water. Mary's hand was gentle. She hummed as she pressed the brush up and down Catherine's dirt-smudged arms and legs.

"Such a lucky one, you are, dear one," Mary said, her words lilting, reminding Catherine of the Irish apple seller back home in her village. As she was dried, Catherine's fears returned. Was Mary really an elf in disguise? Would she be like old Rumpelstiltskin in her uncle's story and demand a reward, or blind her? These thoughts began to grow until Catherine was shivering. "What's this?" said Mary. "Here, take this. You shake like a frightened pony." From her pocket, Mary pulled out a toffee wrapped in red paper. "Go on, silly one, take a chew. You're thinking it's poisoned?" Mary laughed. She went to a chest and pulled out a fresh white under-frock and helped Catherine put it on before buttoning up the back.

"Follow along now, by me."

Mary lifted a ring of keys and opened a door leading into a dark passageway. Onward, up a set of stairs, she led Catherine into a room full of cupboards. "Sit down, dear." Mary pulled open one of the cupboards. She pulled down a box. Walking across the room, she whistled as if she were merrily sewing. *How cheerful she was,* thought Catherine. Her heart quickened. What was this room? Mary opened the box. Catherine gasped. She began to shiver again. Mary turned to her with a sweet smile:

"Oh, dear one. You shall look so fine in one of these. I can imagine the tears. The moans. Such a lucky one you are. So very lucky."

Chapter Nineteen
Soldier's Pay

What preoccupied Endersby's thoughts at this very moment was a counter-idea. It acted like a mirror "held up to Nature" — as Prince Hamlet says. To test himself, Endersby challenged what he knew and what he had surmised. Had he been rash in his initial conclusions, he wondered as he jostled from left to right behind the trotting horse pulling his cab.

This morning he faced another dilemma. Were all his gathered facts illusory? The confessions, the clues, deliberately misinterpreted by his need to tag a culprit? How could the lace seller in Rosemary Lane have recalled accurately the man culpable of killing the two matrons? Rum had blurred his mind; the desire for a sale prompted him to say anything to receive a coin. For that matter, was the sketchy description given by the children and the matter of the lace only coincidental? And Malibran! Let alone his pity-man — was he nothing more than another scarred denizen of London's underworld population? How many men bearing the so-called culprit's facial features could be found in the city? What other proof was there but words?

"Old fool," Endersby whispered to himself. "Strutting about with your feathers ruffled." *All of detective work,* he sadly reminded himself, *all of it is misapprehension and fickle luck.*

The broad gate to St. Pancras opened. Here stood London's largest workhouse, north of St. Giles and near to the slum called Seven Dials. It reminded the inspector of one of the new steam ships he'd seen docked at Land's End: two large black chimneys in a row spewing smoke, a long lean central building like a great hull, and two small additions to its sides. To the east of the building flowed the Regent's Canal, while to the west spread the trees and grand passages of London's pride, Regent's Park. Endersby had forgotten to bring his cane and while stepping down from the cab he felt as if poor Caldwell's dental agony had transferred itself into his large toe.

"Sir?" The timid voice belonged to Constable Rance.

"I beg your pardon, Rance. My thoughts were elsewhere," responded Endersby. "My mind *is out of joint.* Let us proceed."

Flowing out of the windows of the workhouse came the sounds of clashing dishes, gongs being struck. A low murmur succeeded the initial racket, that of rote prayer. St. Pancras housed families, the mad, boys, girls, teenagers. Some criminal, many simply poor or lost. One wing held boys whose violence had to be checked with hard labour. "It's the alcohol in 'em," a master had once explained. "Suckled from their mothers' tits — gin-soaked milk. Makes 'em restless, bullying."

The present visit of the inspector and his two constables took place not in any wing of the huge structure but outside in the stable yard under a canopy covering the horse stalls. Ten feet away, the grey stone washhouse emitted steam and the clacking of the hand-driven paddles used to agitate the water in the washtubs. Accompanying Inspector Endersby, besides his two constables and the gaunt master, was a fine-boned woman dressed in blue. Her bonnet rode atop her hair somewhat like a helmet might upon the brow of a warrior. However, when the woman spoke, a wistful voice issued from her throat. A south county accent shaped her vowels: "A live body most certainly, Mr. Endersby. A soldier, if his tunic be true," the woman explained. "Please be so kind as to address me as Head Matron Dench. Rhymes with bench."

Endersby smiled. His fatigue had slowed his pace. But the head matron's touch of humour enlivened his spirit. "I am born a Dorset gal, sir," the head matron continued. "But a mere country girl as you see. Parents drowned and set me adrift and here I came, first as orphan. Fate carried me forward into the position of a captain of all she surveys. If you follow my track, sir."

"Indeed, I do, madam," Endersby answered. He brushed away his dark thoughts. Surely if this woman, whose life had been one of loneliness and terror, had raised herself to manage a workhouse, he could spare some energy to admire her.

Sitting on a chair next to a pile of straw was the man himself. Endersby watched him closely as he and the group approached. The man was short, scruffy. His filthy hands were black with smut. His high military boots revealed their age — cracked and uncared-for. The man's hair had grown long, quite out of regulation length required of a member of Her Majesty's Military Service. He was un-shaven. Across his face a long red slash of something — the dim light of the stable tricking the eye at first. Was it a scar? Had this red inflamed streak been *perceived* as a scar in the dark of night? Standing closer now, Endersby watched the man raise his head toward him. How belligerent his eyes; how pinched his turned-down mouth. On closer inspection, the red slash now resembled a ragged birth mark. The man's hand rose toward his cheek. Its long black nails began to peck and scratch at the scabs on his skin.

"Stand up please, sir, and step forward into the light," commanded Endersby.

"Wot for? I be plenty comfortable here, thank you. Who are you? "

"Sir," replied Endersby, "I am Detective Inspector Endersby of the Metropolitan Police Force. I understand you paid St. Pancras a visit last evening. One which quite alarmed those who run the place."

"That so? Wot pigeon told you that? Nay, I am with Her Majesty's. Just takin' a bit of holiday here in London. Stopping here, as is my wont, on public property to rest my weary legs."

"You have tales to tell, I am sure, sir," Endersby said, quietly amused by the man's bold insolence. A thought flashed: could this belligerent man be fond of disguises? A bandaged street beggar one day, a soldier out of pocket the next?

"Now if you please. I wish to return to my slumber." With that, the man got up from the chair and lay down on the pile of straw. Endersby came up to him. "My good fellow, you are a fine soldier, if your boots and unpolished buttons are an indication. But you are under command, sir. To step up and rightly so."

The man stirred. He sat up. He spat at the ground and wiped his palm across his chin. "You, Mister Inspector, I take no orders from you. Leave me be, I say." Endersby was so tempted. His heart began to thump, his fists clenched. If he could, he would have breathed smoke and fire. But to his credit, he held his "demon" in check. Stepping back, he calmly instructed Rance and Tibald to lift the soldier and walk him into the light. What followed was worthy of a fight scene in one of the Coburg Theatre's melo-dramas. The soldier jumped to his feet just as Rance and Tibald arrived with arms outstretched. A shout, a warning, a grabbing for a sword in its scabbard, a sword no longer in evidence nor attached to its belt. Then a show of fisticuffs — feints, strokes and full left hooks put into motion. Rance, the braver of the two constables, took off his hat, handed it to Tibald and raised his arms, fists held in tight ball formation. "Onward, sir," the constable shouted to the soldier.

Gin, however, soon slowed down the fighting spirit in the intruder. Fists faltered and knees soon smacked down against the wooden boards of the stable. While watching the soldier's pathetic attempt at boxing, Endersby wondered about the man's early life: a brutal, hardscrabble childhood, restlessness rather than disciplined routine leading to drink, fighting, whores, cheap cures, and finally recruitment in the land army of Her Majesty's. The uniform was only a cover, a thin veil hiding an indulgence in profligate ways.

"Come, Sergeant," commanded Endersby. "At attention, sir. Inspection."

Into the morning light the soldier was dragged. He stood slumped, head forward. Looking him over, Endersby noted his calves had been rubbed raw by his military boots. On closer view of the soldier's face, the red slash was neither a birth mark nor a wound. It was an angry rash. Pustules and welts, a symptom perhaps of the pox. It blared red. Was this, then, the "pink worm" the second young Catherine had described yesterday morning? The barkeep in Rosemary Lane had hinted at a rapier wound, but this redness resulted from some force inside the man's body. From the soldier's clothes there rose a stink of dung and horse piss.

"You have been staying in the finest inns, have you Sergeant?" Endersby quipped.

"You, sir, you bastardly gullion," the soldier replied, spite returning to his voice. "A beefer you are. I ain't no runner, I got papers."

"Surely, sir, Her Majesty's has been just in its judgement and fair in its payment to you as a stalwart fighter?" Endersby was starting to enjoy his baiting of the man but another pang in his foot told him he must retreat into calm reason. "I imagine, Sergeant, you are no deserter."

"Relieved, I was, of duties, gullion. Papers are in m'tunic if your beak's snout needs to sniff 'em out." The soldier spit and teetered a little. Constable Tibald was ordered to go to the wash house and find the soldier's tunic. "And any other items, Constable, he may have carried. A sack, perhaps. A gaff, a weapon."

Head Matron Dench stepped forward. "Inpsector, I have taken the liberty to have food brought out for the chap. He is sore hungry after his journey." Entering the stable yard came a parched-looking woman carrying a small bowl. The soldier stood at attention as if to mock her. "Allo, young peach," he said. "You here for some splittin'?" he smirked, raising his arm in a vulgar gesture. The woman moved cautiously toward him. He snatched the bowl from her outstretched hand and set to gulping its contents. He spat out a grey stream of fluid. "This be pig slop, you slammy scab." The man threw the bowl down, smashing it on the yard's cobbles.

"Matron Pickens," said the head matron. "I thank you for your pains." Matron Pickens curtsied to the head matron, her face marked by a sneer. "Come, Sergeant," said Endersby, an edge of impatience lining his words. "I been on a wee walk," the soldier then said. "From Scotland north; ten toes to every mile and a split or two on the way." He laughed and rubbed his crotch. Constable Rance was commanded to take hold of the man but the soldier stepped away. He thrust his hands on his hips and began to swagger. "Devil's arse-hole be my name, gulls. A fancy man am I. Can split any wench who's willin!'" He guffawed.

"You, Bobby, and you Ladybirds. Here stands a fellah for you. Beau-nasty before you, smart if soiled." Stumbling, the soldier lost his balance but after a twirl of his arms, stood firm again.

"Yes," he cried. "To your liking. My military leathers? In my brass, the scrags called me Buckle-beau. Nay, uncle, 'tis true. A fine turn I was!"

"Your name, sir," asked Endersby. His mind rapidly fitting together the gathering puzzle before him.

"Bingo Boy to you, gull. Or if it sits, Beezlebub."

"Perhaps," Endersby said, hesitating a little, "Mr. Buckle-beau?"

"Nay, git," replied the soldier. "I ain't neither fop nor beast. *Uncle Beau*. Now there's a ring." Constable Rance took hold of the soldier's arm and led him back, limping, into the shade of the stable. "Matron Dench," said Endersby, his mind now keen with anticipation. "What drew your attention in the night to alarm your guards?"

"Inspector, I had word of the murder in St. Giles and thought it best to set up masters on watch and to secure all doors and gates. Such banging at the front door after midnight caused us all to rise. The children became restless. Then, worse, a great clanging."

"T'was this beast at the coal chute, ma'am." Matron Pickens stepped forward. "Master Cox ran into the yard and saw this fellow hitting the iron lid of the locked coal chute."

"What occurred next?" Endersby asked. He looked up and saw Constable Tibald approaching from the wash house, a large sack and a soiled military tunic in his arms. Master Cox, the gaunt man, answered: "Me and two other masters gave chase but the intruder locked himself in the washhouse."

"Inspector, sir," said Tibald, now standing at attention. The group moved closer together to view the items the constable had carried from the wash house. Endersby turned his eyes first to the soiled military tunic, its sleeves torn, many of its buttons missing.

"What a tangle," said Endersby. "Before we examine your papers, sir," said Endersby. "Tell us how long you have been on your journey."

"Fortnight, add one or two days."

"And in London, sir?"

"A night or three. No penny for lodging house, slop, nor straw."

"You know London well, do you?"

"Curious git, you are. I know it well enough. Been up to the Foundling Hospital and to other houses." The soldier then began to hold his head in his hands and rock back and forth.

"What is the matter, sir?" Matron Dench asked, signalling to Pickens and Cox to take hold of the man's arms. "I shall die," the soldier howled. "There, Inspector," said Master Cox. "There it be, so I told you, crying out to die." *What a sudden change of face*, Endersby thought. From a mocking bully to a blubbering child. "Speak up, Sergeant," commanded Endersby, who at this juncture believed a sharp word from a person of authority might cause him to confess.

"'Tis she, my little one. Oh, I was wrong to do it. To leave her. Up and down, I been. I been lookin' for you, my sweet. I don't remember where I put you ..."

"Who, sir?" prompted Endersby.

"My little Catherine."

"Your daughter, sir. A niece?"

"Daughter, ill begot by me in a flurry," came the sad response. "Sweet Catherine."

Head Matron Dench pulled lightly at Endersby's elbow. The two stepped aside.

"At first I was not certain, Inspector," Matron Dench began.

"But then, setting aside the dreadful infection on his features, I finally came to realize who the man is. He came in January with a young blonde female of ten years. A daughter he said she was. Paid a three-month stipend to me — most unusual. To guard her and find her work. Back in the winter, not three months hence, he struck quite the dashing figure ... red tunic, sword, full hat and plume. I recall he was as drunk and belligerent. But not so downtrodden as now."

"His name, Matron?"

"Smeets, I recall. Sergeant Peter Smeets."

"And his daughter, young Catherine? Is she here in St. Pancras?"

"I shall have Pickens fetch her at this moment."

Returning to the huddled group, Head Matron Dench commanded Matron Pickens to bring young Catherine Smeets into the stable yard. Matron Pickens bowed her head. "What is it, Pickens?" asked the Head Matron.

"She's fled, ma'am. Run out."

"Are you certain, Pickens? She's not hiding in the yard or the latrines?"

"No, Matron. Her bed was left empty, most of her rags still in the bundle. The cripple-girl, Mag, shared the knowledge with me that Smeets had bolted."

Sergeant Smeets leapt to his feet. His face contorted — his eyes wild. He rushed at Matron Pickens. "You filthy slag," he screamed. "You let her flee. You killed her, scab." His fists found their mark: the nose, then the matron's right cheek, and finally the sagging breast. The soldier grabbed the woman's throat. Blackened fingers squeezed hard. His right hand pressed down upon her mouth and nose. Rance and Master Cox leapt into the fray. Eventually, after much wrestling, the two combatants were parted. Matron Pickens stepped back, sniffing, and wiped her bloodied nose.

"Pickens, take your leave at once. Get to!" shouted Head Matron Dench. The dazed woman dashed out of the shade into the stable yard. Meanwhile, the writhing Sergeant Smeets was thrown into the chair in front of the horse stalls. Constable Rance ran behind and took hold of the man's elbows and pulled them back. Smeets stamped his feet. *What rage and injury,* Endersby thought. *Here, indeed, was a man who could kill in an instant.*

Endersby returned his attention to the items Constable Tibald had brought from the workhouse. He offered to spread the contents of the bag on the ground before them. As he began to take out each piece, a silence fell over the witnesses. First appeared a narrow piece of knitted cloth. It resembled a belt and on it were blotches of dark colour. Next, a small packet of papers. These were hastily unwrapped by the inspector with the head matron reading over his shoulder. "Indeed, we have a legal document. Sergeant Peter Smeets dishonourably discharged for insubordination and petty thievery." He read on. He lowered the papers. He requested Rance lift up the back of Smeets' shirt.

"We shall attend to your wounds, presently, Sergeant," Endersby said in a calm voice.

The shirt was lifted from the man's back. Scoring the soldier's back, from shoulder to buttock, were huge scabs — formed over welts made by a flogging. "Flogged twenty lashes," Endersby read out, returning his gaze to the papers. "Insulting a senior officer; inciting a riot in a tavern."

Endersby requested Tibald to cover the man. "Sergeant Smeets, you are a fortunate man. The gallows is the more usual punishment for such acts."

"Inspector, what should we make of this item?"

Constable Tibald now drew out a new-looking frock coat of fine weave. Endersby felt its sleeve. The puzzle now formed a complete picture in his mind, its contours fitting Smeets into the facts of the case. Such a number of matching pieces allowed Endersby to draw a conclusion of dire consequence. "Search the pockets. Turn the bag inside-out, Constable," said Endersby. Tibald did so. A razor, a smudged towel. "Shake it hard, sir," Endersby said.

"There is nothing left, sir," was the constable's response.

Endersby now took a stance."Where is your hat, Sergeant Smeets?" The distracted man felt his head. "My hat?" he sputtered. "Lost, lost," he mumbled.

"Matron Dench, I wish to speak with Matron Pickens and the cripple-child to discover, if possible, other pertinent facts to support my fear that this man before us, Sergeant Peter Smeets, may in fact be a villain of a more heinous kind." A groan rose out of Sergeant Smeets's throat. "For the meantime, Rance and Tibald, kindly escort Sergeant Smeets to Fleet Lane Station House on suspicion of felony — the murder of two matrons: one at St. Giles, the other at Shoe Lane." Head Matron Dench gasped.

"Murder?" screamed Sergeant Smeets. "I ain't killed no one, git."

Endersby pointed his finger at the two constables and they moved with great speed to haul the swearing man toward the street, cuffs now locked to his wrists.

"Are you certain in this action, sir?" asked the head matron once they were alone in the quiet of the stable yard. "Would this man murder," she asked. "Would he risk punishment and lose the chance to see his only daughter?" Endersby thought carefully about what her words implied. Here was one byway into the criminal landscape of Sergeant Smeets's mind. Smeets had motive for killing — his anger at Matron Pickens proved he was capable of violence like that of a bear protecting her cub. Could this same fury have killed two other women?

"The criminal mind, Matron Dench," replied Endersby, "is myriad, maze-like. I cannot disagree nor at the same time agree with your words about love of child and punishment. Men act on their hearts and guts. There are dark sides, however, which we representatives of the law often cannot fathom. And so, I must decide for the moment if a man is a *possible* suspect given all signs. In the case of Smeets, he resembles the culprit in many ways. Note, as well, his attack on Matron Pickens at the mention of his daughter. It is my duty to investigate Smeets if only to prove myself mistaken."

"Admirable in your tactics, sir," replied Head Matron Dench. "I shall lead you to Pickens and the child we call Little Mag."

Chapter Twenty
A Fine Frenzy

The beadle stood in the doorway and raised the tip of his hat.

"Oh, Beadle," cried Mrs. Bolton, morning sun dappling her doorstep. The clock by the front door began to chime eight o'clock. Yesterday, Mrs. Bolton had been a contented woman. Twelve hours ago she was looking forward to the village being fully awake: wagons and pedestrians with market baskets flowing along the high street. But now, ill fortune had darkened her view.

"Mrs. Bolton," said the beadle, holding up his staff of office. "Run off, you say? Please, good woman, explain how." The beadle stood six feet, narrow in frame, precise in diction. Ever polite, he was most charitable to those in his parish needing his assistance.

"Come in, sir," Mrs. Bolton said. Into the bedroom she led the man in his long coat to the bed where her ill sister had once lain: the walls had been stripped of all lace samples, the bed abandoned. "Beadle, my Jemima has fled. As you see, the walls bear none of her handiwork. She was so proud of her lace."

"Fled! To where do you imagine, Mrs. Bolton?" The beadle removed his hat. He moved efficiently about the sick room. His head leaned close to the walls to inspect the spaces where items had been removed. Investigation was but one of his responsibilities as a parish official. Eventually, he would have to sit down and write up a brief description of the morning's events — including the flight of one Jemima Pettiworth.

"Oh, Beadle," cried Mrs. Bolton. "I have discovered more."

Around the cosy house the two of them went. One trunk had been ransacked — all lace items removed. The dining table lay bare of its lace cloth. Near the backdoor to the yard, a handsome hanging of flowers in a vase — Jemima's masterwork, according to her sister — no longer covered the water stain in the wallpaper. "Oh, dear," moaned Mrs. Bolton. "Where would she go?"

"My precise question, Mrs. Bolton, is *where* and *how*. Once we determine this, we may discover Miss Pettiworth's whereabouts."

These last words struck Mrs. Bolton directly in her heart. The blow was such that she had to sit down and fold her hands in her lap. "I cannot imagine — I am afraid to do so — what has happened. I fear she may be mad."

"This shall be our tactic, Mrs. Bolton. We will effect a search. Come along, good woman. We can look for witnesses around the village."

As she shut the door, Mrs. Bolton remembered one item. She ran back through her cottage, into the sick room, and looked in the cupboard. On greeting the beadle again, she said: "My sister was writing a confession, Beadle. On what subject or for what reason I do not know. The pages have disappeared with her, along with the lace."

"A confession? Did she have a secret to hide? A feeling of guilt for a crime of some sort? Proof of a guilty conscience, Mrs.

Bolton," said the beadle. "Therefore, if this be true, we have a reason for her flight. Now this may prove disastrous."

"How so?" asked Mrs. Bolton, locking her front door.

"From what I know of the human heart, the guilty tend to search for recompense or punishment. If indeed your sister has committed a wrongdoing she will need to confront her feelings of guilt and remorse. The conscience is somewhat like a bladder, if I may be vulgar in my comparison. Once the bladder is too full, it can only relieve itself, it can only let out its contents in a rush. This same principle of 'rushing,' as I deem it, applies to the guilt-racked mind. It is forced to free itself of the pressure, if you will. Thus, madness, flight — or worse ...."

"Worse, Beadle?" Mrs. Bolton's eyes were on the verge of tears.

"We shall not entertain such a thought, my good woman. Your sister is a Christian, a soul of the parish." *Village folk up at an early hour would have seen her,* thought Mrs. Bolton, *some kindly farmer tilling his field spotting a woman in a nightdress carrying bundles, her voice humming a mad song.* Up and down the village the beadle and the widow walked side by side. The church warden shook his head; the baker shrugged, the hat maker, the blacksmith — each gave a sorrowful glance and a shake of the head. After an hour touring the village, the beadle led the widow to the nearest farm near the roadway. Neither farmer nor wife nor any of the farmer's nine children had seen a woman rushing by in a nightdress.

The road home seemed long to Mrs. Bolton. Her feet were heavy, as if she wore shoes of iron. At her front door, the beadle promised to spend more of his morning asking in the market if any pedlars had seen the mad Jemima. "Good cheer, Mrs. Bolton," he said, tipping the edge of his hat.

Mrs. Bolton went toward her back door. "My goodness," she said. "What is this?"

Conspicuous on the chair by the back door was an object. It was square in shape, wrapped in a pillow cover. On top there lay a number of ink-stained quills. "Jemima?" said Mrs. Bolton. She picked up one of the used quills. She slipped off the pillow cover. To her delight she found a neat collection of notepaper. On every page lay her dear sister's precise handwriting. "Her confession, perhaps?" Mrs. Bolton wondered and took the bundle toward the hearth. Her eyes were eager and fearful at the same moment as she picked up the first of the sheets of the confession her sister had left behind.

Down Fleet Street he scampered, his high boots rubbing his ankles raw, the rhyme and chaos of the city like a stiff breeze mussing his thoughts. Mud from the still-wet pavement spotted his frock coat. What Geoffrey Grimsby wanted were wings. Falcon, eagle — his peace of mind for a pair of feathered arms! Behind him, the ominous clack of a policeman's wooden rattle. Before him, men in hats, women in bonnets. Morning sun glowered off church steeples.

"Halt, sir!" A commanding voice rang out. Another shouted: "Stop, villain! In the name of the Metropolitan Police Force."

As ever, the gin on his breath tasted sweet — even after a night of drinking and trying to wash away his sorrows. The sweat forming on his brow glistened as he ducked into an alleyway. To his dismay, a wall suddenly rose up to meet him and stopped his stumbling footsteps. How his head ached! How fatigued he had become with his life, his failures, his need for secrecy. How he wished he could be loving to all even though he had done so much harm in his desperation.

A hand from behind took hold of his right shoulder. He refused to buckle under as he struggled to wrench himself free, forcing his breath to puff. The hand held hard. On turning around he saw the ruddy face of young man in a top hat, his hands gloved in white leather. Another man in similar clothing held a rattle and a wooden truncheon.

"Stand, sir," said the first man. The policeman's gloved hand moved the sweaty hair from the brow. The second policemen held up a piece of paper. He read it in spurts, looking up into the face and nodding, then reading again, slowly, checking out features — a scar, frock coat, boots.

"Your name, sir?" asked the policeman.

The answer slid forth in a gin-slurred jeer: "The Devil himself, sir."

"Come now, sir. Your true name."

"Mr. Geoffrey Grimsby. Undertaker. Son of Mr. Tightwad Grimsby himself." A drunken giggle issued forth with these words. "I ask what this commotion is all about. It is most inconvenient for a man of my station to be chased and accosted in such a vulgar manner."

"Mr. Grimsby," the policeman said in grave tones. "I am to arrest you, sir, on suspicion of a felony."

"A what?" Grimsby spouted.

"Your scar sir, your manner, your appearance fit this description given us by the chief detective of Fleet Lane Station House." The other policeman waved the paper at Grimsby who snatched it and read it quickly, his eyes squinting in gradual horror at the details arrayed before him in neat official writing.

"A felony? This is most ridiculous," young Grimsby announced. He thrust the paper back into the hand of the policeman.

"One of serious consequence," came the policeman's reply.

"*Serious,* Officer?" enquired Grimsby, trying to pull forward the tails of his frock coat.

"We are to arrest you on suspicion of murder most foul. Come along, Mr. Grimsby. We ask no trouble."

"Murder?" whined the young undertaker, his arm held by the first policeman as the other clapped a set of iron cuffs on his wrists.

"Murder, indeed, sir."

❦

Chapter Twenty-One
New Clothes, New Faces

"You do look fine indeed," the older woman said. Catherine turned again. In the looking glass she saw herself. Long blonde hair combed and pulled into a knot at the back of her head. "She's a lovely face, mum," said Mary, her Irish lilt like a song in Catherine's ears. The long black gown spread out at the sides as Catherine made a pirouette. When Mary placed the sheer veil over her head, Catherine felt as if she had become like the young Queen Victoria. What amazed her even more was the feeling of goodness in the air. These women were so kind and patient. Three months in the workhouse had deprived her of the delight of a tender hand. The older woman stepped up to Catherine and stroked the veil. "I wish you well, my child. Your deportment is most gracious. My foolish son can behave like a brute, it is true. But he has a good heart. I do apologize for his cruel way of snatching you up from the street."

"Thank you, Mistress," Catherine said, her voice direct and strong. She refused to weep. She had told Mary she had lost her mother, been abandoned by her father, and seen her loving uncle arrested and sent to a ship bound for a far away land. Now, however, as she told the story again to the older woman, tears formed. "Sent from my village forever. Dearest Uncle, I miss him."

"How do you mean, my child?" asked the older woman. The two sat down side by side on a black settee. "He was my mother's brother. They grew up together in a terrible workhouse outside of the village. Uncle moved in with me and my mother while father was soldiering in the North. The day my mother died, he held me in his arms. Then my father came home. Uncle and Papa got angry at each other. Uncle hit Papa. The bailiff came. He said Uncle was a felon because he struck a soldier. They arrested him. He was all alone. I wrote him a letter because he said letters make people happy."

"You poor creature," said the older woman. Her arm lay around Catherine's shoulders.

"Uncle was sent on a ship with other bad men. Away to a country with elephants."

"The prison ships," said the older woman with a shudder. "The hulks."

"You are the only people I know now," Catherine said drying her eyes. The older woman took Catherine in her arms. "There, there, child. You have touched my heart." Catherine felt like singing. "You may call me Mrs. Grimsby, child. You shall find comfort here, Catherine Smeets, with me and Mr. Grimsby."

A maid entered the room. "Mistress," she said. "Mr. Grimsby asked me to tell you he wishes to speak with you."

"Tell him I am here. Tell him I have found a perfect mute for him." The maid curtsied and with a look of doubt in her eyes she left to fetch her master. "Dear Catherine," Mrs. Grimsby said. "We have a funeral at three o'clock this afternoon. This shall be your first. You shall head the procession. Walking in front of the hearse in your dress and veil. You do not speak, of course, or utter any sound since you are the mute. By no means must you smile. Keep a strong gaze and hold your head high. I shall have you carry a black candle as well. It is very effective."

"How shall I keep it lit, Mistress?"

"Oh, dear one, we do not light it. In fact, you carry it turned upside down, the wick held toward the earth. It is what we call a symbol. You shall see."

Catherine took hold of Mrs. Grimsby and held her. As the door of the room flew open, Catherine turned to see an old ruddy-faced man enter. She held onto Mrs. Grimsby even tighter as the man came near. "Good morning, girl," the old man said in a gruff voice.

"Oh, dear Mr. Grimsby," said his wife. "We have found an angel. She is to live with us from now on. Like a daughter."

"Is she, by Jove?" the old man said, his voice sour in his throat. "How fortunate for us, Mrs. Grimsby, to have an unlimited number of mouths to feed."

"Whatever do you mean, sir?" Mrs. Grimsby replied, somewhat peeved.

"We shall need to bury half of London in the next fortnight if we wish to afford food and lodging for the victims of calamity in this world."

"Mr. Grimsby, sir. You are most unkind. Dear Catherine has suffered a terrible lot. She will be my ward. You need not bother your selfish self with her matters."

"Well, dear wife," replied Mr. Grimsby, "you may alter your song once you learn of yet a graver situation at hand — one concerning your favourite offspring, young Geoffrey." Letting go of Catherine, Mrs. Grimsby rose quickly. Her hands flew to her mouth as if to block a sudden scream from escaping. "Dear, sir," Mrs. Grimsby pleaded. "Do tell me. Is my dearest boy safe?"

"Hardly a boy, Mrs. Grimsby," her husband replied. "Not in the matter at hand. Come with me. Bring along Miss Catherine. No need to shelter tender ears in this house of ill fortune." Holding onto Catherine, Mrs. Grimsby followed her husband out of the parlour. The three made their way into the large front hall. Standing at the door was a square-built woman wearing frills and bows. By her elbow, a younger version, her daughter, a face puffy from weeping. Between mother and daughter, held fast by both hands, a short female child with a round face. She was no more than three years old. Her blonde hair was curled and stuffed under a straw hat.

"My good woman, allow me to present to you my wife, Mrs. Grimsby," older Mr. Grimsby said in a flat manner.

"How do you do?" said a puzzled Mrs. Grimsby. She tightened her hold of Catherine's hand. "To what do I owe the pleasure of your morning visit? We normally do not receive until between one o'clock and three in the afternoon."

"Visit?" said the woman in frills. Her voice reminded Catherine of the creaking of an old door. "Beg yer pardon, Missus. A visit of need, I dare say."

"Oh, please, do not hold me in suspense. A mother's heart cannot bear bad news to be withheld so," cried Mrs. Grimsby.

"Well, mum," replied the woman, her left hand rising to tap the elbow of her daughter. "This be my own flesh and blood, Miss Hilda. Born respectable, I might add, and once a fine girl. Father bolted when she was but thirteen. The Devil took her then, in mind and spirit. Soon enough, as I reckoned, the demon grabbed hold of her body. She danced a good 'un with one gin-fool, no other than yer son, Master Geoffrey."

"This is most vulgar," said Mrs. Grimsby. "You are surely mistaken. Show her out, Mary, and be quick."

"No mistakin', missus," countered the woman in frills. "Even if yer be so high and mighty. But Hilda and me, we been traipsin' around town for nigh two years to find the whereabouts of you, the parents of Master Geoffrey. Bills and expenses, sir, to be recompensed. A slippery one he is," the woman said, a broad grin breaking over her face. The woman in frills was once a pretty woman, Catherine could tell on studying her face. Though plump now and wearing clothes too tight, she had handsome eyes despite her voice. Her daughter's features carried the pink of youth; she had blue eyes and a hangdog look that reminded Catherine of Matron Pickens.

"He did it," blurted Hilda. Daughter Hilda stood forth and looked into Mr. Grimsby's eyes. Catherine watched her pouty mouth push out a little and her eyes flutter. "Oh, kind sir," she began, "you find me a sad woman, sir. Used, forgotten and abandoned to my singular mishap. Here, beside me, is little Margery. Such a likeness to your kind face, sir. As you can see. The Grimsby chin, here, and the brow, so like Master Geoffrey's." Hilda stepped back, her speech over and done, her head once again poised at an angle to show shame.

Mrs. Grimsby was led to a chair where she sat down, her hand still grasping Catherine's. At the same time, old Mr. Grimsby walked in a slow circle. Hilda brushed a bit of fluff from her skirt. The child began to kick the floor with one of her scuffed shoes. The mother in frills opened a cloth bag she had hanging from her wrist. Out of it came a penny, which she held up to the light in the foyer. Mr. Grimsby halted. He leaned forward to peer at the penny. "I'm very glad," said the woman in frills, "to have the pleasure of meeting you, kind sir. I have great respect for the funerary profession and no one who practises such a fine art can be an object of indifference to me. Such a fine house. What shall one imagine of young Geoffrey? A son of great importance to you, I am sure, sir." The woman spoke directly, the penny held up as if it were a talisman to protect the restless child at her feet.

"He did it, it was him," repeated Hilda, her voice puncturing the air still ringing with her mother's well-turned phrases. "Hush, Hilda," the mother said in a firm voice. "We can sees well who was the father."

Mr. Grimsby stood at attention: "You find me, Mrs. … but I do not know your name."

"Barraclough, sir. Mrs. Henry Barraclough, maiden name of Jimson, sir. From Surrey south. Hilda my one and only. Now, too, our sweet Margery."

On hearing her name, the child broke free of her mother's grasp. She stood her ground. She put her two little hands on her hips. "Mammy," she yelled. "I want to *go!*"

By this time Mrs. Grimsby had regained her strength. Catherine let go of her hand as the distraught mother of Geoffrey rose from her chair. Catherine watched Mrs. Grimsby's back straighten. Her head lifted and, with a voice full of feeling, she said to Mrs. Barraclough: "Mistress, your behaviour and your appearance at our respectable front door is not to be borne. You have come into our home bearing lies. You have displayed *your* shame to perfect strangers, using my son's good name to further the disgrace of your own failings. I have nothing to say, nothing to give to you but a word of dismissal. Leave my house on this instant or I shall call for a policeman to escort you to the nearest station house."

Mrs. Barraclough did not show any sign of retreat though she lowered her hand holding the penny. She addressed Mrs. Grimsby in a voice held low in her throat: "No need, mum, fer threats. We ain't here to rob you. But to get what's fair. What's comin' to Margery as yer own flesh and blood. Hilda, here, she's with a milliner lady. Makes good hats. Not a slack-child, no indeed. I sees to that. But me, I must stay at home, you sees? To feed and tend my lovely grandchild here. So I come only fer help, missus."

Mr. Grimsby moved between the two women. He bent forward and lifted up the child's face. He studied its features; he asked the child to remove her straw bonnet. She did so, dropping it to the floor. Her blonde hair tumbled out, ringlets falling to either side of her face. On seeing this, Mrs. Grimsby let out a little moan. "Oh, my goodness," she said. She rushed into the parlour. Pulling open a drawer, she lifted out a small paper envelope. She returned to the foyer, her face now pale with anxiety. She stood before little Margery and fluffed the child's light curls. From the envelope, Mrs. Grimsby drew a lock of light hair. A wisp of child's hair, fine and blonde. Kneeling down before little Margery Mrs. Grimsby looked into the child's face. "Oh, my," she mumbled. With her right hand she pulled forward one of Margery's ringlets. It had been recently cut with what appeared to be a pair of blunt scissors. Holding up the lock, Mrs. Grimsby matched it to the end of the cut ringlet. Miss Hilda gasped. So did her mother. Mrs. Grimsby stood up.

"Mr. Grimsby," she said. "Will you kindly escort Mrs. Barraclough into the parlour; I am feeling somewhat faint and will retire." Mary led the visitors into the parlour as Mr. Grimsby placed his arms around his wife's shoulders to steady her. Catherine stepped forward. "My dear one," moaned Mrs. Grimsby, "please be so kind as to return to your room. The one I have shown you. There is too much here that is vexing for a child of your sweet nature." Catherine Smeets curtsied to her new-found guardian. A rattle of a hansom cab outside the front door distracted her as she was about to leave. Hard knocks from the brass knocker forced Mr. Grimsby to release his wife and open the door himself. In the flood of morning light pouring into the foyer, two men stood at attention in top hats and gloves.

"Mr. Richard Grimsby, sir?" asked one of the men.

"Good morning, officers. I am he. How may I be of assistance?"

"We have been sent, sir, from Fleet Lane Station House on orders from Superintendent Borne and Inspector Owen Endersby of the Metropolitan Detective Police."

Mrs. Grimbsy fainted to the floor. Little Margery dashed into the foyer waving her arms, her mother Hilda in pursuit. Mrs. Henry Barraclough cocked her head.

"On what account, sir?" said a shaken Mr. Grimsby. "On suspicion of murder, sir" the officer replied. "A felony, sir. Your son, Mr. Geoffrey Grimsby, has been arrested and is being held in custody. We have been sent to inform you and to enquire if you would accompany us to Fleet Lane Station House to procure an identification of said son." Hearing those words, Mr. Grimsby looked down at his feet. There he took a moment to look at his prostrate wife.

"I shall, sir," Mr. Grimsby replied. "Miss Smeets, please attend to Mrs. Grimsby. Mary, help Miss Smeets. Mrs. Barraclough, I beg of you a few words in private." The shaken Mr. Grimsby took Mrs. Barraclough aside into a second parlour. Catherine watched their faces. Mrs. Barraclough spoke at a quick pace as if she were suddenly asked to recite a memorized passage. The woman's hands flew up and down to emphasize a point, the older man listening with great concentration, widening his eyes on occasion, then bowing his head. He stood for a moment and seemed to blank out his face, losing all shape of sadness or anger. An instant later, he slowly walked back into the foyer. "Good day to you all," he said politely.

The women bowed in respect to Mr. Grimsby who took his hat, gloves, and walking stick and followed the two police officers toward a waiting hansom cab.

Chapter Twenty-two
Forms of Things Unknown

Sergeant Thomas Caldwell struggled. His knuckles turned white. He lay back, mouth open, and felt the pincers take hold. A stab of pain racked the left side of his mouth.

"Steady, sir," said the barber. "One yank and one shilling and you will be free of pain."

"Arrrrghhhhhhhh!"

The barber held up the rotten tooth. Caldwell took a mouthful of gin and spit it into a basin next to the barber's chair. The sergeant knew the man and trusted him. He cut his hair, shaved his chin and occasionally yanked out a tooth. Another swish of gin and payment of the shilling, and Caldwell was out to the street, a bloody handkerchief pressed to his face. At a public house he took a glass of Scotch whiskey and winced. In the mirror in front of him he gazed at his face: pale, drawn from pain, tired. *I am a half-orphan in this life,* he thought. *No parents left. Only my Alice.*

The faces in the workhouse haunted him as he walked toward

Fleet Lane Station House. He had spent much time thinking about them. *Their sad eyes; their lost families. Family.* A word he rolled over and over in his mind. A sudden joy brightened the grimy street in front of him.

Why not rescue a young one from St. Giles? Or Shoe Lane? Alice and me could raise him. Love him like our own. Or her. A daughter. If Alice cannot have a baby we can choose a child from so many. Would Alice agree? This way she could be saved the toil of childbirth. Gain her strength. Love a needy child.

These thoughts rested lightly on Caldwell's mind as he spat blood one more time into the gutter. He wiped his mouth. *Time to set aside wishes and hopes for a happy domestic life,* he thought. Be prepared to report to his superior.

The day would go well. He had solid facts to relate. And he could toss away his tin box of cloves and relieve Inspector Endersby of the offending smell.

Inspector Endersby looked out of the window at the soot-filled air. *An afternoon of confusion ahead,* he thought. He stood in his jacket and waistcoat, hands held behind him in a pose of reflection. Though his early luncheon had been satisfying, he did not feel contented. What to make of the present situation two floors below in the cells of Fleet Lane Station House? "What indeed!" murmured Endersby. And, now, a packet of letters found by a surly matron in the St. Pancras Workhouse. All written by a ten-year-old named Catherine Smeets. *How do these fit?* he wondered.

"Ah, Mr. Caldwell," greeted the inspector as his sergeant entered. "I see you have paid your barber for your pain. By the way, how was your visit with Malibran? Did you 'tail' him? Follow him to any lair?"

"Unsuccessful, Inspector. I waited in the street, called to his landlord, and was shown into his room — but there was no sign of him. Two witnesses in the area had seen him leave very late, return, and then go out again before dawn. Seems I missed his comings and goings."

"Pity, sir," said Endersby.

"I then walked to the Strand to look for him," Caldwell continued. "I questioned a number of street folk. They told me Malibran has been out singing and earning his money in other streets. He does his one-man act on the Strand only at night, however, sir."

"And so this evening we shall pursue him along the Strand, Sergeant," replied Endersby. "All is not lost for the moment. We have a surprise at present, awaiting us below, Mr. Caldwell."

Sergeant Caldwell's eyes brightened. "Yes, Mr. Caldwell," Endersby continued. "Let me recall to you our present situation. Two matrons, two murders, two workhouse Catherines as first witnesses, and now in the pens below, two likely felons. *Two*, sir. One for each murder, if you wish to be equitable in assigning guilt!"

"Two felons, sir?"

"Most remarkable they are in likeness as well — height, color, facial mutilation. Twins, perhaps, in action and motive."

"And alibis, Inspector?"

"None as yet. And both refusing to divulge information. In fact, Sergeant, both claimed innocence at first. Our task is to strategize, sir."

On their way down to the lower floors of the station house, the inspector showed his sergeant the packet of letters. "Written to an imaginary uncle, it seems, Caldwell. A felon sent to Australia for a minor crime. Seems *this* young Catherine refused to believe he was dead." Descending farther they found themselves in a broad stone corridor. On either side were heavy wooden doors. Each had a large handle and keyhole made of iron. The rooms behind them were low-ceilinged and without windows. Once they had held political rebels when the original structure was built hundreds of years before. Endersby did not like the lack of space or light. He believed the darkness oppressed men, made them too fearful to speak out. On approaching the cells of Sergeant Peter Smeets and Mr. Geoffrey Grimsby, the inspector ordered two large lanterns to carry into the gloom of each wretched space.

"Now, Sergeant. Let us play at doubles, if I may borrow from the noble sport of lawn tennis."

Caldwell nodded. He stood at attention. Such was his relationship with his superior that Caldwell knew an adventure of some kind might soon take place. "Sergeant, I wish you to visit the cell of Mr. Grimsby. I know naught of him. He was arrested on the street this morning in a state of drunkenness. A fellow in a frock coat. A scar on his face. Much about him resembles the description we sent out. Kindly go to him, show him kindness, then begin to ask who he is, where he was ... well, you are familiar with our routine. I shall effect a similar discussion with Sergeant Smeets. I will use these letters if need be. After a half hour or so, let us convene here by the stairwell."

"Certainly, sir. If I may say so, sir, a fine opening manoeuvre."

"Cannons ready, then, Sergeant?"

"Primed, Inspector."

Endersby checked his coat pockets one last time. In them he had gathered a number of items, including Catherine Smeets' letters, the sergeant's release papers, and the lace found on the two dead matrons. As the constable opened the door to Smeets' cell, Endersby greeted him: "Sergeant, I do hope you are comfortable."

Smeets looked up as Endersby entered. One simple bench

lined the far wall; it served as seat and sleeping platform. A foul-smelling chamber pot sat in the opposite corner. One candle stayed the deep gloom. The lantern carried in by the inspector threw shadows upon the gritty stone.

"Rum-gull," mumbled Sergeant Smeets. "Why I 'ave to wear fetters in this bog?"

"Irons," replied the inspector, "are a necessity, Sergeant, for keeping both prisoner and guard at ease."

"Cheeky git you are," came the sergeant's reply. He was sober, now. His eyes were ringed with dark circles. His ankles had been washed and bandaged and his hands no longer resembled those of a coal carrier's.

"Sergeant, I read in your release papers that you were stationed at Dumfries, just north of the Scottish border."

"Wot of it?"

"Sixteen days ago you were discharged after a lashing. Given two shillings as leave pay." Endersby held the papers up while reading them by lantern light. He folded the soiled sheets and put them away in his pocket for the time being.

"Enough fer drink, Bobby."

"You made good time walking from Dumfries to London. All effort for the sole purpose of finding your daughter."

"None of that be yer business, rum-dog. Splittin' wenches is all I cares about," the sergeant said, his leering smile showing a number of lost front teeth. Endersby had instructed a constable to bring food and there was evidence on the bench of a half-eaten lump of bread. Sergeant Smeets wiped his eyes and lay down on the bench, stretching out his legs and placing his head on his folded-up frock coat.

"A fine frock coat, Sergeant. A better fit than your tunic?" questioned the inspector. Endersby was now leaning his frame against one of the stone walls, his face in shadow.

"Won at cards, pup," came the tired reply.

"How so, Sergeant? You claimed you lost musket and scabbard at cards. How came you to procure a coat of such good weave?"

"Killed a man-slag for it," the sergeant then said, his voice low and lazy.

"I presume your murder of the man took place after he had removed his coat?"

"Ha, sir. A wise goat you are."

"No blood on it. No sign of musket powder. Or perhaps I am being a fool," Endersby said, playing his game of questions. "Of course, you were more clever than I first thought. You, sergeant, strangled the gull once he was in his cups. Took the coat right off his back."

"Hi ho, Bobby-dog. Such a tale-spinner you are. I killed 'im with bare hands *and* a knife *and* my musket, all for a weave. A good'un!" The sergeant's voice had fallen into a whisper. He was beginning to doze and Endersby feared he might lose his attention. On impulse, Endersby leapt out of the shadows. He grabbed hold of the sergeant's shirt front, lifted him up to sitting position and shook him vigorously.

"*Murder*, Sergeant. You have admitted to a crime of great import. Drawing, lashing and hanging await you. Now speak up, where did this happen? I will trace it down if I must. I will send constables into the cities where you stopped and enquire of gravediggers and police officers about a strangled man."

The sergeant tried to break free. Endersby shook him again. He slapped the sergeant's left cheek. He hauled him up to his feet. Nose to nose he stood, fighting the soldier's stinking breath. The sergeant began to cough, forcing Endersby to hold him at arm's length. Once again, the inspector shook Smeets, this time until his coughing let up. "Gull, dog, wot do it matter?" sputtered

Sergeant Smeets. "I killed 'im. Or I didn't kill'im. All the same to me."

"You, sir, are a liar. Jests are but forms of lies," Endersby hissed, his "demon familiar" rising, his fists ready to strike. Wisely, the inspector took a breath. Chin raised, he let his body and anger calm. *No more fisticuffs,* he warned himself. "Where did the killing of this man take place?" Endersby asked, letting Smeets go. The soldier sat down. He shrugged. He then began to rub his head with his hands and rock back and forth. Here again was this agitated action of remorse Endersby had witnessed earlier at St. Pancras.

"What is the matter, Sergeant?" Endersby asked. The sergeant wailed: "I shall die now. I will die and ne'er see my sweet one again." Endersby sat down on the bench beside the sergeant. One of his methods of investigation was to unsettle his captives by showing them first brutal authority then brotherly kindness. Such an approach often placated the criminal mind, Endersby would argue. Reaching out, Endersby squeezed the sergeant's shoulder. Bending forward, Endersby could see fear and doubt in Smeets's eyes. Would this give way at last to a truthful confession?

Endersby remained quiet beside the rocking man. After a moment's reflection, the inspector considered the discharge papers: these were proof of Sergeant Smeets's whereabouts in the last two weeks, given the state of the man's boots and his haggard appearance. Taking a new tack, Endersby instead showed Smeets one of the letters written by his daughter to her uncle.

"Glance at this, sergeant," Endersby said. Smeets sat up and took hold of the letter.

"Well, what do you make of it?" Endersby said.

The soldier looked bewildered; he turned the letter over a few times, peering at the writing and tracing out some of the words with his finger. "I ain't no letter writer. Canna read much beyond a dot."

"Allow me to read to you what I have." Endersby took the letter and bent close to the lantern. He read the contents out loud, slowly, emphasizing each single word.

"Ow, ow," the sergeant moaned, remorse filling his throat. Smeets sat up boldly. Endersby finished by repeating the last two words: "Your Catherine."

"T'was my temper, Bobby, that done it," the sergeant said. He wiped his eyes. Endersby noted again the man's capacity for tender feeling.

"How do you mean, Sergeant?" Endersby asked, folding the letter.

"He was my dead wife's brother. A good fellah. Good to my sweet Catherine. We all lived in the village near Frogmore. He struck me one night for hittin' my own daughter. I was a looby lout. All he wanted was to protect her. I was jealous of 'im. I charged 'im with hittin' me, a sergeant of Her Majesty's. Arrested he was. Poor gull. T'was him taught my little one to read."

"What happened to him?"

"Sentenced to the prison ships, the hulks. The judge sent 'im off to Australia. Gone forever. Or dead of fever." Endersby knew the hulks were pitiless places. Old navy ships refurbished to house felons since the land prisons were overflowing. The prisoners were sent to work on canals and roads where many died of disease.

"Could a man escape the hulks, Sergeant?" Endersby's question hung in the air.

"Not him. Too frail he'd be. He'd die soon enough like some starved dog. Poor scag, he and my wife raised in a filthy workhouse. He ne'er forgot that place."

"When was the uncle condemned to the hulks, Sergeant?" the inspector asked.

"Christmas last."

"Did your daughter Catherine know anyone in London, Sergeant?"

The poor man resumed rocking. "I left her here. All alone. God curse me, sir." Endersby waited for a moment: "Is your daughter a strong girl, Sergeant. Will she survive on the streets?"

The sergeant gazed into the dark emptiness of the cell. "*Please*, find her, gull. Rotten I am, but I'd do anything for my sweet." Through the flickering lantern light, Endersby looked hard at the broken man. Words of Prince Hamlet jumped into the inspector's mind: *a countenance more in sorrow than in anger.*

"You say you'd do anything, Sergeant. For your daughter."

"Yes, gull. Anything."

"Does killing come easy to you, Sergeant? You are a trained soldier. Do you find it a simple act to accomplish?"

"Wot you mean?"

"If you saw, say, Matron Pickens, the tall woman you met today at St. Pancras. Let us picture her beating your Catherine. Hurting her, making her ..."

"I'd cut her slaggy throat. Choke her if she give me reason."

"Have you ever been in a workhouse, Sergeant? Ever there as a child?"

"But once. For a fortnight when a lad. Them matrons were demons. The scags gave the whip every morning and night if you spilled a bit of porridge."

"Can you remember Tuesday last, Sergeant. Where you were? At night, what did you do?"

"Sleepin', gull. You try settin' foot after foot for a fortnight, livin' on bits of bread and drippin'."

"When did you start to look for Catherine?"

The sergeant fell silent. He began to enter the trance-like

state Endersby had seen moments before as if it were a recurring fever in one afflicted by consumption.

"Sergeant?"

"Leave me be, Bobby-gull. I can take no more. I killed the fellow, I killed 'em all, if that be the truth you want to hear."

Realizing he had come to a standstill with the sergeant, Endersby decided to allow the fellow a moment of peace. He paced as the sergeant lay back, exhausted, on the bench. A tap, and in the doorway, at attention, was Sergeant Caldwell. "Half hour, sir." The inspector walked quickly toward his sergeant. "Carry on with this suspect, Sergeant. Here, take one of these pieces of lace. Show it to him. Ask if he knows of Rosemary Lane. He is tiring. Bring him some hot coffee. Push him. He needs a new voice to keep him awake. Get more about the uncle, especially his *full true name* if the man can remember it. He is a hard one, Caldwell. I have not as yet nudged him into a confession. I shall go to Mr. Grimsby."

"Beware, sir," cautioned Mr. Caldwell. "Grimsby is a fighting fellow. Denies everything. He is open to suspicion and yet, sir, there is remorse in his voice. He seems a man playing a part."

"I thank you, Sergeant, for your warnings. I will stoke the engine, full steam ahead!"

"Thank you, sir," smiled Mr. Caldwell.

Endersby walked a few paces. He let his mind take a rest on the present maze of thoughts about Sergeant Smeets. Forming a plan, he entered the cell where Grimsby was confined. Young Grimsby sat on the edge of the prison bench inside his dim cell. He was wearing a stained frock coat, his face covered in stubble, his scar like a stretch of red ribbon flowing across his face. Endersby introduced himself and asked the young man to give his name.

"Grimsby, sir, Geoffrey. Son of Richard Grimsby, undertaker, in Marylebone. What the devil have I done to place me here, sir? I demand you call for my father at once."

"To answer your first question, Mr. Grimsby, you have been arrested on suspicion of murder. Second, your father has been sent for and may arrive at any moment."

"Preposterous," chimed young Grimsby. His breath smelled of gin. "Never raise my hand to touch a bee nor a fly for that matter."

"Neither bees nor flies are the law's concern, Mr. Grimsby," came the inspector's sharp reply. "Rather, we are more concerned with the death of two elderly women, strangled to death by a villain in the night."

"How *dee*do?" smirked Grimsby. "None of my taste, sir. The sordid underworld of Bow Street is beneath my purview."

"Indeed, sir?"

Young Grimsby sat forward and rubbed his forehead. Endersby looked into his face. "You have a scar, sir," he said. "How did it come about?"

"A tree branch. Cut me while riding."

"On Tuesday last, where did you spend your time?"

"I refuse to be badgered, Inspector. I wish to speak with my father."

"Two women were murdered, Mr. Grimsby. Brutally, in fact. One in the St. Giles Workhouse and the other in Shoe Lane."

"Never been there, not in my life. Oh, yes, once to Bethnall Green Workhouse to fetch a boy for our mute. Sickly one he was. Scummy places, Inspector."

"It would suit your present situation to tell me about your comings and goings on Tuesday last, Mr. Grimsby. I suggest you try and remember."

Grimsby coughed. He stood up. "You remind me of my mammy, Inspector. Always *at it*, always wanting to know who I know, where I go. Cannot a young man have his pleasures without endless questioning?"

"Murder is what we are speaking about in this instance, Mr. Grimbsy. A hanging matter in deed and in outcome," Endersby quipped.

"Betrayed I was, Tuesday night last," Grimsby began. "To the gin house, then to my Hilda. Then out into the street with a firm shove from her wicked mother."

"And then?"

Young Grimsby laughed. He shrugged his shoulders. "Cold on Tuesday late, as I recall."

Endersby could see the man was fearful. But he was holding back. What secret was he not willing to reveal? "Hilda?" Endersby said, prompting the bedraggled young man. Grimsby raised his face. "This be a sordid den, sir. Too damp for my liking." Grimsby kicked the floor with his cracked boot. He looked toward the cell door, which stood open behind the inspector. A young constable was standing by it and with him in shadow was another gentleman with a top hat and a cane.

"Father?" cried young Grimsby. Inspector Endersby turned and commanded the constable to come in with the other gentleman.

"Good day, Inspector," said the elder Mr. Grimsby. "A fine place for you, son, I see," he said, his voice hard with sarcasm.

"Father, sir, this lot have me caught up for murder. A lark, sir. A false accusation," pleaded young Grimsby. Endersby noted immediately how young Grimsby had changed. Indeed, it seemed he was playing a series of parts, like an actor in repertory. How well he could show disdain; how masterful his sudden switch to pleading. And yet the inspector also noted a vulnerable air about him.

"I beg your pardon, sir," Endersby said to the elder Mr. Grimsby. "Your son was arrested on suspicion only. His appearance matched precisely to that of a culprit who we believe is running loose in London, having killed innocent women in two workhouses."

"A new sport of yours, son?" the stone-faced father replied. "Gin addled your senses, then? Forced you to indulge in greater violence to drive you further into crime and cruelty?"

"Father?" young Grimsby wailed. "Father, please help me. You know I am not ..." The young man's eyes were full of sadness. The father, in response, lowered his head so as not to show the flicker of emotion distorting his features. Endersby wondered if this were a case of "like father, like son." Was the father also playing a part at this moment, straining to hide his real self?

"My son, sir," the elder Grimsby said turning his attention toward the inspector. "My young Geoffrey is a reprobate. His character does not speak well of my own efforts to raise him properly. I offer you and your professional colleagues an apology. My whipping cane, sadly, has had no effect whatsoever."

Endersby considered the man's hard words. Was this a jest, perhaps? More ominously, were these words to be understood as a father's condemnation of his own flesh and blood?

"Capable of murder, you believe, sir?" Endersby said, his voice cool. Mr. Richard Grimsby did not flinch. "Foolhardiness leads to a decadent state of mind," the father replied. He then turned to his son. "Empty your pockets, sir. On the double." Young Grimsby was shaking. He tore into his pants pockets and turned them out. The same procedure was applied to his frock coat, pockets both on the inside and the outside.

"Where is the licence I sent with you to the workhouse?" enquired the older man. "Where is the two pounds I trusted you to carry to procure a child to play the mute for our processions?"

"Lost, Father," the young Grimsby replied, his low tone full of contrition.

"Not lost, son. Tossed by you, both the license and coin into the hands of a gin seller."

"No, Father, no," the young man said. He sat down. Shoulders forward, a short series of sobs started gurgling in his throat. The elder Grimsby stepped close to his son and reached out his hand. He was about to touch him, but then he stepped back. It seemed to Endersby, the older man was torn between disdain and compassion.

"What would you have me do, Inspector?" the elder Grimsby then said. "I know so little of this scalliwag's adventures. He was refused by Her Majesty's military service on account of his weak foot. I am at a loss." As he spoke, the elder Grimsby moved closer to Inspector Endersby. He leaned toward the inspector and said: "There is a matter I best speak to you about out of my son's earshot. If you will indulge me, sir?"

"Indeed, sir," Endersby replied. He showed the older man out and followed him into the corridor. Young Grimsby stood up frantically and dashed toward the door: "Father, you are a brute, a stingy cruel old man!" he shouted. The constable caught young Grimsby as he tried to bolt out the door. "Keep him under lock and key for the time being," commanded Endersby.

"Father! Father? Oh where is my mammy?"

"Come, Mr. Grimsby. We may speak in the offices upstairs."

The older Grimsby nodded in assent. He had grown ashen as a consequence of the encounter with his son. "Are you feeling ill, sir?" Endersby asked. The older man took hold of the inspector's arm for support. "I am ill at heart, sir. Most perturbed! I cannot stay and witness this scene a moment longer. Please, take me into the open air or I may fall prone at your feet."

"Constable, kindly lead this gentleman upstairs to my office." At the same moment, another young constable arrived from the far end of the stone corridor. He stood at attention in front of Endersby.

"Yes, Constable," the inspector said.

"Sir, following your orders. We have secured a gentleman earlier this morning who closely resembles the description of the culprit you have set down in your description."

"*Another?*" said Endersby. "Indeed. Lead on, Constable."

Following the young man down the corridor, Endersby came to one of the wooden doors which the constable swung open. Taking up a lantern, Endersby stepped into the cell. In front of him was a man sitting in ragged clothes, with filthy hands, the air about him full of human stink.

"Your name, sir?" Endersby commanded, lifting up the lantern to grasp a better view of the man's dirt-covered features. He could see the face, shadowed by a soiled hat. It was hard in the lantern light to determine if the mark upon the face was a scar or a defect in the left cheek.

"Lardle, sir," came the croaky response. "Mr. Henry Lardle. At your service."

"You were arrested this past night?" asked the inspector.

"Done my duty, sir. Done it. And on my ways to home by the St. Giles Workhouse I stood. Took a piss, you see by the gate. Wot then? A Bobby shakes his rattle, arrests me, holds a lantern to me face, looks me over and drags me in here."

"On what charge, Mr. Lardle?"

"Bobby says, I am in suspicion of a murder," came the response. "I say, stuff and nonsense. I work hard for my livin', hard enough to keep me runnin' about and no time for murder. No, sir. No time at all."

"Tell me more, sir. Explain yourself," coaxed Endersby, moving into the cell and standing next to Henry Lardle.

"Well, sir," said Lardle, "it be a long story, but an honest one."

"Please indulge me."

Chapter Twenty-three
A Discovery

It was the appointed hour of three o'clock. Catherine Smeets pulled on a pair of clean stockings. "There you be, lovely as ever," Mary said, lowering the black gauze veil over Catherine's face. Mary led the way out of the dressing chamber and into the courtyard. The crepe gloves Mary had given Catherine scratched her skin but they made her hands look so regal that she imagined herself as a young princess. Before her stood a magnificent coach, its sides and ends made into windows of glazed glass. When the driver came forward with his whip, he was dressed all in black with a tall hat trailing a scarf of the same gauze, which masked Catherine's face. Each of the funeral horses wore a head-dress of purple-tinted plumes.

Out of the courtyard hall, four men carried the coffin of a tailor. Catherine felt her heart jump. She was an important part of this solemn ritual. She was the symbol, after all. After a moment of prayer the coffin was slid into the hearse, the door shut. The groom climbed into the driver's seat along with the driver. Both men looked to Catherine, bowed their heads, and Catherine took her cue.

Holding the long black candle given her by Mary, Catherine walked slowly to the head of the procession and led them on toward the graveyard. Afterward, back in Mrs. Grimby's parlour, Catherine felt happy. Mary held her in her arms. "Oh, lucky one. Such a mute I ne'er seen before." Catherine felt warm all over. She stood up. "Look at me, Mary," she cried. Spreading out her arms, Catherine twirled. "I wish only for one thing," Catherine said and looked out the window at the afternoon light. "What is that, dear one?" Mary said.

"I wish my dear uncle could come back to see me. How happy. Oh, he would be so happy."

"But has he gone for good, dear?" Mary said as the two of them gently rocked together on the settee. "Yes, I fear so."

Mrs. Grimsby came into the room. Mary and Catherine stood up. "My lovely child," Mrs. Grimsby said. "You behaved so well. Come, embrace me. You bring me such peace, my child. You are now with your new family."

⁕⁘⁙⁘⁕

The elder Mr. Richard Grimsby struggled up from the chair in Inspector Endersby's office at Fleet Lane Station House. The old undertaker had told a long tale about his son. "His present state of mind is not good. Discontentment with his lot has warped my young Geoffrey's behaviour." Putting on his hat, the older man said to Endersby: "I thank you for granting me more time to resolve this confusion. I believe the two of us can readily prove the nature of my son's innocence in this matter with the facts I can present to you on the morrow." Endersby accompanied the man into the foyer of Fleet Lane Station House. On his return to his office he found Sergeant Caldwell. His trustworthy colleague was seated in a small chair under the window. Bent over, wearing his spectacles, he was writing in his notebook.

"Sergeant, please finish your sentence," said Endersby. His gouty foot burned; his injured hand itched; his mind felt heavy with facts and doubts.

"I would love some biscuit and tea," Endersby mumbled.

"I beg your pardon, sir?" said Caldwell, checking his last paragraph.

"Musing, Caldwell," came the inspector's reply. "Gathering wool."

"I have details, sir, to report," said Caldwell. "I can have these notes re-written in ink by the supper hour."

"I thank you for your efficiency, Caldwell. I, on the other hand, am at a loss. I have been bargaining with a father over the life of his son. A most curious phenomenon in which all will be made clear, I am assured, at eight o'clock tomorrow morning."

"Unusual, indeed, sir," Caldwell said.

"Did Sergeant Smeets stay awake long enough to afford you reliable information?" Endersby asked.

"He is a dour fellow, sir," said Caldwell. "In need of much prodding. Claimed he did not recognize the bits of lace. Most of the time he denied any knowledge of anything, sir."

"I had much the same experience with him," said Endersby. By now, the inspector's mind had revived somewhat and a curious hunch took shape among his gathering thoughts. "Did you ascertain the name of the uncle?"

"Yes, sir." Caldwell underlined the name and handed the sheet to his inspector.

"Most curious, Sergeant. So, this name may clarify a number of our clues. The puzzle is beginning to form a picture." Endersby placed his hands behind his back and started to pace. "I have heard a most intriguing story from one Mr. Henry Lardle, who once worked as a dredgerman."

"Yes, sir," said Caldwell.

"I will tell you en route, but let us investigate this business a little longer before I come to any conclusions. We have a number of hours left of this particular afternoon so we must take full advantage. I need to look again in St. Pancras. We must also take a moment to visit a fine house in Bedford Square. For now, let the two of us make haste before the sun sets this evening."

Within moments, the two men were sitting in a hansom cab. In his satchel, the inspector carried his square magnifying glass and his ear trumpet. Streets heading north were lined with purveyors of all goods, from bird's nests and brass parrot cages to trombones and hot muffins. A rain squall pelted the hansom as it crossed Euston Square, then sun dried its canvas roof as the driver turned into the large court of St. Pancras Workhouse. The two men descended and went in.

"Ah, Inspector," smiled the gregarious Matron Dench. "We are at your disposal — if I may use such a vulgar term in the presence of a professional gentleman."

"I thank you, Matron Dench."

"Come, sir," said Endersby. "The March light is fading. You take the west and I shall take the east side of the outdoor court and stables. Mind the washhouse and the quarters for the blacksmith." Endersby did not stir for a moment. It was his custom to look around a site, to picture himself as walking in a suspect's boots, conjuring up his mood and his terrain of feelings. Endersby imagined Sergeant Smeets coming into this darkened court searching for a doorway, the coal chute — any entry — to effect a rescue of his daughter. In the case of Smeets, gin and deep fatigue might have undermined the man's abilities to make judgements.

"The byways of the criminal mentality always astonish," Endersby said aloud, to remind himself never to draw a conclusion before proof was established. He then began to walk. He kept his eyes to the ground. He circled the stables. He passed by the stalls where he had first encountered Sergeant Smeets. Looking toward the east side wing and the latched gate nearby, the inspector started thinking that perhaps this gate might have been chosen as the most convenient way out for Smeets. It was close to a fallow field; it was far from the entrance to the courtyard. What prompted the inspector was a hunch—similar to an itch. This was a feeling familiar to Endersby: this singular urgency always seemed to appear when he believed an important clue was about to turn up. His eyes slowly scanned the dead grass in front of the gate.

Endersby paused, a thin smile lighting up his face. "Ah, so you are hidden here, are you?" he murmured to himself. Endersby stepped forward, pulling off one of his suede gloves. A dredgerman's gaff with its curved metal hook lay against the brick of the wall. Taking out his square magnifying glass, Endersby examined the hook's metal surface in the fading light. "Orange," he whispered. He scratched the surface of the hook. "Rust flakes," he said. "So, monster, you have dropped this in haste?" Endersby stepped back.

"Caldwell! Sergeant Caldwell!"

In less than a second, his sergeant was by his side.

"A find, sir?" asked Caldwell, eyeing the gaff.

"No doubt, Sergeant," Endersby said. Sergeant Caldwell took hold of the wooden handle and turned the gaff in his hands. "A worn piece, sir. Rusted. Does this throw suspicion on your Mr. Henry Lardle as well as Sergeant Smeets?"

"Perhaps, Sergeant. Be not too hasty, however. Whoever it belonged to, it was abandoned. Was the villain in flight?"

"We do have a puzzle, sir."

"But if we are clever we can match its pieces. I think we may have before us an unusual turn of the tide." The two men continued their search until the light faded. "On the double, now, Caldwell," the inspector said. "A doctor named Benton needs to tell us a story."

Chapter Twenty-four
A Secret and A Dream

A short man opened the front door to Number Sixteen Bedford Square.

"Good evening, sirs," he said. When he learned his callers were gentlemen from the Metropolitan Detective Police, he stepped back, wary but polite. "Please come this way, sirs," the butler said. "May I take your hats?" The butler walked ahead and led Caldwell and Endersby into a small parlour with a fire in its grate. Presently, an ample woman appeared. On her face was a frown of concern and Endersby wondered if she might prove an obstacle, indeed a great wall to climb to get at facts.

"Mrs. Wells," she replied to Endersby's first question.

"You are well acquainted with Dr. Josiah Benton?" Endersby asked. Caldwell in the meantime had taken out his notebook and was quietly writing down all the questions and responses. "Well enough, sir. He is my employer," Mrs. Wells reported. "Ten years now." Endersby sensed tightness, hesitation. Was Mrs. Wells, like many guilty people, unable to disguise their fear of being found

out? Earlier, while questioning Mr. Henry Lardle, Endersby had
learned of the peculiar tastes of Dr. Josiah Benton. Might Mrs.
Wells prove to be an accomplice in what seemed to be a horrific
type of adult behaviour? "I know nothing of such, sir," Mrs. Wells
replied when confronted with Lardle's observations. She blinked
twice and twisted her mouth on hearing the wretch's name.

"Sir, my position here is as cook," she announced. "I manage
the larder and the kitchen and I prepare each of Dr. Benton's
meals. That is all I am paid to perform, and it is all of what I am
paid to know about. As to this Lardle man, I have no acquaintance with such a person."

"How odd, then, Mrs. Wells," the inspector continued. "He
mentioned you and your name and the delights of your pastry — handouts he claimed — for he said he often came to the
back entrance of this fine house and was met not only by the
butler but frequently by you. In fact, Mr. Lardle felt quite at
home here in Bedford Square. He praised Dr. Benton as a firm
but fair-minded employer whose sole interest in him was his
ability to search out, find and then procure a regular selection
of *young innocent girls*."

The stress the inspector put on the last three words brought
a sudden blanching to Mrs. Wells's face. Not a second later, her
hands covered her teary eyes. "I cannot say, sir. I cannot say at
all," she said. "Is your employer at home, Mrs. Wells?"

"He was, sir. But he has stepped out at this hour for one of
his daily strolls."

"Do you know which way he has gone?"

"I cannot say, sir. I cannot," the woman dried her eyes and
puffed out her chest. "He is a good and honourable man, sir. Mr.
Lardle does not know Josiah — Dr. Benton — as well as I do; he
is kind and gentle and without fault."

"I must insist, then, that you show me a room which Mr.

Lardle stated had been set aside in this very house for Dr. Benton's assignations with the young girls brought to his back door."

"Oh, my, sir. Assignations? You make Dr. Benton sound like a reprobate. He is nothing of the sort."

"Nevertheless, Mrs. Wells. I demand to see this place as proof of some kind to support Mr. Lardle's claims."

"A scum man, no question, sir," Mrs. Wells blurted out.

"You admit then, you know of Mr. Henry Lardle?'

"I admit it," Mrs. Wells said, giving in. "And I can say with much fervour that Lardle has somehow enchanted Dr. Benton." The woman blew her nose and crossed her hands in front of her.

"With your permission, Mrs. Wells, I shall ask my sergeant-at-hand, Mr. Caldwell, to search the rooms of this house. I ask that you have a servant stand by the front and back doors and to call out if anyone — Dr. Benton in particular — wishes to come in or go out."

Reluctantly, Mrs. Wells nodded and gave the orders. She then asked Inspector Endersby to sit down in the foyer by the stairs, where he continued his questions.

"Tell me, Mrs. Wells. What facts do you know of Lardle?"

"Little. He is unwashed. He was once in the army up north. He has poor lodgings and he wanders the streets at night."

"Has Dr. Benton ever mentioned anything about his background?"

"Yes, Inspector. Mr. Lardle was once accused of murder. It seems he was found innocent of the charge. A woman, sir, I believe. A washerwoman."

"Can you describe any of his features you can recall. His face, for example."

"But, sir, you have met the man. You have seen his face."

"His face has an odd mark, I agree, Mrs. Wells," replied

Endersby. "At least it is all I can see in the dim light of a prison cell."

"Well, Inspector, it seems he was born with a puckered muscle in his cheek. Dr. Benton explained to me it was the result of a midwife's poor skills."

"This is all you know?"

"He is not violent so far as I can tell. And he has a woman."

"A sister, a wife?"

"A woman, sir," said Mrs. Wells, her mouth turning down. "He says she lives with'im, says she puts up with 'im and loves 'im."

"Do you know where they live?" asked Endersby.

"I believe in a court on Drury Lane. Short by the St. Giles Workhouse. The butler knows for certain."

"I thank you," Endersby said politely. "Now, Mrs. Wells, difficult as this may be, I wish you to lead me up to this room Mr. Lardle has told me about. He has never seen it but he imagines it is a place ..."

"Come this way, sir," Mrs. Wells said. "It is a most decent and sweet room, if I may venture my opinion." Up the central hall stairs and onto the second floor, Endersby noticed fine wallpapers, a carved desk, a short passage leading to a little bedroom. The door was unlocked. "Please, Inspector," Mrs. Wells said showing him in.

On the little pink table one of the teacups still sat half full of cold tea. The inspector looked about. The room indeed was unusual, but neat and suited to the tastes of a child, particularly a girl. "I have sometimes brought tea to Dr. Benton's young visitors," Mrs. Wells confessed. Endersby now watched the woman's eyes. They shone with pride. Was Mrs. Wells in thrall to Dr. Benton and refused to see what his actions might imply? Was Henry Lardle correct in claiming that Dr. Benton, like many men of his station, was fond of physical pleasures with virginal girls? And was it therefore true that Lardle — a man once suspected of murder — had stolen girls from alleys and workhouses and killed any person who stood in his way of his weekly fistful of coins?

"I thank you, Mrs. Wells. In the best interest of Dr. Benton, I strongly suggest you do not tell him of what we have seen and heard today. I wish to discuss these matters with the man himself." With her eyes tearing up again, Mrs. Wells nodded and led the inspector downstairs where Caldwell was waiting in the foyer. "Rooms empty, sir. No doctor hiding in closets or cupboards," said Caldwell.

"Thank you, Sergeant. Mrs. Wells, please gather your servants and the butler here as quickly as you can." The woman rushed into the kitchen. "A most intriguing place, Caldwell. I am somewhat at a loss at this moment to figure out how this Dr. Benton thinks."

"In what way, sir?"

"Is he a miscreant? Is Lardle a true procurer of whores or is there some secret we have yet to uncover."

Before Caldwell could comment, Mrs. Wells reappeared with the butler, a footman and three housemaids. "Thank you, all," said Endersby, his voice gentle. "I must ask all of you to stand on your honour. Dr. Benton and his accomplice, Mr. Henry Lardle, are under suspicion for a crime."

Two of the housemaids uttered cries of alarm. "My sergeant and I are members of the detective police and we now ask you to send us word when your employer returns home. I will ask you, Mrs. Wells, to be certain Dr. Benton is comfortable and not alarmed and that he stays indoors over the next twenty-four hours. You believe he is a good, honest man. Please advise him, then, on the matter of his safety and be aware that if he escapes for any reason, the law in its pursuit may be harsh." The small group all bowed their heads. The gesture touched Endersby and he wondered about the nature of Dr. Benton and whether he was, indeed, capable of criminal activities. Mrs. Wells then ushered him and Caldwell out to the street. Bedford Square gleamed in the light, the brick fronts of houses shining with polished glass windows.

"Caldwell," said Endersby. "First, please return to Dr. Benton's and ask the butler for the address of Mr. Lardle. We shall take up the matter of his 'woman', if she exists. Then, to the station house nearby, and on my orders have two constables sent immediately to guard the front and back of Benton's house. Explain the matter to the desk sergeant and be sure to counter any refusal by telling about the murders and our present case.

"Yes, sir. I will in haste."

"I believe, Caldwell, we can rely on Mrs. Wells and her servants. I have an inkling that Dr. Benton will not bolt. For there seems to be something odd in this clean house."

"Certainly, sir," Caldwell answered.

"And Caldwell. This day has passed and we have yet to locate Malibran. He claimed not to know where his 'pity-man' has fled, but my gut tells me differently. Send a constable to relieve the present guard at his lodgings in Nightingale Lane where we met earlier this morning. Tonight, Malibran might sneak out. Come to Number Six Cursitor Street at midnight. I will by then have returned from the theatre. We can attempt to locate Malibran along the Strand — if he is there singing."

Still, though his mind could endure much turmoil, Endersby was unable to relinquish his mood of uncertainty. The hansom he hired had broken free from London's ever-growing river of early evening vehicles and found a path of quiet through back streets out of Bedford Square. Endersby meditated on his day: the gaff discovery was fortuitous — no question. But what of young Grimsby? What "matter to prove innocence" did his odd father hold in secret? *Do not jump so eagerly to a conviction, old gander,* Endersby thought. The cabby had to knock twice on the cab roof to awaken the dozing inspector on arrival at Number Six Cursitor Street. After a quick sponge bath in his study, the inspector joined his beloved Harriet at the dinner table. For this evening's repast, Mrs. Endersby had requested that Solange, their young French cook, prepare an English-styled supper rather than the usual soup, fish, and fowl *a la francaise.*

"Ah, splendid," cried Endersby, napkin tucked under his chin, knife and fork raised.

"Dear Mr. Endersby," Harriet cautioned. "Be gentle, sir. We have time to eat. Do not gorge yourself."

"Madam, I thank you for your admonitory words. You shall not see a repetition of my 'demon appetite' as you witnessed earlier this morning."On one platter set before them and fried whitings and potatoes; on another, suet dumplings; two plates of mutton cutlets with parsley, and one of the inspector's favourites, cold calf's tongue in a small dish with the boiled brains arranged around it. A light Spanish port was followed by a slice of Hampton cheddar.

"Delicious indeed," said the inspector, smiling, when they had finished. "And penny-wise," added Mrs. Endersby. The two stood up from the table and walked arm in arm down to the street. A cab was hailed and the journey started toward Covent Garden Theatre. A fine breezy evening. "Lovers tonight," Harriet said, looking into his eyes. "Confused but soon reconciled."

Endersby blushed a little. "Lovers?" he asked. "Not *Macbeth*, then?" Endersby looked confused.

"In fact, not," Harriet explained.

"Forests and fairy glens are the fare." With her profile framed by her bonnet, Harriet Endersby looked as lovely at forty-one as she had at twenty. *A fine first mate, indeed,* the inspector reflected: *she weathers storms, bears the doldrums without complaint, steers a clear passage through roiling wave.* Endersby lifted his arm and placed it snugly around Harriet's shoulders.

Sitting down in Covent Garden Theatre, Endersby noted to himself how this aristocratic theatre had changed. Boxes and private rooms had become much cheaper; the pit was always full now of clerks and salesmen rather than the cheroot-smoking dandies in silk Endersby had once seen as a boy. As always, the galleries resounded with the laughter and stomping feet of coal carriers, footmen and their wives, and large families eating their cold dinners on their laps."Here, take two for now," Harriet said, handing Endersby an open tin box full of homemade sugared almonds. Endersby's back soon relaxed and by the time the drum rolls had finished and the baton of the conductor was raised, the inspector was in an open-hearted mood to watch the dream of a midsummer's night.

After the theatre, over late-evening tea by the hearth, Endersby looked into the eyes of Harriet, who was at work with her sewing kit.

"I am at sixes and sevens, Mrs. Endersby," the inspector mumbled.

"How so, dear?" Harriet said, not looking up.

"It is a piece of lace that bewilders me most," he said.

"Lace? How curious."

"Yes. It was found stuffed into ..."

"Please, Owen. Spare me," Harriet pleaded.

"I beg your pardon, my dear," he replied. "What concerns me most is 'why?' Why lace?"

"What would possess a villain to choose such a particular item?" asked Harriet.

"Malice, perhaps. Sporting cruelty."

"Retribution," came Harriet's word. "Lace is a special kind of cloth. Used in churches, on wedding gowns. It has a sacred quality. Perhaps the lace was used to bless or to mock a blessing."

"Mrs. Endersby," the inspector said, delighted. "What a novel thought."

"Do you think so?" Harriet said, leaning forward to tap her husband's knee.

※

Chapter Twenty-five
A Goose Chase of Sorts

Resting in his study near midnight, Endersby sat at his games table and clicked together a wooden puzzle. *Tonight and tomorrow may turn the world around,* he thought. *Like the final tableau of the play.* Eventually, with Harriet sound asleep, the inspector went down to the street. Sergeant Caldwell was waiting below at the front door, a hansom readied to drive toward the Strand. "I venture to say Malibran may have outwitted us, Sergeant," Endersby said sitting back on the carriage seat.

"Outwitted, sir?"

"If he did not perform on the streets today, he has had a head start scouting out where his pity-man has gone."

"If I may, sir. I would claim Malibran is too eager for coin to pass up a day's work. Might he then take advantage of the night to search for his man? He knows where his pity-man likes to lodge since he helped him escape."

"Ah, Caldwell, a wise take. The escape was to a purpose, I wager. Malibran may have suggested a strategy and a new place for the man to go. In this fashion, he would then be able to secure his chap for more lucrative work."

"In the north, do you imagine, sir?"

"Sergeant, much as I delight in our ruminations, my powers of deduction lead me only so far. Did the constable you sent to Nightingale Lane see either hide or hair of our man?"

"He told me, sir, the dwelling of Malibran showed a light in its window. Malibran had returned just before nine o'clock and then went out again."

"Anyone with him?" Endersby asked.

"He said he was alone."

"You are keen, sir," said Endersby. "The Strand may offer us some good luck tonight."

The hour was five minutes to one o'clock in the morning. The wide street known as the Strand was still rushing with men and women. Jugglers and musicians clustered on corners under the gaslight. After asking a few of them if they had seen Malibran, Endersby learned from one of the fiddlers where Malibran had gone. "To a public house. There, he takes a late meal," the fiddler said.

"Come, sir," whispered Endersby to his cohort.

Through the crowds they found their way to the public house and by chance caught sight of Malibran as he marched up an alley northward.

"You may have to stay ahead, Sergeant. My gouty foot will drag me down. Keep him in sight. I will try to keep up."

The trail became long and arduous. Malibran had slow legs, much to the relief of the inspector who was able to keep huffing along, sometimes ducking into doorways to escape detection. Endersby remembered, from his violent confrontation with the man, that the district of Seven Dials was where they most likely would end up. For an hour more the inspector and his sergeant kept out of sight. Malibran, meanwhile, began stepping into open gin shops and fish houses as the streets wound toward Holborn and the Seven Dials. He chatted with men sitting at the tables before carrying on his way. Gradually, as the darker slums presented themselves, Malibran spoke to faces in the dimly lit streets. What had begun as a walk had turned into a search: Malibran seemed in earnest to look around, ask questions of every other man he encountered, often shaking his head in response. Finally reaching the hub of Seven Dials, he took a penny ale at a corner public house and then moved on.

"What in Hades, Caldwell, is the man up to?" The two policemen trailed Malibran along lanes that eventually gave way to a narrow square where a night fair was taking place. Booths selling pies and porter were set up in a circle, while in the centre of the square was a huge iron brazier full of dancing flames. Crowds of people watched a dog trainer and an acrobat. Malibran went into one house and immediately reappeared, playing his green concertina. His voice rang out as he entered the circle of light.

"Sergeant, we have a show to watch," Endersby said. Caldwell went around the brazier and stood to Malibran's left, while Endersby circled to the man's right. Malibran sang a foreign melody, his eyes shut. Finishing his display, he bowed to the crowd, passed his hat for coin and moved on. Close behind him, Endersby and Caldwell speculated on the final destination. "Malibran has led us on a fine goose chase," said the inspector. "And I fear our monster may be running loose." As the three men wound their way through the seven streets leading back to the hub of Seven Dials, it became clear that Malibran was going in and out of lodging houses.

"Caldwell, pull down your hat. Here, take these spectacles." Endersby opened his satchel and handed his disguise spectacles to his sergeant. "Play the fool. Go in behind Malibran as if you were looking for a room. Keep your face down." Into one, then another, then a third, the tireless Malibran enquired of the lodging house managers.

Caldwell reported back as he and Endersby resumed their trail, keeping steps behind their quarry. "He questions, Inspector, but Malibran receives a 'No' in every instance." Malibran entered the hub. Endersby pulled his sergeant into a dark archway. "Go on, Sergeant," he said.

"Well, sir," said Caldwell, "it seems all the lodging houses — so far — are full. Regulars mostly. Malibran asks after rooms. He never enquires about any particular person and never mentions a name." Endersby watched Malibran walk into a large lodging house in the centre of the Seven Dials hub. He and Caldwell waited and were about to give chase when Malibran came out the door, lighting his pipe. He moved onward, heading south and east toward Nightingale Lane. "He's going into that gin house, sir," said Caldwell pointing to a small door with a red sign.

"Go in, watch him, Sergeant. I will meet you there in a few moments." The two men parted and Endersby pulled out his head wrap, wound it into a turban, turned his great coat inside-out and took a bit of dried cobblestone muck and smeared his cheeks. He crossed the hub and went up to the front door of the lodging house where Malibran had made his last stop.

"In a jiffy. In a jiffy," came a woman's voice.

The peeling green door of the lodging house creaked open. Endersby assumed the woman was the owner. Her lined face proved a dependable witness of her life of toil.

"Ah, goodly sir," she smiled. "No need to knock. We ain't formal 'ere. Step in, sir. Step in."

"I wish to find lodging, Missus," said Endersby affecting a Scots accent.

"Oh, sir. You be a moment too late. The last gentleman who

stepped in rented my only empty place. An attic room. We've no dormitories 'ere, sir. None like down t' the river. But our prices is fair. You shall have to go elsewhere."

"Ah, Missus, what's a fellah to do. This last 'un, he that took the final room ..."

The owner broke into an impish grin. "You looks, sir, like yer have a fine appetite if yer belly tells its story." She chuckled and slapped her knee.

"Well, Missus, if you needs know, I am not what I am!"

"Come agin, yer. What foolishness. I have two strong scullery gals who could chase you out if my needs call for it."

"Ah, Missus, make no mistake. I am a good chap."

"I reckon you knows your business, sir," the woman said, her face blushing a little. "Wot is't you want, sir? I provide vittles if y're hungry."

"Can you keep a secret, missus?"

The woman broke into a loud toothless laugh. "I be as tight as a tomb." Leaning toward the inspector, she pulled him into a small room near the front door of the lodging house. The house itself was small, a domestic dwelling once used by a family, and not like the large, warehouse-styled establishments down near Nightingale Lane.

"I am looking for a special place, Missus. For my cousin, you see. Ach, he's been in a bit of trouble up north, in a wee tumble with his penny-pinching sister, and needs to keep his head down for a time. I figure to find him a respectable place here in London. Do you see?"

The woman raised up her chin. Her eyes lost their merriment. She clamped her hands onto her hips as if she were about to elbow the inspector out the door. "Wot yer up to, sir? Yer and that other chappy?"

"I beg your pardon."

"Nay, I am no fool, sir. Been in the lodging profession for twenty years. This has the stink of a scam."

"Missus," pleaded Endersby. "I hope I have not offended. No, Missus. I am looking for a safe haven, you see."

"Enough, sir. You and that other chap, the one here not five minutes afore you tapped at my door; he comes in hoity-toity and says much the same wash as you! Lookin' for a room for a relative. Cousin in a bind. Wot you two on about?"

Endersby scratched his head. He shook it. "I be an honest Scot, Missus. I do not know this other man you speak of, not at all. And you persecute me, Missus. Persecute!"

"But —"

"Here, good lady. Here stands afore you an honest son of the North. And you —"

"I beg pardon, sir. It was the coincidence of it, you see. That other chap, he says he has a cousin in trouble with his wife." The woman winked, her eyes sparkling once again. "This bolter cousin needs a room for three nights or so. The other chap hands me three pennies to hold the room. Says his cousin will come by late afternoon tomorrow to move in. Now who can I believe?"

"You can believe in me, Missus. As sure as sunshine."

"I can only trust the man with coin, sir. And you two are in *cahoots*. You be the relative come early, I wager. Come to get *a free night*. Out with you."

The woman pressed her bulk against Endersby, who gave in and tumbled into the hall where he found the door to the street. "I take no guff from a man such as you. Out." Endersby tried to say another word when Caldwell stepped in. He recognized Endersby playing a role, grabbed him as if he were a lost child, ushered him into the street and pointed toward Malibran, now making his way along the street, his balance a little off from the gin he had taken. "Come sir," said Caldwell out of earshot of the woman.

"I thank you, Sergeant. We may have an easy chase on our hands. Seems Malibran has secured a room in this particular lodging house. No doubt this is part of his protection plan to keep his pity-man as a money-making companion. If he warned his pity-man about us coming after him, most likely he has also arranged for him to have this as his new place. The landlady of the lodging house tells me his so-called 'cousin' moves in tomorrow night. In fact, Malibran will get word to him with the address. We have a fine chance of greeting this pity-man face to face if tomorrow's sun rises."

"I hope so, sir."

For the rest of the hour the inspector and his sergeant-at-hand followed Malibran out of Seven Dials, down Drury Lane, and then toward the river until, at last, they ended up once again in Nightingale Lane and watched their lead enter his tenement. The two policemen waited before they crept into the building and heard footsteps going up to the fourth floor. Caldwell tip-toed ahead. When Endersby arrived, somewhat out of breath, the door to Malibran's room lay open. Lying flat on his face on the floor was Malibran, sound asleep and snoring. The inspector stepped in, took a quick look into the one cupboard, lifted the foul sheets but found no paper, no name, no address of any man or woman. Going downstairs, the two men heard Malibran moan in his sleep.

"It is very late, Caldwell," Endersby then said, "but London never sleeps and we have one other stop. We will need sharp eyes and patience."

The two of them got out of a cab near the river. The Thames reeked of rotted fruit and wet hemp. "Do you think me mad, Sergeant?" The two men stood amazed: a long line of steam wheelers and sailboats were moored; men were hauling barrels, swinging nets full of chests; whistles from ship to shore created a cacophony of half-human sounds. "Here is where William More has been working. I have no other description of him other than what we know of our culprit. There is a curious problem with him. He calls himself by a dead man's name."

"Yes, sir," said Caldwell. "Do we call out for him on our first round?"

"No, Sergeant. Instead, let us just look. Wander. I learned he works in the early hours of the night. But let us ask if any of his fellow labourers know of him. Or if they can tell us where he lives. These men can have no idea that I am a policeman given this turban on my head. Take me along by the arm as if you have me under arrest. That way we may become the butt of laughter, but we can ask questions. Play the wronged lender looking for his money back. But if the 'pity-man' proves to be an innocent, then we will suffer a great set back. By this walk-around we can afford ourselves a head start."

"A clever idea, sir, if I may say so."

"Only if it works in our favour, Caldwell."

The dock stretched for a mile and a half and the two men walked its length, examining workers' faces by dim lantern light and asking after William More. No one at this hour knew of him. Many had worked since sundown but could not tell if More was a familiar face. Public houses were full; men of all shapes and sizes were eating, downing pints of porter. Jokes about Endersby losing money afforded the men some relief, but once again no one had heard of William More.

"But listen up, covey. If you say he works early or late, come early, look for'im then. I say, you'll get your money." The other men laughed beside the worker who had spoken. "I heard of him," one of the labourers at another table said. "He's on mostly at sundown. Cripple fellah. Not much to say, but he pens a letter or two for a ha'penny."

"I thank you, friends," Endersby said affecting his Scots accent. "Off you go, wee Geordie," the men laughed as Endersby and Caldwell left the public house. After an hour of further searching, Endersby pulled his sergeant aside. "As I feared, Caldwell: the old proverb come to life. "Finding a needle in a hay rick." Endersby bid his sergeant good night. He stood alone amidst the chaos and then went home. In bed, he could not sleep and so stared at the ceiling.

What a blank expanse of plaster, he thought. He knew the name of the uncle, but was it of any use if he were impossible to find? Or if he were dead? *Lardle, at least, has told a tale that bears analysis,* he mused. Is there any sense to sending out warrants for the escapees from the hulks? Most would have vanished into the crowds by now, or were dead. And now the 'pity-man' and William More were new challenges, new blockades to the truth. Who, then, did the lace seller and the barkeep from Rosemary Lane actually *see*?

Pondering for a time, Endersby crawled from under his cover and went to stir the embers in the hearth. As he stood up, an idea took shape in his mind. "What if...?" his inner voice asked. "Two are actually one. One by day, one by night." The tumbling of names and suppositions grew so forceful, Endersby felt himself propelled toward his bed where he sat down on the edge. "But this makes sense," he whispered. A memory crowded into his consciousness; it nudged the names aside; before the astonished inner eye of Owen Endersby four confused figures stood: young lovers, their faces lit from below as if by a row of gas jets along the edge of the Covent Garden stage. "Of course," Endersby now said. "Confusion, mixed and mismatched. Then the juice of magic and all is made right. Such was *A Midsummer's Night's Dream.*"

Endersby lay back. Like one of his French puzzles, the final section of the case clicked into place and presented a whole landscape, complete and balanced. "Ah well," the inspector sighed. He now could plan his final campaign. Caldwell and he would have to play roles. A fight might ensue. But Superintendent Borne would have his conviction — if all efforts ended up with logical results. Endersby heaved one last breath as his eyes began to droop. Was it too much to hope sleep would come upon him before dawn broke on the third and last day of his investigation?

❦

Chapter Twenty-six
New Facts for Old

Superintendent Borne raised his eyebrows. He thrust his fingers into the pockets of his waistcoat but as it was new, and the pockets too tight, he had to struggle. Pouting, he gave up and stood before Inspector Endersby with his hands clasped behind his back. Fog pressed against the office windows and clocks through city struck the morning hour of eight; the damp, rainy weather had obscured London beneath a foggy shroud, turning it into an invisible city. Grey everywhere; muted voices and the slushy clip clop of horses were all that could be heard, as if the entire metropolis had sunk into the sea during the night.

"Three felons captured? That is excessive, sir," complained Borne, his face sleepy at this early meeting.

"Proof pending, sir."

"Fine work, Inspector. Diligent labour. A conviction by sundown, do you think?"

"Most likely, Superintendent."

"Likely? 'Certainly' is the word I'd prefer."

"There is as yet the matter of a confession from each. And a witness."

"As yet, you say? Endersby, you confuse me. Felons, proof, then I hear hesitation. We are men of action, sir," Borne announced. He looked out the window at the fog as if gazing into a far horizon. "*As yet* are two words I do not understand. Caldwell and the other two, Mance and …"

"Rance and Tibald, sir."

"Yes, yes. Industrious, hardworking?"

"Most precocious, sir."

"Three felons. Three hangings, then?"

"If it be so, sir."

"Do not depend, Inspector, on 'ifs' and 'buts.' We are not in the profession as a city detective police force to depend on haphazard surmise."

"How true, sir."

Borne began to pace. This action was familiar to Endersby: it was a sign that his superintendent was growing bored. There was not much else to report to him on this third and final day. The ultimate confrontation with Sergeant Smeets was to take place in an hour. The matter of the Grimsby affair remained unsettled; the guilt of Dr. Benton, Mr. Lardle and the pity-man had yet to be established. And a long shot — the dredgerman named More, if he were fact rather than fancy.

"Carry on, then, Inspector. By tonight, a conviction. Or more," Borne said, stifling a yawn.

Endersby left the superintendent, went down the stairs, across the courtyard and up two steps to his own office. Entering, there appeared before the inspector a group of people arrayed in black, the tallest of which was Mr. Richard Grimsby. The man had come, as promised, at eight sharp. Beside him, seated in a chair, a woman in veils sat weeping. To Mr. Grimsby's left stood a fine woman in a large hat; a younger version of herself slouched to her left, and between them, attached to both women's hands, a blonde female of three years whose little mouth worked on a stick of yellow treacle.

"Good morning, Inspector," said the solemn-voiced Mr. Grimsby. The inspector bid all good morning and introduced himself using his full title and name. Caldwell stepped forward from behind the door. "I have taken the liberty, sir, to escort the family to your office."

"Thank you, Sergeant."

The weeping woman raised her tear-stained face. "When may I see my dear one, my sweetest Geoffrey?"

"I shall oblige you presently, madam," replied Endersby.

Mr. Grimsby presented Mrs. Barraclough, who curtsied, then her daughter Hilda, who raised one eyebrow in contempt. Hilda pointed down: "Little Margery." The female child yanked the treacle from her mouth and greeted the inspector with a yellowish tongue.

"Good morning to you all," the inspector repeated.

"I am here, Inspector, to exonerate my son of the suspicion of murder," explained Mr. Grimsby. To which words, his wife moaned and spoke into her handkerchief, "Oh, dear. Oh my." Sergeant Caldwell had his pencil poised and a clean page of his notebook open. The inspector sat down; the shuffling group of Grimsbys deposited themselves on chairs brought into the office by Rance and Tibald. It was Mrs. Barraclough who began the proceedings. She cleared her throat. Her knowing smile filled the grey morning with a sense of righteousness.

"Plain and simple, sir. My Hilda, is in love with young Grimsby. Scar and all. A total of three years. In the beginnin' my Hilda was open to suggestion. In particular, my Hilda was unwilling to take my stern advice. Nine months later, little Margery."

The child yelled out: "No!" Hilda smacked the child's knee. In retaliation, little Margery threw her treacle stick to the floor.

Mrs. Barraclough continued, her smile of triumph broad. "Three years or more, sir. Free vittles for young Geoffrey. A leech without parallel. But now I needs recompense, you see. Hildy works at hats, milliner. But I am left to guard the child with little money to clothe and feed the issue of yer son, Missus Grimsby."

Mrs. Grimsby moaned. Hilda interrupted: "Not true, Mama. Geoffrey is kind and good as gold."

"I ne'er saw any gold, Miss Hilda. And precious little goodness," snapped the mother. Mrs. Barraclough steamed on, plowing through her story, descriptions of night entries to her flat on the part of Mr. Geoffrey Grimsby, fighting looks exchanged, love letters opened and a weeping daughter confronted.

"No, mama," sniffed Hilda.

"A fine spectacle of appetite, sir," Mrs. Barraclough resumed. "Nothing but trouble, strife, and now lovely little Margery."

Margery scowled at her grandmother and stamped her foot.

Mr. Grimsby spoke up: "This is the history, Inspector. The facts of Tuesday last are of greater importance."

"Most certainly, sir." Endersby said. "Facts need verification, however. Lack of bias. An observer of events whose interest in such is incidental."

"I may only speak for myself, sir. But here in my hand is a recommendation of one of my servants, a man of honest disposition who may speak for young Geoffrey's character."

"I shall consider it. I wish to hear what you observed on Tuesday night and early morning, Mrs. Barraclough."

"Me, Inspector?"

"You were at home during the day and night, were you not?"

"I was, sir. I saw much. Not all of it to my liking."

"Please, take your time," Endersby said, putting on a patient voice.

"As is *his* habit," the woman began, "Tuesday being no different from any other day, Mr. Geoffrey Grimsby arrives drunk after our supper. It being *his* usual hour. Demands to see *his* child."

"Mama," said Hilda. "He comes to show her he loves her."

"Loves? Well, if yer in love with yer kin, you should —"

"At what time did he arrive, Mrs. Barraclough?" Endersby interrupted.

"At seven. As usual. Beats at the door," the woman said, moving her arms in a theatrical gesture of knocking. "Curses me, as usual. I'd none 'f it. Took the broom to 'im when he gets particular loud. He come again at eight, then at nine, more gin in 'im. Impossible chap, sir. I am a workin' woman as is my Hildy. He, well, he is a scoundrel, right n'ready."

"And then?" queried Endersby. Caldwell flipped over a page of his notebook and waited, his pencil poised.

"Well, Inspector. The ruckus keeps up. All the evening. Him at the back door, the front door, the side. Him up a ladder. Him down. Hilda shouting out the window. Scamperin' about on my floor above. I takes to my bed by half ten of the clock. Still the ruckus and racket. Bless me, sir. I chase him again with the broom from the ladder. 'To see his little Margery,' he says. Fool's so gin-sodden he can hardly climb a rung."

"Do you keep a servant, madam?" the inspector asked.

"A day woman. Cleans, cooks at *her* leisure."

"Is there another tenant in your building? A flat in the back, downstairs?"

"Mr. Leech, sir. A peculiar gentleman."

"Might he have seen or heard the commotion you have described?"

"Hardly, sir. He travels. Monday to Friday to Manchester. Then into the wilderness for all we knows."

"During the late night on Tuesday, you say you *saw* young Grimsby, given it was dark, as well as heard him?"

"As if 'twere sunshine. Most disagreeable."

"What was he doing?"

"Mounting ... climbing a ladder up to Hilda's window."

"After midnight?"

"Precisely, sir. Then afterward on the hour, so it seemed. To Margery's room, as well. The fool thought I was to sleep."

"And later on. You were awake?"

"Oh sir. Wot's a poor abandoned woman to do? Young Grimsby invades my house. He romps about all the night and steals my sleep. He appears in the morning, down the ladder. Ruckus then, too. I sees and hears him at dawn, or just afore. If I scold, my Hildy will leave me behind. Give all her money to *him*. Send me to the workhouse, sir."

"Mama?" Hilda cried. "Do you believe —?"

"*Ingrate*," Mrs. Barraclough blurted out. From her frilly pocket she pulled out a handkerchief and blew her nose. "You will betray me. I knows it."

"Where and when did you last see Geoffrey?"

"In the yard. In the stable in the lane. At dawn, then he begs me for a bit o'bacon and coffee. Oh, sir. I have enough to feed ..."

"Thank you, madam," for your frankness. "It is necessary in a case of murder to ask all nature of pertinent questions."

"I can see, sir. Painful they be, too, for some of us." Mrs. Barraclough shrugged her shoulder and threw a glaring look toward her daughter. "And Hilda?" the inspector asked.

"He is kind and innocent, sir. You shall see," Hilda replied softly. "He puts on acts, he does. But he is good in his heart when he feels loved."

Mrs. Grimbsy sat up. She lowered her handkerchief and looked into the eyes of Hilda. "He is that, young woman. He has his mother's love."

With eyes then blinking into focus, Hilda turned back to address the inspector. The young woman began to relate her knowledge of Tuesday night. "Miss Hilda," the inspector interrupted. "Please stand up and follow me."

Mrs. Barraclough grew pale. "What, sir? My daughter be innocent," she said, pointing her trembling hand.

"Caldwell," Endersby said, his voice a sudden blast. "Take Miss Hilda to the cells below, on the double. You, sir, Mr. Grimsby, please come along. This is a matter of life and death. This is a matter of truth over sentiment. Your son's life hangs in the balance."

Silence ensued. Faces paled. Hilda marched out on the arm of Caldwell. Rance and Tibald were commanded to stand guard. Mrs. Grimsby began to look faint, but her theatrics were cut short by her husband, who yanked sharply on her arm as he passed by. Below, in the corridor of cells, young Hilda took on a brighter air. She held her head high. She pulled off her bonnet to show a fine head of hair. When the inspector caught up to her and Caldwell, she turned to him with a gleam in her eye. She spoke out with conviction. "Thank you, Inspector, for relieving me of my mother!" she said frankly. "I can only tell you I love Geoffrey despite his many faults. He is innocent sir. That I can only prove by my own words, to which I will swear upon our holy book — I carry it with me in my reticule." She pulled out a square, leather-bound volume. It was the size of a block of butcher's butter. She opened it to show her name inside, the pages of thin paper. She read aloud a prayer from the section of Psalms and, with no hesitation, held the volume to her heart and swore she would tell the truth.

"Most commendable, Miss Hilda," the inspector said. "But I have to ask you to be patient. Come, and we shall test together the veracity of your love." Hilda frowned. The inspector rephrased his reply ending with the words, "the ardency and truth of your affection." Hilda smiled. "He is my love," she said. "Through thick or thin," she said, her voice trembling.

To the elder Mr. Grimsby, the inspector said, "Now, sir, please be honest and address your son with respect and be diligent in your observations of him."

"I will, sir. I admit to you and to Miss Hilda that I am beginning to see why my son has been so distracted, or shall I say, so melancholy over the past while. Hard it is for me to reconcile my needs as a father and a professional with the behaviour of my son who so often has appeared as a ... well, as a ..."

"A man without his loved ones, sir," said Hilda. The elder Grimsby nodded and Endersby could see his face was full of remorse. The cell of Geoffrey Grimsby was opened by the guard. A lantern was carried in by Caldwell who stood aside as the two young lovers fell into each other's arms. Much unrestrained kissing and hugging ensued. Hilda sat down next to Geoffrey on the narrow bench. His sober face grew wet with tears. "All is known, now, dear one," Hilda said, her gentle attention reminding Endersby of the same tone of voice his beloved Harriet used when giving comfort. Hilda placed Geoffrey's right hand on her heart. "Do you feel it beating, my love?" The tired young Grimsby nodded. Hilda then took her small bible, placed it under her lover's hand, and held both together to her heart. "Now swear, dear one. Let us clear up this prattle."

"Drunk I was Tuesday night last," young Grimsby began. "I am sorry for it. Sorry to you, Hildy and to you, Father. I have been most vexed. I am gin-sodden most days of the week." Hilda patted his forehead. "The old crocodile would not let me see my Hilda nor my little angel. 'Twas past supper, I recollect."

Hilda said: "He came at ten. He hammered at the door. Mama would not unlock it." Geoffrey then told of circling the two-storey building; finding the fire ladder, which lay in the narrow yard behind. "He climbed up half way to my window, but Mama shooed him down with a broom."

Geoffrey cleared his throat. "Waited for two hours in the dark till the crocodile went to bed. Climbed in my Margery's little chamber. Hilda was there with the scissors. I wanted a lock, you see. I wanted a bit of my Margery to carry round with me. I even have the locket somewhere."

"No, dearest, I have it," replied Hilda. From her reticule she lifted out a chain and locket. "I cut another lock for you. See?" The lock was shown. Old Richard Grimsby held it for a moment and then on giving it to his son, he suddenly took hold of him and embraced him. The old man tried on this occasion to find words but he retreated instead into silence. Geoffrey Grimsby sat forward. "Hildy then took me in."

"For the night, sir," the woman said boldly. "I let him out by six as Mama awakened. He promised me ..."

"I promised my Hildy a ring ..."

"And a ceremony."

"Yes, Hilda. A ceremony. On my way down the ladder I missed a rung. Smashed up my knuckles." Hilda continued. "Mama was at the hearth making breakfast."

"The old croc came out to fetch wood," added Geoffrey. "I had to take refuge in the neighbour's stable, under the straw and horse dung."

"Did the neighbour find you by chance, sir?" asked Endersby.

"No, sir, the groom found me. Said he'd spent his early breakfast watching us from his window. A happy fellow. Laughed when I told him about Margery and the ladder. Name of Balham, Arthur."

"Caldwell, kindly go upstairs. Find Rance and send him to fetch Mr. Balham, the groom. Mr. Grimsby will supply the address. We will need him to write out his witness report and swear to its veracity at the magistrate's."

"He will do it, sir. He is forthright," Hilda said. Suddenly, without warning, she burst into tears. "Oh, Geoffrey, my Geoffrey. How hard done I have been by you, and our little one, too." Geoffrey put his arm around the sobbing woman. Endersby alerted the guard to bring pen, ink and paper. "Miss Hilda. Master Geoffrey. It is not enough to swear to your innocence. You must declare it in writing. Constable, kindly lead these two up to the deposition room. Alert the clerk and have him supervise the writing of their stories. You do understand, that you will be asked to write the truth under oath and appear before a magistrate?"

The two lovers nodded. "Margery is ours, Hildy, my love," young Grimsby said. "You and I, we are together. I swear I will change my ways. Father, please forgive me. I have been a foolish man." The elder Grimsby came forward. "Geoffrey, you are surely forgiven. This has been a trial for me as well as for you, my son. Now, swear to the inspector that you are innocent of your suspected crime, and we'll put this unpleasantness behind us."

"I swear, Poppa, I do swear. I was with my Hildy all the night."

"Dearest one," Hilda exclaimed.

"Nay, Hildy. Hear me out. I have been a scoundrel. A fool, too. Taking gin to soothe my fears. But being in here, in this prison cell, knowing I could lose you and be hanged for murder has brought me to my senses. I survived this so I can show my best side to you and our little one." Hilda wept on his shoulder.

Endersby stood up slowly and left the cell. He told the

constable guard to release the young Grimsby once his confession had been written. While climbing the stairs to the courtyard, the inspector felt a tinge of relief. The mystery was solved. Grimsby had a credible alibi. If the neighbour's groom was honest, his witnessing of the events would stand as evidence in support of young Grimsby's innocence.

The inspector went back into his office. "We have a confession, ladies and gentlemen. I thank you all for coming. Mrs. Grimsby, it appears you were right in your belief that your son could not have taken a life. Indeed, he has sworn to his Hilda to renew himself now that there is enough evidence to support his claim to innocence." Much grumbling issued from Mrs. Barraclough, who snatched up little Margery and carried her outside. The elder Grimsbys rejoiced and thanked Endersby. On the pair's exit, the inspector instructed Tibald to go across the lane to the coffee house and have a server come over with a tray of hot coffee and toast.

Caldwell reappeared. "Constable Rance, sir, has reported there were no disturbances in two northern and one western district last night. No workhouse invasions. No dead bodies."

"Most curious," said Endersby. His face slowly formed into a frown. "And what now of Smeets? I am all at sea with him, the coincidence of his presence in London." The inspector took the gaff he had found the evening before and, with Caldwell, went down to Smeets's cell. On opening the cell door, a cough and a deep moan issued out of the dim light.

"He is with fever, sir," Caldwell said, touching Smeets's forehead.

"Constable," Endersby said to the guard. "Fetch the surgeon, Mr. Reeves, of Number four Farringdon Street. Just up the way." Endersby gazed into the soldier's pallid features. "Exhaustion and lack of food, I reckon, Sergeant," Endersby said to Caldwell. The two men left the cell and returned to the inspector's office to wait for the surgeon to come. Placing the found gaff across the top of his desk, Inspector Endersby started rubbing his chin and letting his thoughts spill into spoken words: "Abandoned because it was no longer needed? Or lost in a panic of escape?"

"The gaff, sir?" inquired Caldwell who had poured out two cups of coffee left by the server.

"I am amused by our find," was the inspector's response. "I have second thoughts about why the gaff was used … if Smeets is our villain."

"How do you mean, Inspector?" asked Caldwell.

"A father in search of a daughter, a distraught man with no means. Why would Smeets take the time or the effort to carry such an instrument? Cumbersome it is; unnecessary in fact, if one considers that he is an angry, violent man. A soldier is trained to kill. Would Smeets have any need for a weapon such as this one?"

"You do enjoy your ponderings, sir," Caldwell said, blowing on his steaming cup.

"I am full of questions, Sergeant, which lead me to more questions and few answers," Endersby replied taking the corner from a bit of toast and chewing it slowly. "And young Catherine Smeets — disappeared. Fled? Murdered?" Endersby stopped speaking and started to pace. "Smeets claimed the uncle had been condemned to the hulks — one of the prison ships anchored in the estuary. We know the uncle's name — if Smeets can be trusted. Tobias Jibbs. We know his sentence. Now, look at this list from the Naval Office. You see, a Jibbs escaped not three weeks ago from the Greenwich hulks. Might this Jibbs have come up to London?"

"To search for his Catherine?" said Caldwell.

"For certain," said Endersby. "And here in two of the child's letters found in the workhouse, she addresses her uncle as Bobo and Uncle Bo. A nickname for Tobias?"

"'Unklebow' or 'Knuckle Toe' or 'Uncle Bobo' are one in the same?" asked Caldwell. Endersby paused and re-read the letter, his brow wrinkled by the turning of his mind. "However, and here is *the rub*, if I may," Endersby said. "Surely Smeets fits the description of our culprit more precisely. He is certainly driven, angry, and capable of murder. He returned to London, went searching, *knowing* his daughter was in the city. Frustrated, he became distraught and violent. On the other hand, the uncle was sent away to the hulks and to his certain death. How would he *know* to come up to London? If he were able to escape the prison ships — highly unlikely — would he not have headed home to his village? If he wished to his Catherine again?"

"Remarkable, sir," Caldwell said.

Endersby stopped pacing: "Listen, Caldwell … just a thought. A leap. Suppose the villain were not Smeets. Smeets comes searching to St. Pancras, shouts, bangs about. At *the same time*, in the same dark hour, the true villain has come — say, William More the dredgerman, or Malibran's pity-man — with his gaff. On hearing Smeets, he escapes out of panic and fear. He drops the gaff running and climbing over the wall."

"Yes, sir," said Caldwell thoughtfully.

"And Mr. Henry Lardle? What of Dr. Benton and his strange room?" Endersby said. "Lardle once killed and could kill again. What I need urgently from *him* is an alibi."

"Proof as well, sir? If we can untangle the strands," said Caldwell.

"Untangle indeed, sir," replied the inspector. "But before we start to cut apart the knots, let us take ourselves to check on Smeets, then go off to visit the place where Mr. Lardle dwells."

Dr. Reeves knelt down beside the sickly Sergeant Smeets and opened the patient's left eye. Endersby admired the doctor's use of a wooden tube, a French invention, one end pressed against the chest while the other end fit against the ear to determine the rhythmic beat of a man's heart.

"Good morning, gentlemen," Dr. Reeves said. "My first recommendation, Inspector, is to have this man moved to a dry warm place. I must remark that his fever is steady, likely caused by an influenza. This red streak across his face is not the pox, nor indeed a wound. Rather, I would venture to say it is a nervous disorder seen more often in the aged. It can *appear* like a scar or a healed wound in its bumpy nature for it swells with fluid."

"Most informative, Dr. Reeves," said Endersby. The morning damp permeated the cell; Endersby requested that Smeets be moved up to a chamber with a fire.

"I would rather recommend the public hospital nearby, Inspector," Reeves said.

"Why so, sir?" questioned Endersby. He had little confidence in public wards. Endersby believed a trip to the hospital was but a cheap farthing ticket to the nearest undertaker's establishment.

"I can supervise the man's recovery there in more amenable quarters for the ill. My assistants I have trained myself."

Dr. Reeves's words allayed Endersby's fears. "I will attempt my best, therefore, to accommodate your preference, Doctor," said the satisfied inspector.

Caldwell had pulled out his notebook and was writing down the symptoms and causes outlined by Reeves.

"Commendable, sir," Endersby said on noticing his

sergeant-at-hand's initiative. "Might we make a habit of this, Caldwell?" Endersby asked. "A thorough record of all facets of a crime case — a doctor's as well as a magistrate's conclusions may set a precedent for us to study in future cases."

"A fine idea, sir," was Caldwell's response, making a note of his superior's suggestion.

"I have a question, sir," said Endersby, once again addressing the doctor. "Sergeant Smeets is definitely an ill fellow. In pondering your remarks, I may conclude he is weak from lack of rest and food. In your estimation, could he have been strong enough in the past two days to have completed a fortnight's walking journey from the Scottish border to London, ransacked his way into a workhouse by using a coal chute, then — bear with me, Reeves — with renewed vigour, taken the life of two struggling women by strangling and thus depriving both of breath?"

"Incredible, Inspector," said Reeves. "I might surmise that if this man had desire to wreak havoc, as you have described, he most certainly could have performed all of those feats. Men survive much deprivation, sir. Circumstances afford men the opportunity and, undoubtedly, the fire to commit many types of actions."

"Thank you," said Endersby.

"Inspector, I will notify St. Bartholomew's Hospital," Dr. Reeves said. "I can arrange for this man's transport. Can the station house provide me with a night guard until this man has had proper rest?"

"Indeed, Doctor," Endersby said, his mind rushing to frame a convincing argument to be presented to his money-tight superintendent. Twenty minutes later, he and Caldwell were climbing steep stairs in a building on Drury Lane. The court where Henry Lardle lived was in fact around the corner from St. Giles Workhouse. Greeting the last step of many, Inspector

Endersby took a deep breath. He and Caldwell first knocked on the door of one Mr. Solomon Graves. "Lardle? Certainly. Good man." Mr. William Graves pointed to the low door across from his on the other side of the attic hall. "Henry works hard for his coin. Nights mostly." Mr. Graves smoked a pipe and, in his long night robe, he smelled of fried fish.

"Fish fryer, Covent Garden, sir," was his prompt response to Endersby's next question about his profession. Caldwell then asked how long he had lived in this locale, how well he knew Mr. Henry Lardle and the woman he lived with. "Years, sir, on both counts. Worked with Lardle once upon a time. Selling laces. His woman is a good gal, not bright, but agreeable."

"Mr. Graves, may I enquire about last Tuesday night. Where were you on that evening?"

"After frying. Here for supper. Sister here can vouch." A red-headed woman in a night robe popped her head around the edge of the door. "Luvly morn, gents," she said. "Tuesday, t'was left over veal chops. Then to cards with Mr Lardle and his Kate."

"Kate is his wife?" asked Endersby.

"His helpmeet, sir," the sister said with a wink. "Good at hawkin' celery. No talent for whist."

"You played cards Tuesday. At what time?"

"We was all late for supper," answered Solomon Graves. "Nine or ten it were. Then we took to some beer. We played for a time, then Henry goes out."

"What time did he leave you, do you recall?

"Late," countered his sister.

"When?" asked Caldwell.

"Oh, very late. Two or half past. Out and gone and not home again 'till light. Henry goes out and comes back at the beck and call of his employer. Night work as I said. Out last night again he was. Haven't heard 'im this morning."

"Do you know where Henry goes at night?" Endersby asked. Caldwell flipped a page of his notebook.

"No sir. Best to ask his Kate."

The inspector and his sergeant bid their goodbyes and crossed the hall. The door opened to reveal a weeping Kate. The attic room had a slanted ceiling and sparse furnishings. Kate told the same story as her neighbour of the veal chops and card playing.

"Can you tell us where Henry went late on Tuesday night?"

"Same place as always. Oh mind, he don't keep nuthin' from me. Off to Mrs. Barnes. Does business with her when she has the time. Poor Henry. Got desperate, no luck in and out, so he went off to Covent Garden."

"Where is this place, Mrs. Barnes and her ...?"

"Nanny house, sir. You chaps go when you have your need." Endersby knew they were the worst brothels — selling young girls to men. "Virgins," they all claimed.

"Here," Kate pointed to a pencil scrawl on the wall near the door. An address, the name of Barnes, other names, too. "Them others, theys the butcher, the pie man." Caldwell copied down the address of Mrs. Barnes' nanny house.

"I thank you, Miss," Endersby said, gathering his energy. Sergeant Caldwell then told of Mr. Lardle's stay at Fleet Lane Station House, the news of which brought a smile to Kate's face.

"Not dead, then? Alive and well?" she asked, grabbing a shawl from a peg.

"Come then," replied Endersby. "Caldwell, take her in. Get a deposition from her — written down or copied if she can't write — about Lardle's whereabouts on Tuesday night. Also, tap on Graves' door again and have him and his sister write out what they told us. I will take myself to Mrs. Barnes."

The village cemetery lay half a mile out, a turn down the road from the gate to the country house where the old princess lay dying in her bed. A day and a night had passed and still there was no news of Jemima Pettiworth. Before retiring the night before, Mrs. Bolton had decided to read her sister's hand-written confession. What a tortured soul her sister had revealed; one that she had kept close to her heart all her waking life. As it was, the confession stirred the imagination of Mrs. Bolton. With the first light of morning, she knew she must investigate what her sister had written about — just to settle her own mind.

At the cemetery's gate, Mrs. Bolton hesitated. Now that she had made the journey on her own, she surveyed the hallowed ground, a place so ominous in its isolation she wondered if it were wise to continue her search.

"Now, don't be timid," she scolded herself. The gate gave out a squeal of rusted metal as she pushed it open. She carefully picked her way through the overgrown cemetery to a corner partially covered with wild vines; in the midst of which sat a tiny gravestone. Mrs. Bolton bent down. Tears rushed into her eyes as she read the name and dates: *Jonathan Pettiworth, Born and Died, December 12, 1808.* "So here is where you rest, little lad," Mrs. Bolton whispered. "Ah, Jemmy." Mrs. Bolton had known only of her sister's broken heart. Never any mention of a child, a stillbirth. Reflecting back to that time, almost thirty-three years ago, Mrs. Bolton recalled how her sister had fled the village for a time, in the early spring of 1808. "Gone to London, she had told me," Mrs. Bolton said out loud to the tilting gravestones. "A lie I did not question back then," she said.

Mrs. Bolton looked up to the sky. What if the beadle had come to her village door with news? Running from the graveyard, Mrs. Bolton kept on down the road, further from town. On the side of a hill stood a wide, three-storey structure with three great chimneys. Its walls of black seemed to have grown out of the hillside stone, and it had always appeared to Mrs. Bolton to be a building of elemental sorrow — for here the abandoned village children, the poor destitute farmers, and the widows of soldiers from the Napoleonic wars ended up living in cold squalor. Mrs. Bolton approached the iron gate to the county workhouse — St. Christopher's Hospital — its old name arched in iron letters above the gate. She rang the bell.

Presently, a workhouse matron met Mrs. Bolton at the gate. The matron nodded in recognition to the kindly village woman. "I am sorry to hear of your sister's disappearance, mum," the matron said, opening the front door of the work-house. "No news as yet," came Mrs. Bolton's reply. A cup of tea was offered and refused. Mrs. Bolton had come for one reason only. She explained her need. Permission was granted cordially; the matron then led Mrs. Bolton down a drafty hall to a large room full of drawers and shelves. "Our ledgers date back to 1799 when the hospital was built. I can bring you an extra candle for better light."

Reading the spines of books numbered for the first ten years, Mrs. Bolton moved along the shelf until she came to the ledger for 1810. She laid the dusty book on the table. There, between neatly drawn lines, were the lists of the inmates of the work-house. Beside their names, ages were recorded along with a brief description: "orphan, abandoned baby, widow ..." In her sister's written confession, the exact names of the three people were not given. But they were described by age and by appearance. What had struck Mrs. Bolton as deeply sad was the cruel treatment Jemima had inflicted upon a jilted woman and her two out-of-wedlock children.

Up and down the lists Mrs. Bolton ran her finger. Three names, just three, she wanted to find, but the ages had to match her sister's descriptions. At last: a single woman who gave birth to a stillborn and died. Her two other children — a boy and a younger girl, siblings — left to the workhouse. Mrs. Bolton stared at the names. *So, Jemima's story was true. No wonder she had felt the need to confess.* More questions bothered Mrs. Bolton: why had her sister not written out the names of the three creatures in her confession? Had she feared recrimination?

Leaving the workhouse, Mrs. Bolton stopped along the way home, sat down on a stump and wept. No more than a few minutes passed and she was on her feet again. As she approached the village square a cold light seemed to cut across the fronts of the shops. Mrs. Bolton hurried her steps toward the great tree by her own snug cottage. It wasn't until she turned the last corner leading to her front door that she saw a milling crowd. Step by step she made her way, the crowd parting to let her walk on toward the beadle who stood by the entrance to her home, his right hand lifting off his official beadle's hat as she came closer.

"Poor dear. Such a pity. What a tragedy." These words were whispered by the village crowd as Mrs. Bolton saw with much trepidation the beadle point toward a cart and horse. In it, a long wrapped object. "I am most grieved, Mrs. Bolton," the beadle said. Mrs. Bolton touched the object. The beadle performed his public duty and lifted one corner of the wrapping. The crowd shuffled; many women covered their eyes. The soggy lace half covered her dear Jemima's left eye. The beadle folded the wrapping back over the body.

"I thank you, sir," Mrs. Bolton said mustering her strength and with as much politeness as possible she added a few more words to the crowd around her. "Thank you. Thank you all. I must rest now, thank you." Mrs. Bolton stepped into her cottage. She shut the door and fell into a chair next to the hearth. Her heart was beating so fast she thought it might leap up into her mouth. Closing her eyes, she whispered a short prayer and then, recollecting her thoughts, she walked unsteadily to the back of her little house. "If it is true, then so let it be," she said, as she lay down on her bed and pondered once again the reasons why her sister had written to expiate her long-ago crimes.

Chapter Twenty-seven
Innocents and Sinners

After much knocking, Inspector Endersby was relieved to see the red door click open. Before him towered a tall, elegant woman with red lips and a cap of fine lace. From her ears hung ruby drops.

"Early, sir," the woman said with a subtle sneer.

Endersby clenched his fist. He removed his hat and announced who he was and why he had come.

"Not again, sir. Who sent you? Lord Harley? The Lord Mayor?"

"Mr. Henry Lardle, in fact, if you are Mrs. Barnes."

"Foolish Henry? Why he runs about like a slave for that sad man. Step in, sir. You look frosted from this morning." The hearth was lit in a small parlour painted in gold. In the next room there was a velvet curtain drawn aside to show seven beds. Each was draped with white tulle and sleeping in each was a young girl of no more than twelve years old. "Business is brisk, Inspector," smiled Mrs. Barnes. She went and pulled the curtain closed and returned to sit by the fire. For his part, Endersby managed to lift his chin and breathe steadily enough to control his urge to yank the woman off her seat, drag her into the room of girls and remonstrate. *But then*, he thought, *a woman of this young age may have been a survivor of just the same kind of establishment.* She acted as if she were twenty-five or more but, on careful examination, Endersby became convinced Mrs. Barnes was no more than eighteen. She had poise; she seemed to have good health, if her teeth were an indication. And she ran a business. *How does one evil balance another?* the inspector thought.

"I will not take much of your time, Mrs. Barnes. I should alert you to the fact that you will be called to the magistrate to account for your acquaintance with Mr. Lardle. And indeed Dr. Benton."

"Have they committed a crime, sir? Shall I act as witness?" she said in dismissive manner as if she were making a jest.

"Or an accomplice," replied the inspector, a sharp edge to his voice.

"How so?" Mrs. Barnes calmly asked.

"Tuesday last, two workhouse matrons were murdered and two young females from their establishments were found abandoned on the street."

"How am I to proceed, Inspector?" the woman asked. "I run a nanny house, not a place of hard labour."

"Mr. Lardle has been arrested, Mrs. Barnes. On suspicion of murder."

"The poor git," she laughed. "I cannot see him ever wishing to return to a workhouse. For any reason."

"He may or he may not have done so. But it is you and you alone who can verify if indeed he was prompted to do so. In search of females."

Jon Redfern

Mrs. Barnes stood up and laughed again. "You, sir, are a respectable man, I assume. Married?"

"Happily so, if the business of my life is of any interest."

"Inspector, it seems to me that the business of *my* life is yours. May I ask why you are enquiring after smelly Lardle? You seem bent on finding out some sordid truth."

"An alibi, Mrs. Barnes. You can do the decent act of telling me the truth about Mr. Lardle and his whereabouts on late Tuesday night last."

"Decent? Can you provide me with recompense?"

"In what manner?" said Endersby, his gut beginning to churn.

"Sir, I am in the business of provisions. Like any honest merchant. Information to you is valuable and if it can help a customer then I am glad to share. But I must have something in return. I live in a world of favours, sir, favours given out for money or assurances."

"What is it you wish?"

"I wish to be left to my living, sir. You may or may not have the power to disturb me here or my girls, but who may I trust? Must I grovel to you or to any official and then bear the rancour of my patrons to safeguard my livelihood?"

"I am not at liberty to grant you any form of protection, Mrs. Barnes. I put no trust in your kind of business. But I am not one to act the moral judge, either, if no capital crime is being committed."

"You are a man of intelligence," she said, her face losing its mocking smile and taking on a more pensive look. "Mr. Lardle, sir, is the working slave of a man. But it is indiscrete of me to mention to you of what our business arrangement consists."

"Do you read, Mrs. Barnes? You speak well, as if you were trained in the Inns of Court."

"You flatterer. You and your kind like to praise me for my wit. How I learned to speak well was hard come by, sir. Let that be enough." Endersby sat back, letting out a sigh of exhaustion. "I want to save the lives of innocent women, Mrs. Barnes. And to protect children. All I can promise you is that if you can provide any information about Mr. Lardle and his actions last Tuesday, I may be able to stop a monster that is killing the females of this city."

Mrs. Barnes reacted by quickly raising her hand to her throat as if to protect it from a murderer's knife. She took a moment to speak; Endersby could see that his words had touched her in a profound manner.

"Mr. Lardle comes here two or three times a week," Mrs. Barnes said, moving away, her back turned toward Endersby as if she wished to hide her features.

"He is employed by a Dr. Benton to procure young blonde girls of ten or twelve. Once or twice I allowed Lardle to lead away girls from my establishment to the doctor's house in Bedford Square. I do not know what occurs exactly between them, but I will reveal the girls are returned to me the next morning untouched."

"Go on, please."

"I admit I became fearful, sir. Mr. Lardle was taking away these members of my house and using my good graces to earn his coin with some payment to me. I accommodated him for a time until I realized it was to my disadvantage. On Tuesday last he came past midnight, his usual hour. He waited until three or four in the morning once my regular clients had come and gone. I do not let him into this part of the house but allow him to stay in the area kitchen below, where he speaks with my cook and maid. At four o'clock in the morning I came down with two girls, not of my prettiest, but thin and young enough for the tastes of

Dr. Benton. Mr. Lardle had been taking porter and was not in the clearest state of mind to accept my offer. He did not become belligerent but he was insistent that I find him two other girls, cleaner girls he said."

"Were the girls ill, sickly?"

"None of my girls are so, Inspector. But Mr. Lardle claimed his employer wanted innocent girls. By that he meant ones whose hair was blonde, cheeks more round and rosy. Girls like *that* are two to three pounds, sir, and poor Lardle had only a pound at best. Whether he kept back more money was of some concern for me. Dr. Benton is a comfortable man with a good profession."

"So you refused him."

"I did, sir. Told him that if his master wished the better kind, he must visit me here. I must reap the reward of my own risks, sir."

"Did you send Lardle away?"

"After some argument, yes, I sent him off. It was close to dawn when he left. I imagine he will not come back here."

"You would swear this to the magistrate?" said Endersby quietly. "And your maid. Is she honest?"

"Do you mean, sir, that she will appear before the magistrate?" The woman laughed. "If you wish it, Inspector. But I assure you Lardle is not a violent man. He has a doxy; he favours cards over any other sport."

Endersby rose. He knew he would have to bring Mrs. Barnes to appear in the court but for now he was satisfied that she had provided an alibi for Mr. Lardle and his actions. On leaving the nanny house, he was at odds and ends. His mind was turning, both with remorse and from his "demon familiar" reeling from its containment. No time like the present, sir, he said to himself. He hired a hansom cab, arrived at Number Sixteen Bedford Square. He spoke briefly to the two constables on guard. "Sir, the man in question returned late. He has not left the house," one constable reported. Endersby thanked the two men and knocked softly on the front door. Almost immediately, it was opened by the butler, who took him straightaway into Dr. Benton's surgery.

"Good morning, sir," the doctor said. Endersby introduced himself. The doctor did not show any alarm. On hearing of Mr. Lardle's arrest he showed some concern and then, with little hesitation, he invited the inspector to follow him upstairs.

"Sir," the doctor began. "I am an honest man. A man without children." He walked on and as he turned the corner to enter the back part of the house, the doctor and the inspector were met by Mrs. Wells.

"Good morning, Inspector," she said, blushing right away and lowering her eyes.

"You are acquainted with Mr. Endersby are you Wells?" Dr. Benton asked.

"I came the other day, Mr. Benton, to enquire after Mr. Lardle," Endersby said. "And about your dealings with him."

"What did you discover, sir?" the doctor asked, no hint of fear or trepidation in his voice.

"I saw the pink room, Mr. Benton. I have also just come from a visit to the establishment of Mrs. Barnes."

"A most unfortunate place," was the doctor's answer. "How ignorant and cruel men can be in thinking that virgin bodies can somehow cure them of a venereal ailment. In Paris, such places are rife and I believe they are now a plague in our own great city."

Inspector Endersby marvelled at the matter-of-fact behaviour of Dr. Benton. He saw no embarrassment in his mien. Was he unaware of his actions? Was he a man pretending to have moral character — in spite of the implications raised by his hiring of girls? "This past Tuesday night, sir, you remained at home."

"Wells, was I at home late Tuesday?" asked Dr. Benton.

"All the night, sir, as I recall. Up and down, if I may be so bold to say."

"Come, Inspector, let me show you something," said the doctor. Mrs. Wells gasped. "Do not fret Wells. You and I have done nothing but good."

Into the pink room, Endersby observed once again the small furniture, the little bed and table. Dr. Benton opened up a cabinet full of dolls and small boxes. "It is here, Inspector, I entertain my guests. Young girls, sir. They are not expecting kindness but I give it to them. I hand them a coin if they ask, I have Mrs. Wells bathe them if they wish. I also have Mrs. Wells tell me if these girls are in any way sickly or injured."

"Is this true, Mrs. Wells?" Endersby asked. The woman whose face was now wet with tears nodded her head. "Dr. Benton does his best."

"You do not favour these nanny houses, Dr. Benton?" Endersby said bluntly.

"Sir, I was a married man. I could not have children of my own. When I suggested to my wife that we indulge our passion — or *my* passion — for having young ones in our lives, she grew appalled and then angry. When I began this practise of 'saving' the young girls, she said I was mad, without conscience. She decided to leave the marital home soon after." Dr. Benton told the story slowly with a hint of sadness. He then sat down on the little bed.

"Please, Josiah," Mrs. Wells pleaded, stepping forward.

"No, Wells. I must reveal. You see, Inspector, I had a great loss as a child. My dear Katherine Helena, my sister." The man's voice broke but he pulled his head up and went on, his throat clearing every so often as he spoke.

"She drowned because of my negligence."

"Not true, sir," Mrs. Wells said, her voice soft. "You must not keep that burden to yourself. It was an accident. Your father told you so in his letter before he died."

"She drowned, Inspector. And since that day I swore I would protect the young when and however I could. Thus, you see around you in this room, my feeble attempts at clearing my conscience. You may think me mad. I know I should go to a judge or a magistrate and demand that Mrs. Barnes and her ilk be condemned. But you and I know the nature of man in this city. How cruel life can be for the sick and poor and the vulnerable."

Endersby stood silent for a moment. "Mr. Lardle is often gruff, sir, as am I with him," admitted Dr. Benton. "But he is not a bad man." Dr. Josiah Benton rose. He shut the door to the cupboard. He then allowed the inspector to see a small book listed with the names of all the girls he had seen over the past three years, their ages, the medicines he had given them for free to cure their ailments. "I have offered these orphans to leave the nanny houses and forgo the streets. Set them up for adoption in the Foundling Hospital. Mrs. Barnes, to her credit, has allowed me at times to do so. Some of the young girls are too frightened, too lost to move from her attentions. She, herself, was a victim of this cruel practise. In fact, sir, I lent her money at one time, thinking she would become an honest woman. But I could not influence her beyond that."

The inspector took a moment. Was there any reason to doubt this man's words? Lardle had an alibi. As did Dr. Benton himself. He, too, would be required to write a deposition under oath and appear before the magistrate. Endersby put on his hat. He shook Dr. Benton's hand. He realized he could not condone nor condemn the man for his peculiar actions. Much good came from this sordid manner of treating the young but Endersby could not do anything but marvel at the fortitude of the man.

"Thank you, sir," the inspector said on leaving. "I shall send a constable to fetch you and your servants to appear before the magistrate."

In the street once again, Endersby gathered his thoughts. *What to make of such a morning? A young woman without compunction selling girls' bodies, a doctor tending to them as if they were his own children? The city is a strange world of the mad and the good,* Endersby concluded. He informed the two constables of their present duty to accompany Dr. Benton and his household to court as soon as possible. On checking his pocket watch, he realized he must hurry. The hours were passing too quickly. The killer could still be at large. Endersby knew that speed and purpose were not enough: there was the moral imperative of life itself. "Onward," he whispered to himself and in spite of his gouty foot, his scabs, and insistent appetite, he moved on.

The hansom cab flew through the streets. It made a turn toward the river with Endersby urging the driver to speed his horse. An hour later, after much bustling, the inspector was standing in the ward of St. Bartholomew's Hospital among a group of familiar faces.

"Was this the man you observed, ladies and gentlemen," Endersby asked of his small herd of curious onlookers from Rosemary Lane. "Nay. The chappy had a wound, not a rash from the pox," argued the barkeep from the Blue Anchor Gin House.

"Hard to say," proclaimed the lace seller. "Wot you think, lovey?" he said to his large wife, her apron sheathed in fish scales. "Perhaps. Not for certain, not for … well, no and yes." All witnesses peered again at the face of Sergeant Smeets lying in his bed. "No," said the boy thief. "Not 'im, no," answered Nick the Hand.

"I thank you all," replied Inspector Endersby. Rance and Tibald led the motley bunch out of the crowded ward of St. Bartholomew's. Sergeant Smeets dozed fitfully, his skin the colour of chalk. "Damnation," the inspector whispered under his breath. How to find proof positive? These witnesses had proved unreliable. Endersby had to admit to having only scant leads despite his wish to blame Smeets. The only truths were the patient's violent behaviour, the found frock coat and Smeets's admission of needing to find his Catherine.

"I say, rum gull," came the sound of a familiar voice. Standing large and florid in the hospital ward doorway was the Duke of the Docks himself, Mr. Fitz.

"How do you do, sir," smiled Endersby. Perhaps Fitz might provide an answer.

"Robust," laughed Fitz. "And you, Bobby-git?"

"I am still a desperate man. Here before us lies a chap who had cause to kill."

"Good on you," said Fitz, coming forward to the bed where Sergeant Smeets lay in sleep. The Duke of the Docks leaned over the soldier's face. Out came Fitz's massive hand; a hard shake to the soldier's arm caused the ward matron to bound forward. "Sir, I beg of you," she said in a hoarse whisper. "Beg pardon, ducks, but I be on police business, eh Jack-boy?" Fitz said looking back at Endersby. "Have you ever seen this man in any of your lodging houses or on the streets where you rule," asked Endersby. Fitz pulled out a silk handkerchief and blew his nose. "Not him, Jack," he said with conviction. "This chappy ne'er saw a street corner in his life. Look at 'im agin, a gin-scum soldier from toe to cap."

"You are certain, sir?" asked Endersby. Fitz laughed: "You doubt old Fitz, Bobby? This fellah's seen prison, e'en the hulks, I reckon, from his fevered looks."

"Damnation," the inspector whispered a second time. He

slipped Fitz a coin in thanks and watched him waddle out of the ward. On his way home to his midday dinner, Endersby attempted to clear his mind. *It is the wayward way of Justice,* he mused. The inspector nevertheless felt proud of his detective work, the thoroughness of Caldwell, Rance, and Tibald. There was consolation in the fact that no workhouse murders and no kidnappings had taken place for two nights. "Yet, a felon still runs free," he said out loud as the cab drove up Chancery Lane.

At Number Six Cursitor Street, the inspector got down. His growling stomach propelled him up to his set of rooms; he smelled the scones Harriet had promised him — a gift from their neighbour, Mrs. McLaren, to be followed by one of his favourites, sheep's trotters stewed in milk. Afterward, Endersby sat down in his study to work on his French puzzle. He could not concentrate. He stood up, paced, and punched his fists together. Time pressed on. He walked into the hall and pulled on his hat and coat.

"You look vexed," Harriet said, bussing him on the cheek as he opened the door. "I suppose you shall abandon me this evening as well. To pursue your culprit."

"Unfortunately, my dearest, I must," replied Endersby. "Mrs. Endersby, I have been pondering your word from the other evening."

"Which one? Was I in some way philosophical?" smiled Harriet.

"I have entertained your notion of retribution."

"This is in reference to your case of the workhouse children?"

"Yes, it was a matter of lace. I question the nature of such recompense in this case. Brutish revenge?"

"Puzzling, dear," replied Harriet. "Surely, the criminal mind is so fraught with wild sentiment we can only guess at what drives it to commit terrible acts."

"In fact," murmured the distracted inspector.

"You look so tired, dear Owen."

"I am lost, Harriet. This case is not coming into the light." Harriet took hold of her husband's hand. "It seems," the inspector continued, "that Caldwell and I have run in a circle. Logic and action are out of match. And tonight, Death may again haunt the workhouses."

"Have courage, my dear," Harriet comforted. "Justice will prevail."

"Do not wait up for me tonight," Endersby cautioned, taking Harriet in his arms.

"The life of a detective inspector's wife, dear one, is often one of waiting."

On his way to Fleet Lane Station House, Endersby diverted himself by reading the new theatre playbills posted on wooden fences. He often thought a detective's work was similar to that of an actor's. Both need to be keenly observant of human behaviour. "Such wondrous figures these players are," the inspector said aloud. "Madame Vestris, Charles James Mathews, and William Charles Macready. Your names will blaze throughout history." At the station house, Caldwell and he gathered together the gaff, the letters of Catherine Smeets, the lace, and the dregerman's hat and placed them in a large sack. "We may need these for bait," quipped the inspector to his sergeant-at-hand. He dictated to Caldwell the story of Dr. Benton and his remarkable charity.

"A man would do that, sir?" asked Caldwell.

"Mrs. Barnes was remarkable in her own way. An odd mixture of decency and disdain."

"Any conclusions, sir, regarding Sergeant Smeets?" Caldwell asked.

Endersby hesitated: "Mr. Fitz claimed he'd never seen Smeets. The other witnesses were not consistent."

"I am sorry to hear that, sir," Caldwell replied.

"By elimination we have isolated ourselves without a firm suspect, Sergeant," Endersby went on, his mood darker. "This is our last day to effect our capture of a villain — Borne will allow us no more subsidy or time. This sack, if used to advantage, may aid us, as I entertain a hunch."

"Chance and coincidence, sir. Like finding a coin on a beach of stones."

"Admirably said, Sergeant."

Chapter Twenty-eight
Mr. Smallwood and Company

As if in sympathy with Inspector Endersby's predicament, the fog lifted by mid- afternoon and allowed a pallid sun to warm the March streets of the great city. "At last some light on this under-world day," muttered Endersby, sitting back in the slow-moving hackney coach. The quarter of Seven Dials presented itself without fanfare. Seven narrow streets formed a star pattern spreading out from a little square. Row houses ran in zig-zag fashion along slim alleys. The hackney pulled up to the Seven Dials Station House on Earl Street. Wild children shouted at the inspector and his sergeant as they paid the fare. A constable rushed out from the station house with a long stick. "Run ya filtee scallywags," the constable shouted. Endersby learned the man's name a moment later: Constable Martin Healey, a burly man with a pair of fists as big as the fattened capons in Smithfield market. "Good aftynoon to yer, Inspectar," Healey cried.

How different Earl Street Station House was from Endersby's home station. Quiet, solemn: a narrow passage led from the front door into a back room, where a large desk occupied most of the square footage. A smell of fresh varnish cut the air. "This way, Inspector." Down a set of stairs to the area below where, in the former kitchen, a long table had been erected. Nearest the door, a wooden stool, and on it with his back toward the doorway, a figure perched in shirt sleeves and waistcoat.

"Owen? Rolly Endersby?" the figure asked without turning to look.

"How'd you guess, Tinytree?" answered Endersby.

"The gouty stomp is unmistakable. And the sway of the Endersby belly. But you are not alone. A thin chap is alongside. Two of you come to Smallwood. Shall you stay?"

The figure stood, turned. Embraces between the two inspectors. Pats on mutual stomachs leading to introductions.

"Sit, sit," commanded the Earl Street detective. "Tea? Coffee?" he asked. "Or port?"

Endersby conceded to port while Caldwell requested coffee. "Here you are, then," said Smallwood. "A bit of trouble, Rolly? A Gordian Knot to unravel?"

"Sadly so, Elias," Endersby said.

Detective Elias Smallwood filled a room, not by girth but by height and loudness of voice. A moustache decorated his upper lip, its strands styled by wax and comb. A pair of black wire spectacles gave him the appearance of a man constantly amazed. The three men drank at leisure. After a time, with clay pipes lit, Smallwood introduced his assistants. "My *two* sergeants-at-hand, Rolly," Smallwood boasted. Two men in plain clothes marched into the room. One, Sergeant Stendebach, born in Munich, raised in south London. The other from Denmark, family name of Ringdahl. "Gentlemen," Inspector Endersby said.

"Now to business," commanded Elias Smallwood. The other two men sat down. Endersby proceeded to review the workhouse murders, describing the culprit's features, the Catherine coincidence. Smallwood held up the written notice sent to all police stations. Endersby continued by outlining the alibis of his suspects and the problem of the ill Sergeant Smeets. "We have run in a circle, Elias," admitted a dejected Endersby. "Another possible suspect is William More, a dredgerman. He works at night for short periods. He shares certain characteristics with the culprit. Above all, we also have a street performer, a pity-man, who fits the description. My deductions lead me to think More and the pity-man may be one in the same man. From our trailing his protector, we can conclude the pity-man is now residing in Seven Dials, in the lodging house with the green door in the main square."

"You expect to nab him?" Smallwood said, his tone expressing doubt. "Elias," replied Endersby, "we have here in our sack two items — a gaff and a hat — which may belong to him. And a collection of letters from a young ward of St. Pancras Workhouse."

"Conjecture, Rolly," Smallwood warned.

"Desperation, rather," said Endersby. "There is also the figure of an uncle, a phantom figure if you will. His name is one of my clues — a Mr. Tobias Jibbs."

"An uncle?"

"I am following a hunch, if you'll permit me," Endersby explained. He revealed what he knew of Tobias Jibbs from Sergeant Smeets. "But can this drunken soldier be trusted in his storytelling?" wondered Smallwood.

Sergeant Stendebach spoke up: "A scar, a frock coat, and a limp? We have our street watchers. We can question them. The soup-house proprietors respect us and will give us honest replies."

"Such cooperation," said Endersby to Smallwood, "is no

doubt a result of the respect with which you treat all folks in this sad quadrant."

"I thank you, Owen, for the compliment. The poor are good people. Trust is always difficult to earn. But once earned, I find my spies are most reliable."

"Commendable, sir," said Endersby.

Sergeant Ringdahl raised a question: "If your suspect has taken refuge here in the 'Dials,' do you imagine he will avoid anyone who looks official, or is dressed like a police officer?"

"No doubt of it, sir," Endersby replied. "Therein lies our problem. If he fears any of us may be on a campaign of question and search, he may flee. Such a calamity would stall our investigation."

Smallwood puffed on his clay pipe. "How do you wish us to aid you?"

"As you are well aware, Elias, I am fond of the theatre. My cohort, Mr. Caldwell, and I often have used disguises to discover clues."

"As is usual with my superior," Caldwell added, "we put ourselves at risk but with ingenuity we have been successful in most all of our endeavours."

"So, you don costumes? Speak in accents?" asked Smallwood, obviously amused.

"Indeed, Elias. It is but one way to gather information. We use coin also, if need arises."

"Or barrels of gin, sir," Caldwell said.

"Indeed, Sergeant," replied Endersby. "In this city of penny-counting superintendents, we must be clever, paying Peter while picking the pocket of Paul." The Earl Street policemen all laughed. "Incognito, then, Endersby?" asked Smallwood. "We dress up, speak like Welshmen and set a trap?"

"If need be," came the inspector's reply. "Such a ruse may

give us opportunity. We have come here because of what we saw while following a chap called Malibran. The logic fits, you see. But since you are well known in this quarter, Elias, it may be difficult for you to join us. How well known are your two sergeants here?"

"Familiar they are, but known?" asked Smallwood.

"If we be in uniform," answered Stendebach, "some folks recognize us. But if we were to dress like street beggars, we might be able to fool a number of people."

"I can trust the lodging house owner to help in our game, if you wish it, Endersby," said Smallwood.

"Most kind, sir. Please follow through. Time plays against us as the hours turn to evening." Endersby stood up as did Caldwell. "May I propose that we, along with these two sergeants, go into Monmouth Street nearby and purchase some second-hand garments? We would need to dirty our faces with coal dust, gentlemen, if you are not adverse to such a procedure. Once we are properly attired we may — under your guidance, Smallwood — begin our search."

"Off to Monmouth," replied Smallwood. "I shall step out of the station and cross the square to the lodging house and alert the owner to our schemes." Stendebach led Endersby, Ringdahl, and Caldwell out a back passage and onto the avenue known as Monmouth Street. In every doorway an eager merchant stood. It had been a few months since Endersby, in company with his dear Harriet, had visited the best known second-hand clothing street in the city. Signs announced who sold goods: from haberdasher's buttons to boots to heavy coats. A constable stood at one corner, truncheon ready to stop any who dared to pilfer. "This way, sir," said Sergeant Stendebach, pointing to a doorway. Down into a basement room where a Mr. Rummage, a name that initially amused the inspector, had his shop.

"Sir, we are in some haste," Endersby explained to the man. "Sore business to be concluded by means we hope you may provide."

"Obliged, sir," came the answer. Mr. Rummage was as tall as he was wide; his hands looked soft from his indoor trade. His son stood beside him, as thin as his father was fat. The three sergeants and the inspector set to work choosing long coats and torn hats, stockings, half- and full-length boots in multiple states of decay, and gloves with holes and missing fingers. "Three shillings for the lot, sir, if you'd be so obliging," said Mr. Rummage. The items were wrapped, coin was given, the men retreated from the cellar to the street and back into the Earl Street Station House where, with much pulling and buttoning, they changed their clothes and smudged them with coal ash from the central hearth, the oily soot applied equally to hands and faces.

"Just in from the gutters, gentlemen?" joked Smallwood, seeing the four men on his return to the station house.

"Shall we be off, gents?" Endersby said, tipping his old hat at the men gathered around.

"A suggestion, Owen!" said Inspector Smallwood. "Stendebach and Ringdahl, you two men meander to the east and west sides of the Green Door Lodging House. Inspector, come with me. Caldwell, I think it best if you accompany us."

"Thank you, sir," the three sergeants replied. "Come along, Rolly," smiled an amused Smallwood. "Perhaps the 'Dials' will afford you posterity in one of its bawdy songs."

Chapter Twenty-nine
The Time to Ponder

At the opening of the green door, Endersby recognized the familiar face of the lodging house owner. The hall led to a back room and an open courtyard. A large window revealed a courtyard packed with old mirrors, stacked upright one against the other. "I do clean-up, sir," the owner explained. "After the funerals of them that has no will and testament. Them mirrors I sell at the auction houses nearby Piccadilly. Turn a profit, I do." The rest of the house reeked of cooking, the walls browned by time and dirt.

"Now, milady," Smallwood began. He led the woman into a side room. She was introduced as Mrs. Kermode. She peered at Endersby with wary eyes. But Smallwood regained her attention and told her directly who the men were in their disguises. "We are in search of a man. My fellow detective, Inspector Endersby, will provide you the details. Most concerned we are to find the chappy, as he is suspected of having murdered." Mrs. Kermode gasped, then composed herself to listen attentively. Endersby related his story. He told of the gaff, the lace, the abandoned girls, the scar, and all other pertinent facts to help Mrs. Kermode form a picture in her mind of the culprit. She lit a clay pipe and pulled at her chin.

"Think, milady," said Smallwood. "Recall the fellows of our district. A rummy bunch some of them."

"For sure, sir," Mrs. Kermode answered. She had a shrewd look about her. "I knows *you*, Mr. Endersby. But where be your Scots accent?" The woman grinned. She slapped Endersby hard on his right shoulder. "This chappy, this Malibran has rented the room for his 'cousin'," she said, raising her voice on the word cousin. "Do you know of this man, Missus?" Endersby asked, teasing the woman with his sudden switch to his Scottish burr.

"Aye, sir. I know of *one*," Mrs. Kermode said. "*He* be right in this very house, for sure. Up in my attic. Rents alone. Came in not an hour ago, I reckon."

"How does he walk?" Endersby now said, pleased to hear that the man had come as arranged by Malibran. If the inspector's efforts were of any value, the case might be drawn to a close before nightfall. To be certain, Endersby asked: "Can you give me a sense of his manner?"

"Ah, Inspector. Limps he does. Stinks of a malady. Ne'er seen his full face for the long hair and a filthy linen binding. Claimed he knew of my house. A gentle sickly sort, for sure. I can see his poor hands all sooty from workin'. Worse of all, he is a shouter. Fights against a banshee, he does."

"How do you mean, madam?" asked Endersby.

"There I be sitting smack in my own hall — just out there — minding my tallies. I hears this shoutin'. Jesus bless me, I runs out to the courtyard yonder. There he is, newly moved into the house, says he is a village man, and he stands shoutin' at himself in one of them old mirrors. Talkin' to his own reflection like it was his brother."

Endersby looked to Smallwood who raised his eyebrows.

"What's the man's name, Mrs. Kermode?" asked Smallwood.

"I ask no name and take none neither. The chaps won't tell the truth any which way in a pinch. As long as they pays me and does no harm to me and mine I let 'em stay on."

"Did this newcomer shout out any name in particular?" asked Endersby. Caldwell looked up at his superior. He had his notebook open at a clean page.

"None I recall hearin', Inspector," said Mrs. Kermode. "He be in at the moment, if you wishes to speak to 'im directly."

"Caldwell, run around outside of the house and warn your two fellow sergeants," Endersby said quickly. "Check the rear entrances and the sides for doorways in and out. Smallwood, will you command one other constable to come post-haste to this spot, here, not far from the good woman's front door. I need him as well as your sergeants to witness the man who matches the description of our culprit. Alert him to the fellow's appearance. If he tries to run, Caldwell, you and the constable must give chase."

"I shall do as you bid," said Smallwood, beginning to move toward the door of the room. "I'll send along *two*, a good Scot lad named McNally and Constable Millar."

"I thank you, sir," replied Endersby. "Have them keep close eyes on the man."

Smallwood and Caldwell opened the door, checked the length of the hall and then made their exit out the lodging house front door. In the mean time, Endersby rebuttoned his newly purchased old coat, mismatching the buttons to the holes so as to give himself a more dishevelled appearance.

"Now Missus," Endersby said, turning to Mrs. Kermode. "I wish to meet this man, if you say he is in." In the lodging house hallway, the inspector followed Mrs. Kermode to a back parlour near the kitchen. In a loud voice, Endersby said: "A kindly good evening to you, Missus. I've come to take me supper if you could be so obliging." Mrs. Kermode winked at Endersby, placed her hands on her hips and leaned back. She thrust out her hand to play her role. "A penny then, sir," she said in a voice too loud, "before you taste me vittles."

At one of the bare tables sat the man in question. Long hair and a soiled bandage covered his face. His ankles were bound in bloodied rags and he wore only tattered stockings. His frock coat was gritted with mud. A necklace of leather holding a small pouch hung from his neck. And his smell, a fetid rot, surrounded him like a cloud. The other eaters — three bent men — had chosen seats at the far end of the room. The man did not look up as Endersby passed by him on his way toward another table. The fellow slurped his soup slowly, as if his teeth ached. Endersby noted his filthy hands.

"A fine good evening to you, sir," Endersby said, addressing the man at his table. The man jolted. He stared at Endersby. He placed down his spoon. "Filth," he said in a smothered voice, his left hand batting at the air as if there were swarms of flies. Endersby tapped his forehead. "Be a night of storms ahead, I predict." A serving boy brought him a bowl. The inspector drank it down in gulps. He kept his eyes on the man; the gestures, the posture seemed similar to those of the figure with the pistol on the night Malibran attacked. Endersby rose and went out of the parlour. "Keep an eye out for him," he said to Caldwell who had just returned through the front door.

"Two of Smallwood's constables are outside at the ready, sir," Caldwell whispered. "Good. Call one in immediately. Have him stand here on guard."

Caldwell ran out to the street and came back with a young constable. His face had a serious expression as he listened intensely to Caldwell's orders. The young policeman nodded his head in respect to Endersby and took his position by the dining parlour's entrance.

"Caldwell," Endersby said, taking hold of his sergeant's arm. "Bring along our sack with the bait and come with me for a hasty look at our suspect's quarters."

⁕⠂⠢⠶⠶⠶⠢⠂⁕

Mrs. Bolton lay alone on the top of her bed. A single candle burned. She got up and went into her kitchen where there were cooked pies and a jug of apple cider brought over by neighbours. She sat down by her hearth. Tomorrow would be sister Jemima's funeral. *Such shame she had taken her own life.* Jemima would not be buried in hallowed ground. "Oh, sad one," Mrs. Bolton whispered out loud.

Mrs. Bolton fetched Jemima's written confession. The sheets were well crinkled by now from handling. At first they had seemed to Mrs. Bolton to be a massive lot. But after much re-reading, she realized there were but a few.

"Ashes to ashes."

Mrs. Bolton read each sheet for the last time; she lay the pages on the embers and watched them blacken and curl before they floated up the chimney.

"Bless you, Jemima. I forgive you," Mrs. Bolton said as the words of her tortured sister filled her mind:

> *I, Jemima Pettiworth, declare that all I have writ-*
> *ten here is the truth. I do not presume to enter*
> *into this state of confession, dearest sister, with-*
> *out due thought, trusting in my own memory but*

269

also in your kind belief that I may be granted by you and my Saviour manifold mercies and forgiveness for what I have done in my early life. I am not worthy so much as to lick up the crumbs under your table, dearest sister. But you are the same woman whose inclination is always to give comfort, to afford allowances, to condescend never to deliberate cruelty or false pride. Those two sins I now openly admit once ruled my sentiments many years ago.

For a time of ten years, as you well remember, I was hired as a ward matron at our county workhouse, a place which still stands not one mile out of our cosy village. My employment was honest; my work diligent. Ruling, feeding, and working young children — both male and female — comprised my duties. When I was but twenty-two years old, I fell in love with a master who, in light of his own sins, could not sustain his affections for me. Beginning from that terrible night when he fled St. Stephen's and abandoned me, I forced myself to hide my sadness. In my pride I believed, dear sister, you would mock me, say I was foolish. How I yearned for him, the cowardly man. I never divulged his name and to remain honour-bound, his name shall remain forever forgotten.

In the spring of 1808, I went up to London to see an old friend and as you remember, I stayed but eight months. A lie you believed, bless you. There in December, all alone, I gave birth. My son was so sickly, he perished within an hour of his

first breath. I arrived back to our village one late
January night. My grief had seduced me to wrap
my baby, cold and dead, and carry him the long
journey home to our village graveyard. My own
hands dug his shallow grave. When you saw me
the next day — you were so kind! — and said I
looked ill, you took me in, fed me, and allowed me
to live under your roof. I went back to the workhouse and was granted a new job as matron of the
family ward. With money I had saved, I eventually
purchased a headstone for my lost son.

In His Great Mercy, God did not grant me
peace. I grew bitter. I felt the world had judged me,
found me wanting, and scorned me. This inner bitterness began to seep out of me as if it were a boil
leaking blood. Like Pharaoh in the story of Moses,
I hardened my heart to misery in myself and in
others. My only relief was lace making. It kept my
mind occupied and my fingers busy. In the family
ward, I began to take delight in punishing innocent creatures. There were three victims — I must
regard them as such — who became my nemeses. I
will not mention their good Christian names. One
was a young mother who, jilted by her husband,
was left pregnant. She came into my ward with a
son and a daughter. The son was young, delicate,
imaginative. The daughter was meek. Their poor
mother struggled in birth and I was unable to aid
her. When she delivered she bled profusely. Her
son stood by watching and crying for his mother. I
had to sop her blood with pieces of my lace while
calling for help.

The boy never forgave me. "Naught to worry, naught to fret," I cautioned him. He railed against me; he leaped at me, blaming me for his mother's death. I beat him numerous times. Then, when I beat his sister to relieve my own temper, the boy struck me. He was very protective of her. Once he tried to strangle me with his bare hands as I whipped her. His tender and vulnerable ways so resembled my own. I whipped him as a way of scourging myself. My worst punishment for him was the gag. To frighten him, I forced bits of my own lace into his mouth and tied a swath of muslin around his face to hold it in. He wept; he fought; I locked him in closets without food. Yet I did not feel relief nor remorse.

Eventually, my ways of sadness abated. The boy lived on and grew, surviving my cruelties. In that time, he hid from me, becoming familiar with the kitchens, the escape doors. Peculiar in nature, he often talked to himself, often imagining he had a friend or a twin. When the two children finally left the workhouse to toil for a farmer, I felt my burden had lifted. All through these years, I have never forgotten them. I do not believe they survived and I cannot recall ever knowing them in the street.

Could my sister have stuffed lace into a boy's mouth simply for cruel pleasure? Mrs. Bolton wondered, and then whispered, "may that poor boy rest quiet in his adult years."

Mrs. Bolton read on. She stirred the embers one last time

and, after memorizing its final words, tossed the last page into the dying flames.

Oh dear sister, as I lie dying, I must release these words to set my soul and the souls of my victims free. I see before me in my penance only the fires of Hell. Almighty Jesus, may Your tender mercies strenghthen those more deserving than I. Take pity upon my dear sister and the three sad creatures of my past.

With this sentence, I end my humble confession ... bowing my head in shame.

Chapter Thirty
A Fall Too Tragic

The tiny window in the attic room of Mrs. Kermode's lodging house showed the first dimming of twilight. "A candle, sir," said Endersby. A single narrow bed, shadow-filled corners, a rumpled collection of clothes too nondescript in the candle's light to afford Endersby any immediate clues. A room barely large enough to house a child.

"Such a sorrowful place," Endersby said quietly.

The inspector went to the window. His reflection in the panes showed a face pulled by fatigue. He unlatched the hook and looked out. "We must not presume our man will give in easily, Caldwell." Tottering attic storeys, broken chimneys, steep runs of roof tile: a challenging above-ground course for any man to run over — or any other man to give chase. Directly below the lodging house dormer where he stood, Endersby saw the dark shape of the courtyard with its stacks of mirrors in their rotting frames. The inspector then began his round, holding up the lit candle, while Caldwell stood close to the door to listen for movement of any kind.

"Do not hesitate, sergeant, if he comes. For he *must* come upstairs eventually."

Slowly, in a circle, Endersby toured the tiny space, followed by his shadow on the dirt-smeared walls. He pulled back the soiled bed linens. Blood stains spotted the pillow. He lifted up the straw- stuffed mattress. The sheets held the stink of the man's body. All along the edge of the single top sheet was oily dirt: coal smut. Under the bed was a pair of old military boots and a small canvas bag. The inspector shook the bag.

"Sergeant," Endersby said. "Look on this."

The contents of the bag lay spread on the bedsheet.

"It is the same lace as we have brought with us," Caldwell said.

"No doubt. Yes, lift it … the pattern, the twists, the cut edge of one piece like the edge of the other. Rosemary Lane lace for curtains."

"And for murder, sir," replied Caldwell.

They fell silent again for an instant.

"Why lace?" murmured Endersby. "Now, sergeant, we begin Act One of our Punch and Judy show." Out of the sack brought from Fleet Lane, Caldwell pulled the rusty gaff found at St. Pancras and the dredgerman's hat and laid them across the bed. Endersby in turn removed from his bulging pocket the letters of young Catherine Smeets. Blowing out the candle, the inspector and his sergeant left the room; they came down the three flights of stairs to the main floor hall. There, Mrs. Kermode sat at her table, counting coins. Smallwood had returned and, to the delight of Endersby, had put on a mackintosh and a squashed top hat as a disguise. Tapping the edge of the hat in greeting, Smallwood lounged by the street door, picking his teeth. Just then, the suspect appeared in the doorway of the dining parlour.

"Coward," he shouted, his eyes half closed. His gait was

uneven as if he had drunk too much gin. The stench from his legs rose in the air of the hall. Mrs. Kermode held her nose: "Sir, I beg of you. To the public washhouse. There be water and soap for a ha'penny." The man swivelled on the spot. His arms flew up above his head and his fists formed as if he were about to strike the landlady.

"Aye, eee, aye, madam!" he said in a ghastly whisper.

Endersby readied himself. The man, however, held his stance as if he were posing for a sculptor. A second was all, then in a quick change, he began knocking his fists together above his head in imitation of a dancer doing a jig. The fellow turned, his stockinged feet tapping lightly in time to his moving fists. "Watch him," Endersby said quietly to Caldwell. Endersby sat down on a chair in the hall and nonchalantly lit his clay pipe. He flicked his match end in the direction of Smallwood, who picked up the cue by sniffing his nose. The suspect danced a little more, oblivious to those around him. Presently, the patter of rain was heard against the window panes. A clap of thunder followed quickly, drowning out the sound of tapping feet. The man halted, his eyes widened in terror. He froze, still as a marble statue. Not a feature quivered.

"Open up! Open up the hatch, for mercy's sake!" he suddenly screamed, his body jolting back to life. His shriek rang through the house. "We will perish!" he howled, stamping the floor with one of his sore legs. Dragging himself toward the stairs the maddened man covered his face. "Devils," he moaned, his heavy steps pounding up the stairs to the attic.

"Now, men. Now!" Endersby hissed. "Our fellow will find the incriminating evidence in his room. Stay on guard. He may come down these very stairs with a weapon. If we hear a clatter on the roof, be prepared to set chase. Caldwell, ready?"

"Yes, Inspector."

Caldwell slipped away from the stairwell, where a slow clomping of feet was heard. "He's coming down," Endersby said, sitting to relight his clay pipe. Smallwood and Caldwell posed, pretending to be passing time. Meanwhile, the rain lightened as the cast of players in the hall began talking to each other. Smallwood stationed himself in front of the street door; Endersby's post was near the other end of the hall leading to the kitchen. Caldwell remained in between the two, resting against Mrs. Kermode's small table. The footsteps above them slowed, as if the man was reconsidering his descent. They started again from the second landing and came down the final flight to the first floor.

The suspect was panting, like a dog after a chase. He held the gaff and wielded it like a walking cane. His pockets in his frock coat were stuffed with papers. "Good evening, sirs," he said in a hoarse voice. The felon did not catch the eye of any of the three men posed in the hallway. He made no sign of demanding how his room had been invaded and objects left there. Endersby could see the man was aware, yet unsure. "Good evening, sir," Endersby said. "A fine evening it is," his accent coming forth. "Wet, I reckon, with the March wind."

"Ah, ah," replied the suspect.

"So, sir," Endersby now said. He tapped his pipe. "You have letters to write, I imagine. I see you have equipped your pockets with paper. But is it not past the afternoon hour, sir? I know of only one mail delivery after five of the clock."

"Ah, ah, a storm at sea. Delays. Must fly, must dash — off to the country, sir, a pudding to purchase." The man pronounced his nonsense in an elevated tone, his head turning from side to side as if he were bothered by gnats. "Devil take'em, I wish," he said, bowing his head. As he stepped toward the front door, Endersby stood up from his chair.

"Mr. William More," he said. "Or more precisely, Mr. *Tobias Jibbs*. Do not go, sir."

"The tide has come in," the man replied. He turned to face Endersby, who now held up the piece of lace found in the suspect's attic room. "*Lace*, sir," the inspector said.

"Ah," cried the man, raising the gaff. "The tide came in as I pulled him, pulled ..." As Tobias Jibbs elevated his weapon further, Smallwood leaped forward, grabbed the gaff from behind and yanked it out of the man's hand. Jibbs dashed back toward the stairwell. His arms were hard and strong. Driven by the need to escape, he struck Caldwell on the chin, the blow sending the sergeant to the floor. Endersby began marching toward him from the end of the hall. Smallwood leaped over the prone Caldwell. He swept up his right arm but found it blocked by Jibbs, who feinted and landed a punch to Smallwood's nose. In the midst of the tumbling, Jibbs reached the stairs, the steps resounding with his boots retreating toward the rooftops.

"After him, chaps," yelled Endersby.

Up the men went, into the empty room and toward the opened window. "Caldwell," ordered Endersby. His faithful sergeant climbed out onto the slanted roof. Smallwood pointed to the figure inching his way along the brick edge of the adjoining building's roof. "There, sergeant," Smallwood said. Endersby stood by as Caldwell slid down and placed his feet on the roof edge. Attached to it ran a dented metal gutter. "Are you safe, sir?" asked Endersby as Caldwell tested the strength of the edge. "And sound, sir," came the sergeant's response.

From his vantage point in the attic window, Endersby watched Tobias Jibbs making slow progress along the next building's edge. Much of the brick and mortar of the houses had long begun to crumble. Showers of broken masonry rained down as Jibbs made his way past two dormers, their windows boarded up. Endersby could hear the man yelling out curses, his thin body making cautious movements. The open courtyard below now flickered with shadows from lanterns lit by Mrs. Kermode and her two kitchen servants.

"Owen, allow me," said Smallwood. He had taken both bed sheets, twisted and tied them in a series of knots. He secured the makeshift rope to the doorknob of the entrance door, tossed the other end out the window to climb down beside Caldwell. Smallwood hoisted himself over the windowsill and slid down the incline to the stone edge. The two policemen began to inch their way toward Tobias Jibbs, Smallwood grasping the sheet line and one of Caldwell's sleeves.

"Filth!" Jibbs yelled at the men trying to follow him. By now he had reached an attic dormer window kitty-corner to his rented room. He had moved along and around the L-shaped angle of the roof edge joining the houses attached to Mrs. Kermode's dwelling. Endersby counted the rooftops to where Jibbs had made his way — two separate houses facing the courtyard. Would Caldwell and Smallwood be able to tackle the culprit on such a narrow ledge? Jibbs grabbed the side of one of the blocked-up dormer windows. With his other hand he pounded hard on the rotted wood until the board fell inwards and he scrambled through the space into the dark interior. "Smallwood," shouted Endersby. "Stay put. Caldwell, can you give chase?"

"Certainly, sir," the sergeant shouted back.

"Careful, Sergeant, go slowly along. Be aware he may attack you."

"Thank you, sir," Caldwell shouted back.

"I shall go down to the street," Endersby called to Smallwood. Endersby hurried through the room and down the flights of stairs. Rushing into the street, he commanded the guarding constable to accompany him.

"At your service, sir," came the young man's reply. "McNally's the name."

The two men left the central square and jogged briskly along the street adjacent to the lodging house. It was muddy, the houses dark and marred by broken windows. Endersby counted out the house fronts and stopped at the one that he believed Jibbs had entered. He told the constable to shine his bull's eye lantern up the facade. The weak beam of light showed only broken timber and shabby windowsills. The dormer on the roof facing the street had been bricked up. "Ah," said Endersby. "He cannot run out to the front roof, then." The inspector ordered the constable to kick down the street door. A swarm of broken bits of wood flew into the air and dust blew out of the abandoned foyer.

"Your lantern, sir," said Endersby, taking hold of the bull's eye. The two men stepped inside. The lantern's beam showed collapsed doors, huge holes in the wooden floors. The dust-smothered staircase looked intact — except for the broken banister bowing out over the hall like the folds of an accordion. The sound of slow footsteps could be heard above the inspector, on the second floor. The constable pulled out his truncheon and inched toward the foot of the stairs.

"Tobias Jibbs," cried Endersby. "We have come to arrest you in the name of the law."

Footsteps crept along the upper hallway toward the back end of the abandoned house. As they did, thin strands of dust filtered down through the cracks "Come down peacefully, sir." The footsteps continued. Endersby heard the man panting, breaking open doors. "Filth!" Jibbs shouted. "Get away."

"Now, McNally. We must set chase," Endersby commanded. The young constable wiped his mouth and leapt onto the first few stairs of the staircase leading up to where Tobias Jibbs was pacing. With a crack, the bottom four stairs caved in, taking young

McNally down into a heap of billowing splinters. His truncheon rolled into the hallway. Endersby watched his body thump onto a pile of sharp ends. The young man groaned.

"Constable," Endersby cried out, pushing through the rubble to grab hold of the young policeman's hand. The inspector helped him stand. Blood streamed from McNally's forehead. "Speak, man," Endersby shouted. "Sir, I ... I can stand." Above, Jibbs had run toward the front of the house. Endersby heard him kick at the rotten mullions. With his constable injured and the way up partially destroyed, Endersby fought back a surge of anger. Jibbs' kicking and cursing increased. "Devil. Fool!" Jibbs shrieked. His words galvanized Endersby's conscience. He could not allow the man to escape. Proof positive was evident: Jibbs' ownership of the lace condemned him. Endersby clenched his fists. He wiped dust from his mouth.

"Sir," Endersby yelled into the darkness. "You are in search of your Catherine. She is alive, sir. She is unharmed."

The kicking and shouting stopped abruptly.

"Catherine is safe, sir. She was found living in St. Pancras Workhouse," Endersby said. An anguished moan filled the air, startling young McNally who, edging closer to the inspector, attempted to stem the flow of blood from the wound on his forehead. "Is the man mad?"

"From grief, sir," Endersby said quickly. "Stay your ground, Constable."

Young McNally stepped forward to resume his place with his truncheon held high. A dark figure appeared and stopped at the top of the stairs. Endersby took hold of the lantern and pointed it up. The sudden illumination showed the figure's left arm rising to cover its face. "Ah, Mr. Jibbs," Endersby said in a polite voice. "Uncle Bo. Your beloved niece longs to see you after all these months." Tobias Jibbs stepped back. His knees buckled to the floor. The pale lantern beams caught his blackened hands. "No child I love shall die in a workhouse," Jibbs cried.

"Mr. Jibbs," said Endersby, "if you shall come down slowly, the stairs will hold you. I will lead you to your niece, for she is close by in Seven Dials."

"Shall you?" the culprit asked, his voice turning shrill. "Stand aside," he chanted, his body swaying. "That be right, Matron. You are right," Jibbs screamed. "Filth you are, not worth a farthing. Squirm all you like. Swallow your handiwork … *eat it, eat it.*"

"Inspector!"

Caldwell's voice rang out from the attic storey.

"Here, Caldwell, on the first floor."

"I shall come down," shouted the sergeant.

"With haste, sir, for Mr. Jibbs is alive and breathing on the second floor, just below you."

Tobias Jibbs scrambled to his feet. He tore off his facial bandages. A long red scar cut over his nose and cheeks. He paced back and forth. Caldwell's footsteps began to descend the staircase from the third floor. "The tide, the tide!" Jibbs screamed. In the next moment, as Caldwell reached the second floor, Jibbs hurled himself toward a back window, smashing through the glass and climbing out on the narrow parapet. "He's out, sir," yelled Caldwell.

"How well can you see him, Sergeant?" Endersby yelled.

"He is on the parapet."

"You won't catch him unless he re-enters a house. Or falls into the courtyard."

Caldwell answered, "I can't reach him, Inspector. He's moved on toward the back of the courtyard. I won't be able to balance and grab hold of him at the same time."

"Come down, then, Sergeant," commanded the inspector.

"He is close to the neighbouring house, sir, to the west,"

Caldwell said. "He's holding the side of the window frame as if … he's moving on."

Inspector Endersby dashed out the broken street door and in less than a minute had made the corner and pushed his way back down the hall of Mrs. Kermode's lodging house, through the kitchen pantry, and out to the open courtyard. An anxious crowd of lodgers and kitchen help greeted him. Smallwood had come down from the attic room and joined Mrs. Kermode; the two of them were at present looking up at the second floor and the painfully slow progress Mr. Jibbs was making along the uneven edge of the parapet.

"We may have him," Endersby whispered to himself. The parapet moulding ran like a band connecting all the houses, a feature of the older houses in Seven Dials. It was clear to any observer that a dormer open to the skies or a second-storey window could afford a way out — except that a problem lay in the descent to an exit door. Watching Mr. Jibbs scramble, Endersby could gauge which door he might use and then have a policeman sent to apprehend the criminal.

"Mr. Jibbs!" shouted Endersby from the lantern-lit courtyard. "Come down, sir, in the name of the London Detective Police. Come out of harm's way, sir."

"Filth and scum!" Mr. Jibbs yelled back.

Jibbs now crouched down, eyeing the slippery tiles lying in wait for him on a walkway connected to an adjacent storey. The women began shouting up to Mr. Jibbs, begging him to come down. Mr. Jibbs slowly stood, determined to take a risk. He took small steps, turning his body to face the roof, his back to the courtyard. He leaned in to give himself balance. He glanced back once or twice at Caldwell, who was still peering out the window of the other house, blocking a retreat. The culprit grabbed hold of a brick chimney flue. He screamed down to the courtyard below: "I shall find her, I shall. I shall put an end to …" His words stopped. His right foot slipped. He retrieved it in time and held on.

Rain began to fall. Mr. Jibbs huddled. His frock coat became sodden and drooped from the pelting raindrops. The courtyard was awash with the sound of murmuring voices and rain droplets. Soon the clouds parted, the rain ceased, and Mr. Jibbs straightened and turned his head toward a far slope. His right hand reached out.

"I am —" Jibbs yelled.

His voice froze; he wrenched his head in the other direction. He tried to regain his footing, but the slippery stone let him go. Mr. Jibbs arched; his feet danced and kicked. Letting forth a piercing cry, his arms flailing in a ghastly parody of flight, Mr. Jibbs plunged through the night air.

"Oh, Mother of God!" cried Mrs. Kermode, covering her face with her hands. "Mercy, mercy," the two kitchen servants gasped, their eyes never leaving the body as it plummeted twelve feet and landed with a shattering crash on top of a stack of mirrors. A sprinkling sound of broken fragments and bits of ornate frame flew up from the body's impact. Jibbs lay spread-eagle; the impact from the body started a kind of avalanche — like dominoes, the remaining stacked mirrors fell over, one against another, frames breaking, the glass splitting and falling to the ground. Not ten feet in front of the astonished group, the body lay prone, mirror ornaments hanging askew amidst a pool of shimmering shards.

"Come, Smallwood," commanded Endersby. "The man is still breathing."

Smallwood and the inspector made their way through the debris. They lifted the injured Mr. Jibbs off the pile of breakage and, supporting his weight, carefully walked back toward the lodging house. Mr. Jibbs' chest was heaving; his contorted face caught the lantern light; Endersby took hold of the miscreant's filthy hand as the two policemen carried him inside to the kitchen. Mrs. Kermode helped her cooks clear off a large table, where the inspector and Smallwood then lay the bloodied fellow down on his back. Mr. Jibbs moaned; his blood had soaked through from his wounds on his spine; his beard was embedded with bits of broken glass. Endersby bent forward, pulled apart the shirt top under Mr. Jibbs' frock coat and pressed his ear trumpet to the chest.

"He is barely breathing. Good woman," the inspector said to Mrs. Kermode. "Can you fetch a surgeon? Does one live nearby, by chance?"

"Close enough, sir," she replied. She wiped her hands and left the kitchen. Caldwell rushed in, his face and clothes powdered with dust.

"Ah, Caldwell," Endersby beamed. "You escaped from that treacherous building."

"Jumped sir, with some hazard, from the top part of the broken staircase to the first floor. A fall of five feet only, I reckon. But what dust!"

Mr. Jibbs opened his eyes. "Sweet Catherine," he whispered. A convulsion shook his body. He lay for a moment, his eyes gazing up at the ceiling. Endersby leaned in toward the man's pale features. There, pink and thick, lay the scar. It ran from the lower part of Mr. Jibbs' right cheek, mounted over the nose, and carried on upwards in a bubbling slant of flesh to rest just under the left eye. *A hard knotted scar,* Endersby thought, *worm-like and certainly frightening in its aspect.*

"Vicious," said Smallwood, who held up the lantern to afford the inspector better illumination. Mr. Jibbs coughed. A great blast of air blew out from his lungs. His mouth trembled.

Endersby leaned closer no more than an inch away from Mr.Jibbs' moving lips. "Caldwell," Endersby said. "Have you your pencil and your ..."

"Here, sir," Caldwell replied bending down to join Endersby. From Mr. Jibbs' mouth, dying words trickled out in a dry whisper: "Not to worry, dear one. Not to ..." A heave, a groan, then stillness. The body grew limp; the head fell sideways; his eyes — half-open — showing only the whites. Smallwood stood back. "Sad fellow," he said. "He is your man, Owen?" Endersby looked hard again at the scar, thought about the gaff, the hat and the lace. "I have no reasonable doubt, Smallwood. I am confident I can present a conviction post-mortem with what clues we have gathered." The inspector, Smallwood and Caldwell stood for a moment in silence, looking down at the body of Mr. Tobias Jibbs. A door shut in the hall and Mrs. Kermode's voice was heard speaking to someone. She entered the kitchen, leading in a tall thin man carrying a surgeon's black satchel. He was in poor but clean dress, his speaking voice, on introducing himself, was amiable.

"Mr. Eamon McClure. Surgeon. How do you do. Mr. Smallwood of Earl Street, sir? A face I recognize."

"Good evening, sir. My colleague, Inspector Owen Endersby of the Fleet Lane Station House. He is in charge of this particular investigation."

Endersby and McClure shook hands. "A dire chase has occurred and concluded with a fall, I understand," said McClure, opening his satchel. From it he pulled out a soiled canvas apron, on which there was evidence of blood splatters from former procedures. The doctor removed his frock coat, put down his hat and pulled on the apron. He rolled up his sleeves and arrayed a number of small wooden instruments, the first of which was a long stick. Dr. McClure pried open the mouth to examine the tongue of the corpse. By this time the kitchen women had resumed their duties. They turned their backs and whispered near the hearth, stirring soups in their cauldrons. "Life continues," mused Endersby, as he looked from one end of the kitchen to the other, where the body lay on the table: all its former dignity now under scrutiny. The other folk in the lodging house had given up their roles as spectators and, encouraged by Mrs. Kermode, returned to their rooms.

"Smallwood," said Endersby. "Kindly lead Mrs. Kermode into the warmth of her parlour; this medical procedure is not one for a lady of business. Then, sir, fetch a wagon and horse. Once Dr. McClure has finished, we must, by law, carry the body to Fleet Lane and prepare for the coroner on the morrow."

"Certainly, sir," replied Smallwood. "Allow me and my sergeants to relieve you of the body once you are finished with the surgeon's examination. We would be obliged to aid you, lending you our wagon and horse."

"I thank you, Smallwood," answered Endersby. Smallwood and Mrs. Kermode left the kitchen. Then, turning his attention back to Dr. McClure, Endersby removed his second-hand disguise coat and pulled off his hat and gloves. "Caldwell, let us observe," Endersby said.

"I am intrigued, sir," said McClure, "by your peculiar uniforms. Are these what the penny crime rags call 'undercover clothes'?"

"Precisely," answered Endersby. "We indulge in many ruses to catch our culprits, sir."

"Most clever," said Dr. McClure. Pulling close two kitchen chairs, Endersby and Caldwell sat down to ask questions of the doctor and to record his answers. Taking a pair of scissors from the small satchel he had brought with him, McClure cut away the tops of the body's boots. A wave of fetid stink wafted as the right boot was slid off to reveal a most foul desecration of poor Jibbs' foot.

"Here, Inspector, here is the source of the terrible stench. Not uncommon among prisoners and soldiers I have tended." The row of toes bent together, black and crusty in colour. On the largest toe, a greenish-hued, scaling mass made the appendage resemble a decayed cucumber. "It is the rotting disease," explained Dr. McClure. "A wound of some kind, one unwashed and then festered, has been the cause. Such an infection kills the flesh, turns it this vegetable-green colour. It can spread up into the limb and cripple a man."

"Painful, I imagine," remarked Endersby. Caldwell wrote. He unfolded a handkerchief from his pocket and held it to his nose.

"At times a pain similar to a burn; my father saw similar infections years ago as a surgeon on the slave ships out of West Africa."

"A terrible institution, the sale of humans," Endersby said, grimacing at the spectre of human suffering raised by the mention of slave ships.

Removing the other boot, McClure pointed to the thin ankles. Upon the mottled skin of each leg were displayed circles of blue broken skin.

"These markings are also familiar to me, Inspector," McClure explained. He had taken a notebook from his satchel and, like Caldwell, was writing down the evidence of illness and abuse Tobias Jibbs had suffered while alive. "These are the blackening bruises from iron fetters, a fetter locked to each ankle like hand cuffs. You see them on the legs of prisoners who are held too long in their cells."

"Such barbarities are frequently used on the hulks — the prison ships for transport — are they not, sir?" Endersby asked.

"In fact, they are used in them as a matter of habit, Inspector.

All prisoners kept in those hellish holds are chained together each night with manacles. When the men are marched out to do labour, the manacles are worn, each ankle clamped. The pull and strain on a line of souls tethered in such a manner creates these internal injuries to the flesh."

Dr. McClure finished his examination. "I officially announce that this man died from his fall, his spine broken. The blood in his mouth and throat suggest there was blood in his lungs, which may have effected suffocation."

Dr. McClure shut his satchel. Endersby stood up and examined the pockets of Mr. Jibbs' frock coat. He then pulled off the leather necklace and opened the small pouch. A rolled piece of writing paper. Endersby recognized it as a letter fragment written in the hand of young Catherine Smeets. He read part of it out loud: "So, dear Uncle Bo, I am to be sent to London. Papa says I must live in a workhouse. I am afraid, uncle. I have no one now to help me." He handed Caldwell the letter to read. "Sergeant, Mr. Jibbs has carried this letter with him all the while. It was the only one he received at one time from his niece." Endersby then explained the rest of the story to the surgeon: "This letter proves how the culprit knew where to search for his beloved niece. You see, sir, Mr. Tobias Jibbs escaped from the hulk prison ships anchored at Greenwich. He may have killed a man named William More and taken his name as a disguise. Perhaps this terrible scar was the outcome of a fight in the hold of those hellish places."

"And what of this sir," asked Caldwell. He pulled out a square of yellowed material from the bottom of the pouch. "It appears to be a soiled piece of lace, Inspector," remarked the surgeon. Half of the lace sample had rotted away. "What shall we make of this, gentlemen?" Endersby queried. Dr. McClure took the lace and held it close to the hanging lantern so all three men could see it more clearly. Endersby compared the lace he had found on the two murder victims: "It *is not* of the same bolt or design as the one Mr. Jibbs purchased in Rosemary Lane."

"Doctor, what has stained so much of this lower section?" asked Caldwell. McClure fingered the strands stained a blackish-brown colour. "Treacle? Rouge paint?" the inspector asked.

"Old blood," responded McClure.

"Blood?" asked Caldwell.

"Most likely used to staunch a wound or wrap an injury is my guess," said Dr. McClure. "The lace itself is one from a practiced lace-maker," added Endersby. "The workmanship reminds me of the pieces done by my wife."

Endersby pondered the piece and the doctor's analysis and then replaced the item inside its pouch and handed it to Caldwell to guard as a final clue. A knock at the kitchen door was followed by the entrance of two constables from Earl Street Station House. They carried a canvass stretcher on which they lay the body of Tobias Jibbs and brought it out the front door to the waiting wagon.

"Good evening, Inspector," said Dr. McClure, extending his hand as the two men prepared to part ways on the street. "I admire your methods, sir. The idea of ruse and play is most engaging."

"Thank you, sir," said Endersby. "Thank you for your professional analyses."

In the hansom cab on his way through London's evening streets, Endersby drew up his conclusions to the case. He planned his strategy to present to the magistrate and to Superintendent Borne. The descriptions given him over the past few days would be recorded; at least one of the children, one of the Catherines, would be asked to testify and then dictate her impressions for the police ledgers. If possible, Mr. Fitz might be persuaded to come and view the corpse of Jibbs. The facts of the case coincided well enough to the findings of the detective and his team: the odour of the legs, the fetter bruises, the frock coat, the letters. *In the end,* Endersby thought, *there is little doubt Mr. Jibbs was the murderer — even if the poor man had died before giving a confession.*

At Fleet Lane Station House, Rance and Tibald met with the inspector. He informed them of the capture and then gave them orders for the next morning to make a full day's round of workhouses to determine whether any incidents had occurred during the night concerning murder or the fate of abandoned girls. "A caution only, gentlemen, in case we have made a *grave* error with Mr. Jibbs," quipped the inspector.

"The coroner and magistrate must decide on the ultimate guilt of Mr. Jibbs," Endersby further explained before dismissing the men to go home. He then went up to his office, where he sat for an hour with Caldwell and wrote up a brief description of the evening's events in language lugubrious enough in tone to satisfy the whims of Superintendent Borne.

"And what of Sergeant Smeets, sir?" enquired Caldwell, closing down his inkwell.

"What indeed?"

"May we still regard him as a suspect, sir?"

"We may *regard* him as such, but we cannot prosecute him in that role as we have no acceptable proof."

"Thank you, sir. Shall I inform Doctor Reeves and Smeets himself?"

"I shall do that in the morning, Sergeant."

Endersby sighed. "Our professional life of detection, sir, is so often fraught with doubt and half-truths. I am sure you would agree that the byways of the criminal mind are myriad."

"As usual, sir, I do admire your ramblings," replied Caldwell.

"I thank you, Sergeant," Endersby said, letting out a tremendous yawn. The two men parted. To ease his foot and the band of tightness in his lower back, Endersby decided to walk home to Number Six Cursitor Street. Arriving at his front door, he was met by a jubilant Harriet. After a wash, a shave, and a change of bindings on his injured hand, Endersby donned his Persian smoking robe and sat down with his beloved Harriet at the dinner table.

"What delight," sighed Harriet. "I always sleep more soundly on hearing your case is closed. But then again, I must warn myself that new cases will appear."

"A life of sorrow, madam?" Endersby quipped, patting his lips.

"Worry, sir. Honest concern. It is the lot of a public servant's spouse to forbear the trials of her mate." Later, by the fire, the tea table was crowded with hot toast and fried mushrooms. Harriet had prepared a black Indian tea, a blend saved for occasions of joy. When the two retired to their bed, candles extinguished, Endersby could not fall to sleep. He rubbed his knee; he scratched his head. Harriet sat up. She lit a single candle.

"Tell me," she said gently, showing no impatience.

"Nothing at all, dear one, I swear."

"Tell me of nothing, then," she said, taking his large hand in hers.

"Why lace?" the inspector asked.

"Indeed," mused Harriet.

"Still very puzzling," Endersby then said.

Harriet stared into the tired eyes of her husband. A great yawn sprung forth from the inspector. "I do beg your pardon, madam."

"Pardon granted," Harriet said, pinching out the candle light. "By the by, a most curious-looking letter arrived for you in this evening's mail. It appears to be from the French embassy."

"A letter?" Endersby replied, plumping his pillow.

"Important, I would imagine," Harriet said.

"Best it wait until morning," Endersby said, his eyes closing.

"Very wise of you, dear," Harriet said. "Good night."

"Good night, indeed," said Endersby, his right arm slowly circling the shoulders of his wife as she lay back to rest her head close to his.

Of Related Interest:

Trumpets Sound No More:
An Inspector Endersby Mystery

by Jon Redfern

*Winner of the 2008 Arthur Ellis Award
for Best Crime Novel.*

In 1840, the theatre world in London is shocked by the brutal killing of one of its youngest and most successful entrepreneurs, bludgeoned in his house. The discovery of a contentious theatre contract, a collection of promissory notes, and a walking stick, its bloodied ivory head in the shape of a dog, are the only leads. Inspector Owen Endersby, of the recently formed London Detective Police Force, is called upon to apprehend the culprit before Christmas Eve. The inspector has six days to chart the byways of the Criminal Mentality. The case soon involves street vendors, downstairs servants, money lenders and the greatest performers of the stage. Who had motive to batter the young man to death? Without the techniques of the modern-day detective, Inspector Endersby must root out the villain any way he can: by disguise, break-and-enter, bribery, mail-tampering, and physical force.

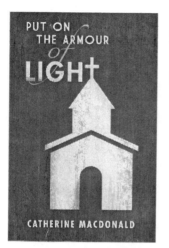

Put on the Armour of Light

by Catherine Macdonald

In June 1899, the Reverend Charles Lauchlan's industrious life as a young Presbyterian minister is knocked off the rails when he learns that his former university roommate has been arrested on murder charges.

The chief of police says it's an open-and-shut case, but Sergeant Setter — labeled as a misfit by his fellow officers — disagrees. Lauchlan and Setter become uneasy alliances in a search that takes them from the sleaziest bars to the most sumptuous drawing rooms of turn-of-the-century Winnipeg. On the way, Lauchlan uses his pastoral skills in ways never anticipated in the seminary. As time runs out he must risk everything, even his heart, in order to find the real killer.

Available at your favourite bookseller

DUNDURN

Visit us at

Dundurn.com
@dundurnpress
Facebook.com/dundurnpress
Pinterest.com/dundurnpress

CPSIA information can be obtained at www.ICGtesting.com
Printed in the USA
BVOW02s1903290315

393818BV00001B/31/P